ALSO BY DALLAS HUDGENS

Drive Like Hell

Season of Gene

A NOVEL

DALLAS HUDGENS

SCRIBNER
New York London Toronto Sydney

SCRIBNER
1230 Avenue of the Americas
New York, NY 10020

This book is a work of fiction. Names, characters, places, and incidents either are products of the author's imagination or are used fictitiously. Any resemblance to actual events or locales or persons, living or dead, is entirely coincidental.

For information about special discounts for bulk purchases, please contact Simon & Schuster Special Sales:
1-800-456-6798 or business@simonandschuster.com.

Designed by Kyoko Watanabe
Text set in Dutch 823

Manufactured in the United States of America

1 3 5 7 9 10 8 6 4 2

Library of Congress Control Number: 2007011578

ISBN: 978-1-4165-4149-3

For my mother

ACKNOWLEDGMENTS

I'm grateful to Joe Regal and everyone at Regal Literary for their invaluable help, and to Brant Rumble for his support and editorial expertise. Thank you to my generous friends Scott W. Berg, Corrine Gormont, Wendi Kaufman, and Robyn Kirby Wright. Thank you as well to Lauren Cerand, Richard Mayberry, Steve Broadhurst, Ray Rimer, Richard Bond, Kelly Justice, Fountain Bookstore, Wes Freed, and Jyl Freed. I also want to acknowledge Robert W. Creamer's *Babe: The Legend Comes to Life* as a resource on the life of Babe Ruth.

Season of Gene

CHAPTER 1

I had always been fond of the bat man's wife. That's not to say she couldn't be somewhat difficult at times. As was the case on the opening night of the Metro D.C. Men's Recreational Baseball League's fall season. There she was, standing in the bat man's driveway, beside the bat man's gold Navigator, busting his stones when the bat man didn't need this sort of distraction, not on game day. And so I politely tapped my car horn in hopes of speeding up the process.

The bat man's wife, Joy, gave me the finger.

"Fuck you, Joe Rice."

I turned off the radio and hopped out of my 'Vette. Thing was, I had responsibilities to attend to. As manager and catcher for the Whip Spa Yankees (the Spa being my car detailing business), I needed to be at the field thirty minutes before game time in order to fill out the lineup card and still have a chance to warm up my starting pitcher. I clattered up the driveway of the new split-level in my Adidas cleats and offered Joy a smile.

"Do you fucking mind?" she asked. "I'm trying to have a conversation with Gene here."

"You think maybe Geno could call you from the car on his cell?"

She looked at Gene and nodded. "Do you see what I mean? You're like a couple of twelve-year-olds. You're a grown man with a kid of your own, and you insist on acting like an inconsiderate asshole."

"And you." She turned in my direction. "Of all Gene's friends, I would expect better from you. I thought you were different."

Geno offered me an apologetic look. He was standing there in his

Yankees uniform: gray pants and the navy blue BP jersey (number 9 like Geno's boyhood hero, Graig Nettles). Big as he was, Gene was tilting to one side because of his bat bag, the Louisville Slugger Deluxe Locker model, a marvel of modern luggage that held four bats (a fraction of the bat man's total collection), a helmet, batting and fielding gloves, cleats, practice balls, two Gatorade bottles, a couple cans of Red Bull, compartments for wet and dry clothes, and still room for a box of baby wipes and half a bird from El Pollo Rico, Gene's sixth-inning nourishment before Joy put him on a low-fat diet and started cramming omega oils down his throat back in the spring when his cholesterol swelled to 360 (and eclipsed his batting average by a hundred points).

Gene tried to be reasonable with Joy. "It's the first game of the season. We can see these people any fucking day of the week."

This was one of the neighborhood clubhouse parties Gene had talked about. Gene usually referred to them as "those fucking snoozefests."

He turned to me. "They got a fucking dance instructor coming in."

"What kind of dance?" I asked.

"Tango."

"That's a very sensual dance," I said. "When you tango with a woman, she should feel like she's in the arms of God."

Joy snorted. "What the fuck do you know about tango?"

"Hey, I saw *Scent of a Woman*."

"That figures. How else would you know about anything? It would have to either be in a movie or a fucking video game."

She'd never gone after me like this before. In fact, she was usually quite the charmer, touching my forearm when we talked, smiling like we shared a secret. I can't deny that I enjoyed the attention. She had the darkest eyes I'd ever seen. They were like carbon monoxide: powerful, but in a way that you didn't notice until after they'd made you light-headed.

"Look it," Gene said, "I told you, I just don't like married people. That's who I fucking am. I'd rather be doing something, not just standing around talking. These people, they've got nothing to say that I want to hear."

Gene had actually heard me say something to this effect in regard to my own marital history. I was full of shit, of course. It was just something to say, as I preferred not to talk about those three long-ago months when I was married. Gene, though, had taken it as some kind of divine wisdom.

"All they do is drink that fucking wine," Gene said. "Two-buck Jack, or whatever the fuck it is."

"You are so fucking ignorant," Joy said.

I went for a positive spin. "This might be fun, Geno. You know, the tango thing. At least you're doing something. You don't have to spend all your time talking to people, because there's an activity involved."

I turned my attention to Joy. "How about I promise you the bat man will there by nine o'clock. Game starts at six, so it should be over by eight-thirty. I'll get Ramon to pick up the equipment so we can leave as soon as it's done. I'll drive your boy straight home, he can take a shower, and you can be in the arms of God by nine o'clock."

She gritted her teeth and looked me straight in the eye. "Fuck you, Rice."

Now I realized the situation was beyond repair, at least by my hands.

Joy crossed her arms and started sniffling.

"Just go." She looked at Gene. "Just fucking go. I don't even care anymore."

Seeing the tears, Gene set his bag down on the driveway. "Aw, come on, Joy. You know I tried. I went to those parties and shit. I did it all for you, but I need a break sometimes. I need to do my thing. That's how I fucking roll."

He took a step toward her, but she fired him a look. It had the effect of a well-timed brushback pitch. The bat man stepped off.

"All that time we lived in a shitty apartment," she said, "this is what I wanted. To be in a real neighborhood, to have friends and to feel a part of something. And now you've fucked it up."

"Nothing's fucked up."

"The fuck it's not. In case you haven't noticed, we're the fucked-up family on the street. Everybody knows it. You're never home, and little Gene bites every kid he's around. Nobody will even have a fucking play date with him anymore."

"What have I fucked up?" Gene sounded totally innocent.

"Don't play stupid," she said. "You know I find your receipts. You're too fucking stupid to throw them away. Paying for your little hand jobs with the Visa—and the Ridge Front Bible Church Visa at that. You don't think that shit hurts?"

She turned to me. I was already backing up with my hands in the air. "I'll just wait in the car and let you two discuss this in private."

"No," she said. "I want you to hear what else he did. He fucking gave me genital warts when I was pregnant. Did he tell you about that? Little Gene could've been deformed. He could've been born with twelve fingers or something."

I knew all about the bat man's propensity for happy endings. I'd never condoned it, but then again I'd also never pointed out to him that Joy might disagree with his belief that hand jobs did not constitute adultery. It bothered me that I'd never said as much, especially now that all this shit was coming between me and opening night.

"Hey, I'm the one who fucking put you in this house," Gene said. "Don't forget that. It's my hard work, not your fucking money from selling that scrapbook shit. And you don't have to go busting my balls about it either."

"What hard work?" she asked. "I never know what you're doing, where you are, who you're with. You come home with your nose broken and some crazy story about being robbed at work. Do you think I believe that shit?"

The broken nose story was pretty fishy. Even I wanted to know the truth about that one. Gene never could lie worth a shit, so I knew I'd eventually get it out of him. For the time being, I'd just be patient. After all, it was his personal business until it affected my business—or the baseball team.

There were no trees in the subdivision to soften the early-September heat; just scalped earth, patchy sod, and a few saplings. We were damn near in West Virginia, despite the fact that Gene and I worked five minutes outside Washington, D.C. Gene had been telling me I should put my money into a mortgage instead of throwing it away on rent, and move out here where there were fewer hassles, less crime. But I just couldn't see it. First off, the traffic was shit, two lanes leading to a string of four subdivisions, including Shenandoah Springs, where Gene lived. No fucking turning lanes, so you get stuck behind people making a left into the CVS or the Food Warehouse, and it takes you twenty minutes to go a single mile and you're still nearly living in goddamn West Virginia, no offense intended.

To the west, out at the edge of the Shenandoahs, a band of storms was stirring, getting ready to roll our way. Half the games had been rained out during the spring season. They were against weak teams, too. We could've had a better playoff seed if it hadn't been for all the rain.

"Come on," Geno said. "Let's go play some fucking ball."

He stomped away from Joy and tossed his bat bag into my car. I stood there long enough to give Joy an apologetic look.

"I'll get him home by nine. I promise."

She just stared at me, squinting into the sun, eyes glistening with tears, arms crossed. They really could have used some bigger trees in that subdivision. I felt vulnerable there, wide open, like somebody could take a shot at me from any direction.

Joy didn't say anything. Another tear streaked down her cheek. A splotch of red shone on her long neck.

"Try to take some deep breaths," I said. "That always helps me out when I'm feeling uptight."

She looked at me like she hadn't heard a word. Her eyes were hazy and sad, all the anger gone from them. "What am I gonna do, Joe? I'm so fucking miserable."

The way she'd asked, it was like she actually believed I might have an answer. But I didn't.

"I'm so fucking miserable," she said again.

She turned to go back inside the new house, and Gene tapped the horn, and there I was standing in the middle, the team manager who had no idea what the fuck he was doing.

CHAPTER 2

Gene came out of the Porta-John following his pregame dump, lumbering up the hill behind the dugout, looking like a bear in a Yankees suit, carrying his box of aloe-treated baby wipes ("a bidet in a box," as he called them). I was sitting in the dugout, holding the scorebook, waiting for everybody to show up so I could fill out the lineup card. We were still three players short with fifteen minutes until game time. I feared that complacency had set in among the ranks. I was always fearing that sort of thing.

Our opponent for the season opener was the Devil Rays, whose roster consisted mostly of assholes who'd played college ball, all of them recruited by their asshole manager, plastic surgeon Harry Funderburk. Their brand of ball relied on speed, taking the extra base at every opportunity, even when they were up by twelve runs, and gloving everything you put into play. They had knocked us out of the playoffs four seasons running, including the previous spring. That game ended in a fight after a beanball war instigated by Funderburk's posing after he hit a pop-fly home run over the puny right-field porch (275 feet) at Shetland High School with the D-Rays leading by seventeen runs in the eighth inning. The shenanigans had prompted the commissioner to threaten expulsion for both teams if we pulled any more shit like that. He had me and Funderburk meet him at IHOP for a sit-down to hammer out a cease-fire. Just to make sure we kept our end of the bargain, he'd paid a pair of off-duty cops to monitor the fall season's opening night proceedings.

Geno reached into his bat bag, pulled out a pack of Marlboro Lights, and lit one. Then he plopped down on the bench beside me.

"Gimme one of those," I said.

He shook out another cigarette and handed me his lighter.

"Is Theresa coming to the game tonight?" he asked.

I shook my head.

Gene murmured, knowingly. "She going through one of her phases?"

"I don't think so. She told me I'd mistaken laziness for contentment. She said we shouldn't see each other anymore."

Gene laughed. "Yeah, I've been meaning to talk to you about that contentment thing."

"She gets ideas from these books she reads. She's got this thirty-six-month theory, too."

"Thirty-six months of what?"

"She thinks that's the limit of most relationships. In some cases it's only twelve."

"So, where were you?"

"Thirty-two months."

Gene nodded. "That's pushing the fucking envelope."

He went into the bag again and pulled out our pregame nutrition: two Red Bulls and a handful of Vicodins. I popped open my can, swallowed the pills, and felt for just a moment that I'd rather be at home on my couch than out on this dusty, piece-of-shit field. My right knee had been aching since February. The doctor said I had a torn meniscus. At that point it was too late to have surgery. I would have missed the entire spring season and been rusty for the fall, which was my favorite time to play. So, I'd been getting by on ice packs and painkillers of various sorts.

The sun was dipping behind the old brick high school beyond the outfield fence. The playing lights were humming, casting a silver light across the rock-strewn infield. One of the cops walked toward our dugout carrying a Starbucks cup. He nodded, took his position at the gate like a guard.

"What about that kid of hers?" Gene asked. "Who's she gonna find to keep that little shit if she stops seeing you?"

"I told her Louis could keep coming over when she was at work."

Gene shook his head. "What's that thing he's got, the defiant dispossessive property, or something?"

"Oppositional defiance disorder."

"Jesus, they got a fucking name for everything these days. You ask me, he's a fucking smart-ass."

"He's twelve. I was a smart-ass at twelve, and I'd lay heavy stakes that you were, too. Besides, you're just pissed that he kicked your ass at *Madden*."

Theresa had lost her babysitter a few months ago, and I'd been keeping Louis for her when she was at work. The kid had his moments. But as long as I kept him busy with TV and PS2 he was no trouble. In fact, we got along pretty well.

Gene touched his hand to his nose, felt the bridge and the bump from where it had been broken. His black eyes were just starting to heal.

"So, tell me the fucking truth," I said. "What happened to your nose?"

He looked at me and shrugged his big shoulders. "I told you already. These black dudes came in the warehouse after you'd left. They had knives, told me to open the safe."

"Yesterday, you said they were Latino. What are you trying to do, incriminate every minority you can think of?"

Gene shook his head, sucked on his Marlboro. "They were wearing baseball caps. I couldn't see their faces so good."

"What about the forty-four I keep in the desk drawer?" I said. "It's loaded and ready to go. I showed you how to use it."

"I was scared. I didn't know what to do. Besides, that flattop's a fucking antique. I bet it'd blow up in your hands if you tried to shoot it."

"Don't try to scam me," I said. "I still remember that time you were screwing around with the cop's wife. He thought I was you, came after me with one of those retractable nightsticks."

"He treated her like an object," Geno said.

"And he wanted to treat my head like a fucking piñata," I said.

Funderburk made a point of walking over with his lineup card before we had our full nine on hand. He was grinning and dressed, as always, like a fucking all-star: the Oakleys atop his hat, extra-length sweatbands bearing his jersey number 8 on both arms, ankle-length pants and freshly polished Mizunos with kangaroo-leather uppers

($129 on BaseballExpress.com). He could play a little, I'd give him that much. But give me a fucking break with the fashion show.

Needless to say, I wasn't in the mood for dealing with him. "What do you want, Thunderturd? You know we don't have nine yet."

I reached out and snatched the lineup from his palm. He made a show of pulling out his cell phone and checking the time.

"You still got ten minutes to field a team, and I'll give you a fifteen-minute grace period after that." He smiled. "I just hope Immigration doesn't get wise and pick up your outfield on their way over here."

"Why don't you get the fuck out of here, before I break that phone over your head."

"Joey," he said. "Where's the fucking love? What about IHOP? Don't you remember IHOP?"

About that time, our right fielder, Joaquin, pulled up in his old Toyota truck. Half our reserves were piled in the back. I was sponsoring Joaquin for his green card. He was the supervisor of my car detailing business.

Funderburk laughed. "Looks like the Taliban just arrived."

"They're Mexican and Dominican, you dumb shit."

Gene was offering no assistance, just sitting there looking uncomfortable. He and Funderburk had become somewhat cordial after the doc had given him a deal on Joy's breast augmentation, the results of which hadn't entirely pleased Gene to begin with. He'd been hoping for double Ds. Instead, Joy went with full, natural-looking Cs.

Gene had told me Funderburk recently botched a nose job, got sued, and was booted out of his practice. For some reason, I'd promised Gene that I wouldn't use this as verbal ammo on the field of play.

Funderburk finally granted us his departure. The bat man finished his smoke, flipped it onto the concrete floor, and ground it under the toe of his cleats.

"What the fuck?" I said. "You couldn't say anything to that asshole?"

Gene shrugged. "So, where we eating tonight?"

"*We're* not eating anywhere," I said. "Your ass is going to dance class."

"Fuck that shit."

"Maybe it'll help your footwork around third base. You're no fucking gazelle out there."

"I can't loosen my hammies anymore."

Our players were mingling outside the dugout; smoking cigarettes, eating pupusas, talking, doing everything but loosening up. Their bags lay scattered around the dugout, stinking of Tiger Balm and a number of other salves and ointments, both imported and domestic, currently being sold online and at health food stores. Gene's bag, which had a hook and clasp, was hanging from the chain-link wall of the dugout. Unzipped, it looked like a full-fledged living space: multishelved, organized, a little hinged door. Slap a recliner in front of it and Barry Bonds would not have been ashamed to use that thing as a locker.

I started filling out the lineup card. We had eight of our starters on hand, and I knew that Willie, our ninth, was going to be running a little late. I left his spot open, set down the scorebook, and told Gene I was going to warm up our starter, Ramon. Gene sat down and lit another cigarette.

"What?" I said. "You're not gonna throw before the game?"

He shook his head. "My shoulder's got a limited number of tosses on reserve. I'm saving 'em for the game."

"You should at least jog around a little, loosen up."

"The fuck is that supposed to mean?"

"Nothing. It just might help you out on the basepaths."

"Once again, what the fuck does that mean?"

"I just want to make sure you can go first-to-third on a base hit to right."

"That was three fucking months ago. You still haven't forgotten. What do you do, keep a fucking log on this shit?"

"With all due respect, I'm just saying. That play probably cost us the game and a decent seed in the playoffs."

"How the fuck is that so?"

"If you're at third, then you tag up and score on Ramon's fly ball. We tie the game right there. Instead, you're stuck at second and we lose by a run and have to face the fucking D-Rays in the first round."

He couldn't defend himself. Geno knew the game, how it was supposed to be played.

"You're dropping me in the batting order, aren't you?"

"I haven't decided yet. We'll just see how things go the first couple of games."

He stood up, paced a few steps. "I can't fucking believe it. This hurts, you know. This really fucking hurts."

"Gimme a fucking break. I'm gonna do what's best for the team. Wouldn't you rather bat seventh and win a trophy?"

Gene pulled back like I'd taken a poke at him. "Seventh?"

He picked up his glove and walked away, shoulders slumped, acting like he was headed out to the field. But then he stopped at the dugout door. Funderburk was pinging grounders to his infielders, calling everybody by name, hollering insincere "atta boys" until I wanted to strangle his fat ass. Meantime, our players were still lounging in the grass like we were having a fucking company picnic.

I told Gene to take it easy. "I'm not dropping you tonight. You're still my cleanup hitter for now. I just want you to pick it up a little bit this season."

He turned, offered no reaction, then went back to watching the pregame activities, his fingers wrapped around the chain links.

"You may have to find another cleanup hitter."

"Don't even start with that shit."

"I mean it. This is probably my last season."

Just then, I noticed Willie making his way up the hill. I went ahead and inked his name in the lineup.

Meantime, Gene was going through his "It's just a game" speech. He trotted it out whenever he was in a slump, threatening retirement. This time he added that I took it all too seriously, which wasn't entirely true. I wanted to win bad enough, but not at certain costs. The team meant something to me, keeping everybody together, thinking about each other before themselves, working as a unit. More than anything, I wanted everyone to be a good teammate. I wanted harmony and longevity, a genuine dynasty, something you could depend on year after year.

Me and Gene had met through his cousin Richard, who owned a limo service up in Cliffside Park, New Jersey. I was working as co-manager at the Palisade Premium Car Wash while on probation for running numbers with my uncle Phil. Richard was an independent driver, owned a couple of Lincoln Town Cars, and came in a lot for the Super Deluxe when customers puked in his backseats. I told him one day that I was about to come off the paper, and he told me about his cousin Gene, who was trying to get a limo service off the ground down in D.C. "Good kid," he said, "but he ain't too hot with numbers. You and him, it might be a good team."

Gene and I had shared a small warehouse space in Arlington, Virginia, for seven years. He ran his limo service, Dellorso Town Car, out of it, and I ran my car detailing business, the Whip Spa, as well as my ticket brokerage firm, Backstage Pass, Inc. It was a good setup for the both of us, seeing how our businesses tended to intersect on a regular basis, leaving us both to handle the same clients. For example: if I sold Redskins tickets to a high-dollar guy, I'd refer him to Gene, who'd offer a discount on transportation to the game. Likewise, he was always steering D.C. lobbyists and high-tech players in my direction for tickets. I sold them the ducats, Gene ferried them to the stadium, and then I'd detail their Beamer, Audi, or whatever, for free while they were enjoying themselves. We got lots of return business from that type of personalized care.

Most of the players on the team worked for us, which made our success—not to mention our state of harmony—all the sweeter. The players were a blend of cultures and playing styles: Mexican, Dominican, Cuban. They washed cars, drove people to the airport, and sold tickets they'd never be able to afford. Despite the Yankees uniforms we were a small-market contender. And I liked to think of myself as a players' manager along the lines of Joe Torre and Bobby Cox. I always raised hell over close calls that went against my guys, and I e-mailed a team newsletter to everyone each Monday, noting stats and good plays. The thing was nobody got the same e-mail. I'd write a draft, and then tweak each version to point out the contributions that each of them had made. I noted each guy's favorite major leaguer and, when it wasn't completely ridiculous, compared their own play to said superstar. I even beefed up everyone's batting average by about twenty points just to keep them confident.

We were looking sluggish in the fall season opener, but so were the D-Rays. Down 2–1 headed into the seventh, we had a chance to steal a win from these fuckers. The meat of our order was due up, with Geno's cousin, Tommy Pumpkin, leading off. Tommy was a spot welder who lived in Salem County, New Jersey. Currently playing a workman's comp scam over a back injury, he commuted three and a half hours each week to our Friday-night games. He spent the rest of his time lifting weights in his basement. Tommy was our shortstop, a former junior college player who'd apparently had a tryout with the Pirates during the Bonds/Bonilla era but was deemed only a warning-track threat. He could've dominated in our league as a hitter if he hadn't insisted on trying to pull everything. The tall lefty on the mound for the Devil Rays was well aware of this deficiency and had kept the ball on the outer half of the plate against him, resulting in a pop-up and a strikeout thus far.

Gene was parked beside me on the bench, in the hole and wearing his helmet and batting gloves, squeezing the handle of his red alloy bat. Ramon was on deck, standing in the dugout doorway, sorting through the bat selection. The dim, half-assed field lights reflected off his helmet like aspirins.

"Hey, bat man," Ramon said. "Let me use Big Red."

Gene handed him the bat. It was a $300 club, supposedly exploiting the benefits of magnesium-enhanced alloy. Everyone on the team, even those mired in slumps, regarded the bat as if it held mystical powers.

I told Ramon he was pitching well. "Let's keep working off your two-seamer next inning. How's the arm holding up?"

He rotated his ball and socket, wincing. "It's okay, but I'm gonna need the Vike after the game."

Gene gave Ramon the thumbs-up. He always had a stock of pharmaceuticals in his bag: Vicodin, Percocet, Tylenol 3. I never asked where they came from. We all had our connections for various necessities, but Gene was everybody's backup plan if they couldn't find what they needed.

Up at the plate, Tommy swung at some junk that was clearly outside.

"Come on," Gene said. "You gotta wait on that shit. This guy's throwing puss."

"Keep your hands inside the ball," I added. "Take one to right field."

Ramon took a couple of practice swings, stepped back inside the dugout. "So where's the post-game meal tonight, Skip?"

I always bought for the team after games. It didn't matter if we had won or lost.

"I'm thinking chicken," Gene said. "Black beans and rice, plantains, about eight or nine Dos Equis."

I told Gene he wasn't eating chicken, he was going home to tango with Joy.

"She can tango up my asshole," he said. "I'm eating chicken."

"You want chicken, I can get you some fucking chicken," Ramon said. "My girlfriend's cousin was flying in from Guatemala today. They sell this bird at the airport there, and he brings it in and sells it at the bodega. Ten fucking dollars for a three-piece box."

Ramon was my number one guy on the ticket end of things, a computer whiz whose grandfather had moved to the States from Cuba back in the forties. He'd designed websites for me and Gene, really helping the business. He also knew his way around a good meal.

"That sounds like some serious chicken," I said.

"I'm talking about a bird that will make your dick hard." Ramon knocked twice on his protective cup as if to illustrate the point.

"Roasted?" Gene asked.

"Pressure-cooked," Ramon said. "Crispy on the outside, succulent in the middle."

Gene looked at me and raised his eyebrows. "I gotta taste this bird."

"You're going dancing, Foghorn."

Before Gene could argue, his cousin struck out on a pitch at eye level. I asked Gene if the guy even knew what a strike zone was. Then I clapped and said, "That's okay, Tommy. Get him next time."

I marked another *K* beside Tommy's name in the scorebook. Gene, who was now on deck, stood up and moved to the door of the dugout. He grabbed one of his backup bats, dropped a donut onto the end, and walked back to where I was sitting. He leaned over as if to tell me something in confidence.

"You know it's over, don't you? I wasn't shitting you about me not playing next season. Me and Joy, it's just a matter of time. Neither of us knows how to end it just yet, but we both know it's over. We're well past that thirty-six-month point."

"What's that got to do with you playing ball next season?"

He leaned in closer, almost speaking in a whisper. "I'm thinking about shutting down the limo business, maybe moving the cars out to Nevada with Tommy, starting something out there."

The hollow clang of the bat surprised me. Ramon had jumped on the first pitch and rifled the ball into the gap in right center, way out in the shadows. He turned on the jets and made it all the way to third with a stand-up triple. The dugout was going nuts, guys yelling, banging the tin roof with their hands. I would have been the loudest of the bunch, but I was still trying to make sense of what Gene had just said.

"Are you fucking crazy?"

Gene didn't say anything, but he didn't make a move toward the field either.

"My name's on that warehouse lease, too," I said. "And about half our business depends on each other. Did you forget that?"

Guys were looking at Gene, wondering why he wasn't heading to the plate. Somebody called out, "You're up, bat man. Give it a ride."

Gene took a deep breath. "I'm sorry, man. It's hard to explain all of this. I'll tell you about it later."

He headed out of the dugout. I couldn't even think straight enough to record Ramon's triple. Our backup right fielder, Artie, came over and took the scorebook from me. "You're on deck, Skip. Let me take care of that."

Normally, I wouldn't have let Artie within twenty feet of the scorebook. He was a notorious revisionist where at bats were concerned, always turning his outs into base hits. I'd caught him doing this on more than one occasion. It was one thing to change a reached-by-error to a single. But this guy would change a strikeout to a double. It was ballsy to be sure, but not in a respectable way.

I grabbed my helmet and stepped out onto the patchy grass. The field was a dog track: beat-up, rutted, and dusty. Only high schools with second-rate facilities would allow us on their diamonds.

Gene was a lot smarter than his cousin. He laid off the outside junk and waited for the lefty to bring something over the plate. He clocked a 2-0 pitch over the left fielder's head and off the chain-link fence. A standup double for anyone else, but Gene made it a close play. It looked like he was running underwater. He slid under the tag, called time out, and lay there for about thirty seconds trying to catch his breath.

Ramon held up his hand as he crossed home plate, but I didn't even think to slap it. And then I stepped into the box and took a strike without taking the bat off my shoulder. Gene was clapping at second base. "Come on, man. Focus. Just like last time."

I felt like I'd been stabbed in the back with some free agent back-room maneuvering bullshit. I took another one at the belt. The catcher flipped the ball back to the mound. "Let's finish him off," he said. "He don't wanna swing."

I stepped out of the box, tried to get my focus. I took a few breaths. *In and feel the pause. Out and feel the pause.*

The next pitch was a breaking ball, a waste pitch, but the pitcher caught a little plate with it. I kept my hands inside the ball, swung, and the bat let out a high, ringing note. The dirty pill streaked into right field for a base hit. A sure run, but Gene was going to make it interesting again, chugging around third, arms pumping, legs struggling beneath his weight. The right fielder missed the cutoff man, but the pitcher, who'd been too lazy to back up the play at the plate, scooped up the overthrow and flung it toward home. The catcher snagged the ball in front of the plate. Everyone in our dugout was screaming "Slide!" And Geno, who should have been out by a step, made a beautiful slide behind the plate, reaching out with his left hand to swipe it. He looked like Jackie Robinson, only fat and slow. The umpire called him safe, and we had the lead.

Geno popped up, clapped his hands, took two steps, and went down like he'd been shot with an elephant gun. Boom. Facedown in the dirt.

My first thought was a torn hammy. But then he just lay there, no movement or nothing, and the umpire and the Devil Rays catcher both knelt to examine him. Soon, the umpire waved to our dugout for someone to come out there.

I sprinted in to see what was wrong. Tommy and Ramon raced out of the dugout. Gene was still lying facedown in the dirt, motionless. It was not a hamstring-injury sort of pose.

The Devil Rays catcher looked up at the three of us. His face had lost all its color. "I don't think he's breathing, man."

Ramon and I just stood there. I wasn't breathing either at that point, but my heart was laying some heavy footsteps against my chest. And then Tommy started screaming, asking if there was a doctor on the field. Funderburk was already running in from center field. He fancied himself some sort of stallion out there. On more than one occasion, he'd pointed to his Mizuno glove and said, "This is where base hits go to die." I longed to see the man fail miserably, but now was not the time. I hoped like hell he was a more competent physician than I'd previously given him credit for.

Funderburk told me to call 911 as he ran past. I hustled back to the dugout and grabbed my cell phone. Naturally, I didn't have a signal when I needed one. Two other guys were in the same boat, but one of the off-duty cops managed to get a call through for an ambulance.

By the time I got back out to the field, Funderburk had rolled Gene onto his back. The bat man was still wearing his helmet, eyes half-open, dirt pancaked on his cheek, his mouth curled into that half smile he always wore when he thought he had the upper hand. It was a tip-off when we played *Madden NFL* on the PS2. If Geno was smiling, you knew he was bringing a blitz package.

I hadn't bartered with God in a long time, but I gave it a try. *Your will be done, but please save the bat man and I won't take this baseball shit so serious anymore.*

Both teams were gathered around the scene in a semicircle, watching Funderburk blow into Gene's mouth and push on his chest. Tommy was down there with him, holding Gene's arm and feeling for a pulse. The tall Devil Rays pitcher sidled up to me. He had his hat cocked back on his head.

"Nice hit," he said.

It seemed like an odd thing to say, but I thanked him.

"That was my cutter," he said. "You stayed on it real good."

"It caught some plate," I said.

Gene still wasn't breathing when the paramedics drove onto the field fifteen minutes later and stepped out into the salty light with their Wendy's Biggie cups in hand. They failed to instill much confidence. One of the guys didn't even seem to be in a hurry to tend to

Gene. He gazed out at the left field fence, smiled, and took an imaginary swing.

After they'd hauled Gene away in the ambulance, with Funderburk and Tommy along for the ride, I went back to the dugout and sat down. Most of the other guys were wandering around the infield like ghosts, talking to one another, shuffling and shaking their heads. We all knew it looked bad for Gene.

Still, a couple of Devil Rays wanted to finish the game. They were worried it might count as a loss if we stopped it. The umpire relayed the info to me.

"Tell 'em they can have the fucking win," I said. "And if I find out who suggested that, I'm putting a fucking bat up his ass."

Ramon and Willie finally came in and sat beside me. Willie was one of Gene's drivers, a tall first baseman who'd been a soccer goalkeeper as a kid in El Salvador. He'd never played baseball until he started working for Gene. He saved our infielders at least ten errors a season with his quick hands around first.

"I don't think we will see the bat man again," he said. "He looked very much like a dead man."

At that moment it was hard to ignore just how ridiculous we all looked sitting there in our Yankees uniforms. Illegal, uninsured, slow of foot, bearing police records. And we were the Devil Rays' bitches to boot. Not that anybody besides us gave a damn.

Poor Gene.

Someone had dropped the scorebook and pen on the concrete floor. I picked them up and dusted off the book. I glanced down at Gene's final line: 2 for 3, a fly out, a single, and a double. He was still on second base in the book. I took the pen and carefully filled in the little diamond, giving Gene his run. Then I made a slash—end of inning—and wrote, "Final Score 3–2."

CHAPTER 3

Me and Ramon ate chicken and split a six-pack of Dos Equis in Gene's honor. We were sitting at the desk Gene and I shared in our warehouse space. It must have been around midnight, and we were still wearing our baseball uniforms, me in the office chair and Ramon tipped back in a folding chair.

"This bird travels well," I said.

Ramon lifted his beer bottle up to his mouth, paused, nodded, and then held it there like he'd forgotten how to take a drink. "All the way from Guatemala, man. No green card or nothing. It's called Pollo Campero. Remember that name. I'm gonna buy a franchise."

"They've got one of those Chick-fil-A's out where Gene lives," I said. "Me and bat man ate there a couple of times. Pretty good shit."

Ramon sat there awhile, his shoulder bundled in an ice pack and Ace bandage. "You know," he said, "we gotta go see Joy tomorrow. There ain't no getting around that."

"You think we should have stayed at the hospital until she got there?"

He shrugged. "Gene was dead, man. What could we do? I'm sure she's got family. She'd rather be with them, right?"

"I don't know. Gene didn't think too much of her family. He said she had a cousin who used to touch her and shit when she was little. Did the same thing to her sister, the one who overdosed. He said Joy told her parents, but they didn't believe her."

Ramon had some idea of Gene and Joy's marital travails. Whenever Gene's porn surfing led to a computer virus, Ramon was always called in to exorcise the demons. He asked when I thought they might be having the funeral.

"Probably Monday or Tuesday."

"True," he said. "You know what the Bible says: after three days, the body stinketh."

The warehouse was small, more like a garage, and it had rarely been this quiet. There was always salsa music playing during the day—congas and guiros and timbales—talking and laughing, the generator on the pressure washer rumbling, and the TV on the wall flickering with the *SportsCenter* highlights. No way around it, this was my favorite place to be. It felt significant in some way, our little team providing these services to people. And now I had this heavy feeling in my chest, like we were about to get contracted out of the major leagues.

I thought about turning on the television, but it felt disrespectful even though I could see Gene checking the scores had I been the one who'd just died. The remote control was sitting there on the desk atop Gene's copy of *Moneyball.* A pile of losing Lotto tickets was scattered around the book, and a day-old *New York Post,* which I bought every morning at the CVS, was flipped over to the back sports page. The headline read BRONX BUMMER, the Yanks having just dropped a series to the Jays. They were stumbling to the finish, and Gene had been worried about their prospects come October.

Ramon said he'd never known anyone who'd just dropped dead on the spot. "My family drags it out. Cancer, emphysema, stuff like that. It can get ugly, you know. But at least you got time to make things right, say good-bye and all that."

"So that's how you want to go? With an oxygen tank and an IV in your arm?"

Ramon shrugged. "If it means getting the chance to tell somebody I'm sorry for something, then yeah, I'll take the suffering. I don't like any loose ends."

"There's always loose ends."

Truth was, Gene had made a beautiful exit sliding into home. Only the timing was fucked up. If it had been forty-five years from now, down in Sarasota during one of those senior citizen games, it would have been brilliant.

I asked Ramon if he thought Gene had prepared a will. He laughed at the idea of such competence. "Who? Bat man? I'll lay you some good odds he didn't."

I told him about Gene's plan to move his business to Nevada. Ramon nodded like it was old news.

"You knew?" I asked.

He shrugged. "Yeah, he and Tommy used to talk about it when you weren't around."

"Why the fuck didn't you tell me?"

"It was a sticky situation, Skip. I mean, I work for both you guys. I didn't want to get caught in the middle of anything."

"You worked for me first, Ramon. And I didn't see Gene floating you any loans for school."

Ramon lowered his chair, took his feet off the desk, and looked down. "My bad," he said. "But for all I knew, they were just talking shit."

There was one beer left. I offered it to Ramon, but he shook his head. I stashed it inside the fridge with all the old takeout boxes and told him we better go. Between the Dos Equis and the Vicodin, I almost felt like I could go to sleep.

"So, what about Geno's broken nose?" I asked. "This bullshit story about somebody trying to rob us. Did you know anything about that?"

He shook his head. "I didn't know nothing about the broken nose. Only God knew what Gene was up to at any given moment. I couldn't have kept up with him if I'd wanted to."

Ramon sat there for a moment, deep in thought. Finally, he began to unwrap the bandage that was holding his ice bag in place.

"I don't mean any disrespect," he said, "but I think you've been approaching this baseball team the wrong way. The thing is everybody's got their own agenda. That shit isn't gonna change just because you pump up our batting averages every week and tell us how good we are."

"What kind of agenda?"

Ramon sighed. "I'm just talking about this place in general. You gotta be more of a hard-ass around here, strike some fear into people. Gene's gone now. He was the unstable one, the resident asshole.

He kept everybody straight, and then we all came to you with our problems. He was Steinbrenner, you were Torre."

"So you think I oughta be like Steinbrenner?"

Ramon hedged. "Maybe more like Billy Martin. Remember what he said about the secret to managing: always keep the five players who hate your ass away from the five who haven't made up their minds."

"Yeah, and he never lasted anywhere more than a couple of years."

I pulled the trash can over to the fridge and started tossing the old food containers inside. Ramon stood up and moved toward the door. He asked what time I wanted to hook up and drive out to Gene and Joy's house.

"Let's go after lunch. I need to swing by here first. We can stop off and get one of those party trays at Chick-fil-A, take it to Joy and little Gene. I think he likes those nuggets."

Ramon stopped at the door and turned to face me. "I'll meet you here around one."

He fished his keys out of the back pocket of his baseball pants. That's when I told him how I'd given Gene shit about his base running before the ballgame.

"It was the truth," Ramon said. "If he'd scored in that game last spring, we'd have won it. No doubt."

"Yeah, but maybe he stops at third tonight if I keep my mouth shut. Maybe he'd be at home right now with Joy and little Gene."

"Fuck that. Bat man did this to himself. God bless him, but he didn't take care of himself. Ate too much. Drank too much. Took too many pills. Joy said his doctor tried to put him on Advicor, but he wouldn't take it. You were just being a smart manager."

Ramon was a good teammate for trying to lift the blame, but I already had more than guilt on my mind. There'd be consequences to Gene's death, and they probably wouldn't include the naming of a hospital wing after him. It was like the bat man himself had tried to warn me of trouble when he was lying in the dirt with that little smile on his face. He was already gone. I could see it. But he wore that smile like he still had a few surprises in store for all of us.

* * *

I switched off the lights and stepped out into the dark lot where Gene's six Town Cars, two stretches, and brand-new Hummer limo were parked. Ramon had already headed out of the lot in his Explorer. When I heard a car engine approaching from the rear of the building, I assumed he'd forgotten something and was coming back for it.

"Gene Dellorso?"

I'd already slid my key into the door of the 'Vette. The other car idled right behind me, a red Acura NSX. The driver had his arm resting on the open window. Across the arm, he'd leveled off a gun barrel. In the dim light, I couldn't tell what kind exactly. But it was enough to make me back up against the side of my car.

"Who are you?" I asked.

"I asked you first," he said.

I ducked my head a little to get a better look at the guy. He sounded like he could have been a college kid. I couldn't quite make out his face, but I could see he was wearing a Dr. J throwback jersey, the blue Nets model. He had a Yankees cap pulled low on his head. A dark goatee covered his chin.

"Are you the guy I sold the Redskins-Panthers tickets to? Because, listen, I said up front those were partial obstructed view. You got no beef, because I gave you a deal on those things."

The first shot hit me in the stomach. It stung like hell. The next two got me in the chest. Same thing. A nasty burn, but I still had my wits and my legs under me. When I looked down, my Yankees jersey was splattered with yellow paint.

"You fucking asshole. You ruined my jersey."

The next shot hit me in the groin. I didn't feel a thing.

"Fuck you," I said. "I'm wearing a cup."

The next two got me in the arm and the neck. It was really starting to piss me off now. I rushed the window of the car and tried to pry the paintball gun out of the guy's hand.

"Give me that fucking thing, you little shit."

We were going at it when I noticed the guy in the passenger seat; about the same age as the driver, only bulkier and sporting a Joe Namath throwback. He got out of the car and came around behind me. I pulled the gun away from his buddy. But before I could turn around, Joe Willie zapped me on the back of the neck. I don't even remember falling to the ground. Next thing I knew, I was lying on the asphalt with my arm twitching. I couldn't make it stop.

It took a long moment for my head to clear. Both of them were standing over me. The driver had traded the paintball gun for a nine-millimeter. He let it dangle casually at his side. Broadway Joe had his arms crossed, paintball gun in one hand and a little black stun gun in the other. The bad-ass pose wasn't helped by the fact that his attempt at growing a Fu had come in on the patchy side.

It felt like somebody was working on the back of my neck with a blowtorch. My mouth had dried up, and I could barely talk. I sat up and leaned back against the side of my car.

"Looks like you two had a hell of a day at the toy store."

Dr. J shook his head. "A deal's a deal, Dellorso."

"I'm not Dellorso. Gene's dead."

The two of them considered each other, looked back down at me. The big one leveled the paintball gun across his forearm and popped me in the stomach with a couple of shots.

"Next time, it won't be paintballs," the driver said. "Now, where's the fucking bat?"

The burning from the stun gun had spread to my forehead. The paintballs were like a hand job compared to that thing.

Dr. J told me to hand over my keys to the garage.

"Fuck you," I said. "I don't know about any bats."

He tugged on the bill of his cap, let out a sigh, and nodded to his buddy.

The big guy held up the stun gun and pressed its button. *ZEET. ZEET. ZEET.* A little blue streak of lightning danced between the prongs.

"Six hundred thousand volts," the driver said. "They call it the Scorpion Six hundred. It's the most powerful stun gun on the market. My friend here hit a guy with it last week, and we could smell his fucking nut hairs singeing. Honest to God."

Needless to say, I handed over the keys.

The guy in the Namath jersey held the nine on me while the other one went inside and tore the place all to hell.

Fucking Gene. There was no telling what kind of shit he'd gotten himself into. First it was the broken nose, and now this. You try to feel sorry for a guy who drops dead unexpectedly, but it can be hard.

I asked Broadway Joe where he was from.

"I'm not supposed to talk," he said.

"You two are from Jersey, aren't you?"

I leaned back to get a look at the license plate on the Acura. It confirmed my suspicions.

"Nice 'Vette," the guy said. "What is it, a '69?"

I told him it was a '70.

"You got an LT-1 in there?"

"Four-fifty-four," I said.

He looked the car over like he was planning to buy it. "There's a little rust under the door."

"Just what the hell did Gene pull on the two of you?"

"Look," he said. "I don't ask questions. I'm just doing a job here. Nothing personal, okay?"

He seemed like a nice enough guy, kind of a laid-back, power-hitting first baseman type. He would have chatted up base runners, always been in his teammates' corner. You wouldn't have minded having him on your team.

"Fuck!"

Dr. J was clomping toward us. Broadway Joe turned and asked him what was wrong.

He handed the big guy a card. "*That's* Dellorso. This shithead ain't him."

Apparently, he had uncovered one of Gene's six hundred personalized baseball cards that he'd brought back from fantasy camp a couple years earlier. He'd had the limo company's particulars printed up on the back and used them as business cards.

The driver knelt beside me. I could smell sweet liquor on his breath.

"You're not Dellorso."

"If you had listened to begin with, you'd already know that."

"So, who are you?"

"That's not important. What you need to understand is that Gene Dellorso is dead. He no longer roams this earth."

He shook his head. "Come on, who the hell fakes their death anymore? You tell Dellorso he owes his business partner that bat. And we will get said bat one way or the other. If he wants a war, I'll bring a fucking war."

"What fucking bat are you talking about? If you'd give me a little information here, I might be able to help you out."

"You already know plenty," he said. "Just give Dellorso the message."

He stood up and snapped his fingers at the big guy.

"Zap him, Andre."

The guy in the baggy green jersey shrugged in an apologetic way and came at me with the Scorpion. I hopped to my feet like I was going after a dribbler in front of the plate. I turned to run, but the sonuvabitch got me right between the shoulder blades again. When my senses came back to me, I was on my knees with my head against the rear quarter panel of the car. My arm was flapping around like a mackerel.

CHAPTER 4

My apartment hadn't changed much in the seven years I'd lived there: same leather sofa anchoring the line, a recliner flanked out wide. The only updates were electronic. I had a 52-inch Sony high-def in the backfield, hooked up to DIRECTV, DVD, TiVo, PS2, and JBL Invaders with surround sound. A Sega Genesis and Mattel Intellivision were parked nearby for old times' sake.

The building itself was what Gene had always referred to as a human kennel; a beige high-rise populated by short-term renters and transitional people in the military or State Department. They came and went, left behind spotty carpeting and garbage smells in the hallway. But I didn't mind any of that. There was plenty of takeout food in the neighborhood strip centers: Thai, Vietnamese, Chinese, pupusas, and three kinds of rotisserie chicken, two being Guatemalan and one Salvadoran. The building management even laid out fresh cookies every afternoon in the lobby. There was a feel of permanence about the place, never mind that the neighbors came and went every few months. Absent a long-term history with these people, we were all free to assume the best about each other.

I went to the computer in my bedroom as soon as I walked in, checked my Roto team out of habit, and then felt bad about it even though my ace, Johan Santana, had tossed a three-hitter against the Royals. I stared at that happy blue AOL screen, a picture of Saddam Hussein in the news window, washing his underwear in some Iraqi prison cell. The first time the U.S. had gone after Saddam, I was sleeping in a cell and working in a state prison laundry room in Camden, New Jersey.

I wasn't feeling sleepy, and my head was pounding from the run-in with the stun gun. Plus, I had all this shit going through my head, wondering what the hell had just happened at the garage and what I was going to say to Joy about it and what would happen to my business now that Gene wasn't around to pull half the rent at the warehouse.

I started thinking about Gene's bat bag, which I'd left sitting beside the desk at the warehouse, about how I needed the bottle of Vicodin in the side pocket. But I couldn't bring myself to drive back to work to steal a dead man's pills.

"Lily Marie Rice." It had been a while since I'd typed the name into the Google box, and the lone hit came up as it always had before, only it was cached now and dated from August of 1999. According to the website, my mother was a yoga instructor at a drug recovery clinic up in Philadelphia. Her photo was on the staff page, her face fuller than when I'd last seen her, hair shorter, eyes and smile still detached like last time, when all she could talk about was a shallow pool of piss in an empty chicken bucket.

Her bio was short, written in first person. It mentioned her go-around with various narcotics and how she was arrested for embezzlement from the little record company she'd worked for in New Jersey. She made a run for it when the police came to get her. I was at school when it happened, serving out the third grade at Cliffside Park Number 3, but she didn't mention that part of it. She didn't mention the other employers she'd stolen from either. I guess it was because she hadn't been caught.

Below her bio, she wrote about how she'd turned her life around when she discovered yoga and the proper way to breathe, or pranayama. She talked about the stages of breathing, namely the transitions from inhaling to exhaling and back again, how you could train yourself to pause. The pauses were important, the *abhyantara kumbhaka* and the *bahya kumbhaka,* because if you learned to lengthen them, you could control your *prana,* or vital life energy. She said she was working on a book about this subject.

All of this had sounded like bullshit the first time I read it. But then we were facing this left-handed pitcher one night that I couldn't get a beat on for the life of me (three strikeouts in three ABs). So, I came up in the eighth with the tying and go-ahead runs on second and third. Fell behind 0-2 on a couple of sliders, and decided, what the fuck. I stepped out, took a few breaths, concentrated on the pauses, stepped back in the box, and hit the next pitch off the cock of the bat for a double. I was a convert. After that, I read everything I could find on the Internet about this breathing stuff.

I'd check from time to time to see if my mother had ever finished that book. I Googled, People Searched, checked Amazon, but nothing. Just the one cached find from the little clinic in Philly.

I stayed in Cliffside with my uncle Phil after my mother got arrested for embezzlement, went back to her after she was released, and then wound up with Phil for good after she stabbed her boyfriend. The boyfriend's name was Nolan Noons, but he went by Nolan Nada. My mother was managing his band, trying to get them gigs in the city. She said they were the next Gang of Four, but they weren't, and something happened, and Nolan got drunk one night, and when he passed out, she took a steak knife and opened a vein in his arm.

I was ten around that time, and we were living in Nolan's dead mother's house in Edgewater. Nolan's screaming woke me up, and he went running out of the house, yelling "crazy bitch" over and over. It was funny how a flesh wound caused him to drop the British accent he'd adopted.

My mother came and got me out of bed. She'd given me speed a couple times before so I could stay up with her. She told me she never liked being the only person awake when it was dark. If there was no boyfriend, the duty became mine.

She said the pill was a vitamin. "It's gonna speed up your blood a little, but don't worry."

The night she stabbed Nolan, we sat up watching these home movies she'd found in Nolan's closet. She flashed them on a blank wall and placed this old Sinatra album on the turntable. Sinatra and The Stooges. That was my mother's world of music. My only hint that anything lay between those two realities was a Johnny Cash album of Nolan's. Any time he and my mother went out and left me alone, I'd play "Folsom Prison Blues" until that chuck-a-chuck beat got stuck in my head.

The home movies showed Nolan's family during a trip to Florida when he was a kid, a dull-looking kid at that, not the sham punk with the glued hair and the dirty sport coat with the green T-shirt underneath. He and his parents and sister had seen a Dodgers-Yankees spring training game, gone to Cape Canaveral, an ice cream stand, and then a broad white beach.

"What a fucking phony," my mother said. "The perfect family on their perfect trip to California."

"That's Florida," I said. "They don't have spring training in California."

She looked at the sunny images on the wall, squinting as if there was a haze. Her voice was sad and slurred when she glanced back down at me. "You're lucky," she said. "Everyone likes you. You could get away with fucking murder."

She closed her mouth tightly as if it hurt to say this, then she reached out for her cigarettes on the coffee table and asked me to turn off the stereo. Somehow, she hadn't noticed that the record had finished playing. Nolan's dull needle swayed and bumped in an empty vinyl groove.

My mother was thin and dark-haired, and she had long bangs that framed her face. I'd heard her mention a few times that she wanted to get a nose job. I realize now that she always thought she was ugly, but she never lacked for guitar players. For a long time, I thought she worked at a doctor's office, even when she was gone overnight. It was Uncle Phil who told me about the particulars of her life, how she'd stripped and worked at massage parlors in the city giving hand jobs. He didn't tell me any of it in a disrespectful way, and not until I was seventeen, working for him and playing on his bar's softball team. He owned Phil's Club Level Bar in Cliffside Park, and he also ran a sub-book for some guys out of the city.

"Your mother was always a wild child. I guess we both were cut from the same cloth, you know. Brothers and sisters, they're a lot more alike than kids and parents."

We were riding in his used black 911, him checking the rearview mirror, paranoid as hell, even in the middle of the day. He drove down a side street, just to make sure we weren't being followed. It was a regular move of his, only this time he parked at the curb instead of doubling back at the next street. He lowered the volume on the Blaupunkt. Kurtis Blow was singing "The Breaks."

"What the fuck?" I asked. "Aren't we going to the batting cages?"

"Nah, forget that. We gotta go see Lily. She's been asking about you."

I felt a tremor of unease. "Where is she?"

Phil stalled, turned up the sleeves on his Mets jersey to show his biceps. The jersey was the gray road model with Mookie Wilson's number on the back. He'd gotten it at Manny's Baseball Land, one of our two favorite stores in the world, the other being Gerry Cosby at the Garden.

"She's in the hospital. But here's the thing. It's not a regular hospital. It's for when you got problems with. . ."

He ran his fingers through his hair, searched for the right words.

"You're trying to say she's in a mental hospital, right?"

Phil frowned. "Yeah, something like that. I just wanna warn you, though. I went to see her a few days ago. She's been through this therapy. Not like they gave Nicholson in *Cuckoo's Nest,* but still a motherfucker of a thing, all right. So, I just wanna prepare you."

You know what you know, and my mother had never been around all that much in the first place. Wherever we lived or stayed, she was always good at talking up the neighbors or the landlord, finding me somewhere to stay when she was off managing a band or doing whatever it was she was doing. I slept on other people's sofas or with their own kids, played with their toys and ate their food and felt the tension build when my mother stayed a day longer than she'd promised, or maybe two days, or maybe a week. People had their limits, even when you were a likeable sort, and my presence eventually became a test of their kindness.

She was different in the hospital, like something had been drained out of her. It was hard to look at her face. She was calm and at ease, but not the same person. She asked if I remembered the time we were driving to Baltimore in the middle of the night and I asked to go to the bathroom.

"I made you pee in an empty KFC bucket," she said. "You wanted to go inside to the bathroom, but I wouldn't let you."

The story didn't ring a bell. I glanced at Phil and shrugged. We were sitting at a table in the hospital cafeteria. The place was empty except for a couple of nurses at a nearby table. The soda machine's motor was humming, and the air smelled like roast beef.

Phil reached over and touched my mother's hand. "I think he's got my memory," Phil said. "Can't remember a fucking thing."

He glanced at his watch. I knew he was aching for a cigarette. I was hoping he'd wrap things up soon. I didn't know what to say.

"I want him to remember." She looked at me and leaned forward. "I want you to remember."

Her sudden attention was strange and oppressive. I couldn't remember her ever focusing so intently on me before. She had always given that attention to guys like Nolan.

All I could do was shrug. "I don't remember peeing in a bucket."

She reached out and touched my arm. I had to fight my impulse to pull away.

"I'm sorry," she said.

It seemed so important to her that the truth of it didn't really matter anymore—remembering or not remembering. So, I nodded.

"It's okay," I said. "A bucket's not such a bad place to take a leak."

Phil and I didn't talk about my mother after that day. He took me straight from the hospital to Modell's and bought me a new pair of Adidas cleats. Then we went to Manny's and looked through the jerseys and caps. I wanted a Yankees jersey with Guidry's number on it, but Phil just couldn't abide. He was a loyal Mets fan.

Phil and my mother were turned loose at early ages, their parents killed in a car wreck after getting back together following a divorce that involved restraining orders and the like. For his part, Phil fit the gambler mold. He lived to acquire the best of everything: women, cars, televisions, all the accoutrements. He bought his clothes in the city at this place on East Sixtieth. He sent me in one day to pick up a couple of suits he'd bought, and Al Pacino was in the store, standing there in front of a mirror looking all slouchy and wrinkled and cool even though he was wearing this black jacket with the tag still hanging from the sleeve.

Phil's way of living was easy to accept. I got to drive his cars, which he acquired and traded about every six months (used 911s and BMWs were a staple), had my own room, TV, and Intellivision in his apartment overlooking the river. I stayed out late with older girls and hit leadoff on the bar's softball team. Everybody I hung around with was older than me. I had no use for kids my own age. They didn't know shit about anything.

I embraced the lifestyle and loved it, but there was an uneasiness, the way that Phil was always looking over his shoulder. This sort of life was real. It was out in the open and could be put to the test at any moment. It gave me this feeling that something heavy was always about to drop on us.

The cops came to the bar with a search warrant one time. It was a Sunday morning, and me and Phil were in the back manning the phones for the NFL bettors. All of a sudden we heard a fire truck's siren and ran to the front to see what was happening. Smoke was pouring out from under Phil's 911.

"Fucking assholes," he said.

I made a move for the door, but he held me back.

"But your fucking car's on fire."

"It ain't on fire," he said. "It's a trick, a fucking smoke bomb. Cops must have a search warrant. They want me to come outside before I can get rid of everything. They think I'm a fucking idiot."

He didn't have to say another word. We both headed to the back room and started drowning flash paper in the trash can full of water that always sat beside Phil's desk. Eight grand in book washed away. The cops came in and didn't find one useful thing.

Wily as he could be, Phil made some lousy bets of his own. To make up for them, he didn't always keep his books balanced. He grumbled about the small cut that he was getting from the big guys, and he took chances playing off bets when he was sure a team wouldn't cover the spread. The older I got, the more often I warned him to be careful.

I was twenty when he fucked up for the last time. The guys he worked for came and got him at the bar on a Sunday. I would have been there with him, answering the phones, but I'd gone down the shore with this girl I'd met in the bar. She was twenty-seven. I came back to the bar that night, surprised to find it locked up. I took out my keys and went inside. Blood was smeared on the floor in the back room. The file cabinets were turned over, flash paper scattered like leaves, the alley door propped open by an Easton softball bat. Phil's Mets jacket lay amid the wreckage, a soft pile of blue satin. I called the cops and sat there with my hands shaking. And I didn't think to drown the paper.

Phil's body never surfaced. The cops rang me up on numbers charges, tried to get me to talk, but I wasn't giving any names. I couldn't. Phil had never let me know that much. He'd done good by me where that was concerned, because I was angry, angry enough to turn over whoever had killed him. I took my year and felt that I'd deserved it. But not for running numbers. Phil was dead, and my mother had bounced from prison to the mental hospital and then back to prison again on another set of embezzlement charges. I suppose it was their job to look after me, but I believed they had been mine to watch over. And though I came to realize that I wasn't all that much like either one of them, that my cloth was somehow different, less needy of recognition, money, expensive suits, or the next Gang of Four, I also understood that they were in my veins, a place where behavior didn't matter but regret chugged on and on like the train in that Johnny Cash song. People were drinking coffee somewhere and enjoying their freedom, but it'd never be my mother and Phil. I had a feeling I was going to ride that train one day, but I didn't always feel too good about it.

CHAPTER 5

More than anything, Joy looked shell-shocked. She was dressed for company, even though no one was there except Tommy Pumpkin and a blond woman named Katherine who lived down the street. Gene had once remarked to me that Katherine's implants looked twice as good as Joy's. Considering the circumstances, I tried to be respectful and not make any comparisons when Ramon and I arrived.

Joy gave Ramon a long hug, then cleared a space on the kitchen island so I could set down the Chick-fil-A tray. Someone had already dropped off a honey-baked ham and a Bundt cake. The house was cold, just like always. Gene had complained that he slept in a hooded sweatshirt because Joy kept the thermostat at 65 year round.

I felt it was best to leave Joy the option of a greeting. And so we stood there for an uncomfortable moment before she finally made a move to hug me.

"I'm sorry, Joy. I don't know what to say. You have my deepest condolences."

She patted my back, made a little noise in the back of her throat. And then, just as I was about to let go, she pulled me tight and started to sob. Ramon and Katherine were facing me, looking uncomfortable. Katherine was wearing a white blouse. And seeing how Joy had her chest pressed against me, I couldn't help making the comparison, and Gene had actually been wrong. Katherine's implants were bigger, but Joy's felt natural and were in better proportion with the rest of her body. I had to grant Funderburk this one unspoken compliment: he did good by Joy.

Ramon and Katherine excused themselves to the den, where Tommy had been planted on the couch watching *Bob the Builder* with little Gene. Little Gene had this cardboard box with a hole cut into the top of it. Every time I came over there he was sitting in that box with his head poking out the top of it, looking like Rommel in a standoff with the television.

Joy finally let go and went over to the sink to touch up her face with a paper towel. "I was so fucking pissed at him last night. And I don't even know why."

"Don't beat yourself up about it," I said.

"I'm a fucking bitch." She said it in a resigned way, like she'd really given it some thought.

"You're in shock right now," I said. "I know the feeling."

She batted her eyes. Based on her curious expression, I'd failed to say anything worth a damn.

Joy had an unusual beauty about her. It was hard to get at beneath the makeup and clothes. She was like one of those cities that redoes its waterfront, gutting the strip clubs and gin mills and bringing in the boring chain stores to take their place. You can still tell there was something there once that was worth seeing, something more interesting and complicated, something with a history. Gene told me Joy had danced at a club in Philadelphia when she was younger, but only for a short time, right after her sister died from the overdose. I could still see that person in her, and I didn't mind it at all.

"He didn't want to dance," she said. "I should have let it go. I should have just let it be. It might have been the stress, you know. That and his weight and the cholesterol. He wasn't healthy. You know, his father died when he was forty-eight. That always worried me. But Jesus, Gene was only thirty-five."

"It's funny with the heart," I said. "You never know what's going on in there."

"I feel like it's bad karma or something," she said. "I didn't appreciate him, and now I'm getting what I deserve."

"Karma doesn't actually work that way. It's more about what you do throughout the whole season. Your life, you know."

She gave me a curious look.

"I read that on the Internet somewhere. It's what the Hindus believe."

"Don't they worship cows?"

"I couldn't speak to that, actually. I wasn't reading too carefully."

I'd never told anyone about my mother's yoga career and how I'd become interested in some different things on account of it. And now didn't seem to be the time to start. Joy fixed her eyes on me for a moment, puzzled.

"Only thing Gene ever looked at on the Internet was porn."

The kitchen was nice, the kind of room that actually made me think twice about apartment living: white cabinets, red paint on the wall, cereal boxes lined up along the counter like classic books—Frosted Flakes, Froot Loops, Honey Nut Cheerios, Cocoa Pebbles, Cap'n Crunch. Gene had bitched about having to brush six coats of that red paint on the wall to make it look even. And even after all that, Joy had still busted his balls about it looking splotchy. Every memory I had pertaining to those two involved one or the other being pissed about something.

I'd decided not to mention the excitement at the warehouse with the guys in the Acura. Odds were, she was as clueless as me about the bat business. It was just something else to upset her. At this point, I felt there were more important things to consider.

"I was wondering, Joy, not to be distasteful or anything like that, but did Gene have a will?"

She was peeling the cellophane back from the Chick-fil-A platter. "I was thinking about that last night," she said. "We'd talked about it, you know—making some plans after little Gene was born. I was worried about something happening to the both of us, and then what would happen to little Gene. I wouldn't leave him with my family, the bunch of fucks. And then Gene's dad is gone and his mother, I think she's got some kind of premature Alzheimer's. It's scary to think that all he has now is me. He's a heartbeat away from being a fucking orphan."

I was worried she might start crying again, but I felt the need to express the ideas I'd been turning over in my mind while I was straightening up the mess at the warehouse that morning.

"I'm just saying that if you want me to take care of things with the limo service for a while, I'd be happy to do it. Understand that I'm not trying to take over the business. I'd just like to keep things together, at least until you might want to look at other options. I'm sure that Gene would want the best for both you and the people who worked for him."

I could tell by her expression that she'd given the business no thought. And then I felt bad for bringing it up so suddenly. It was selfish and hasty on my part.

"You know what I'd like," she said. "If you and Ramon would be pallbearers and ask some of the other guys at work, or from the team, to be pallbearers, too. I think Gene would like that, and besides, Tommy can't do it because of his back. He thinks the workman's comp commission has been watching him."

I told her it would be an honor. That was right about the time Ramon started screaming in the living room. It sounded like he'd been shot.

"Ahhh, motherfucker! He bit me!"

Ramon was standing beside little Gene's box, doubled over and clutching his hand. Little Gene had taken cover inside his makeshift bunker, pulling the cardboard hatch shut. Joy marched over there and knocked on the top of the box.

"Gene Dellorso, you come out of there right now. I'm going to get the hot sauce, mister."

"You should call that kid Jaws," Ramon said. "He almost left me with a nub."

I pulled Ramon into the kitchen and told him to calm down. "The kid's going through a rough time. Show some fucking compassion."

"Look at those teeth marks," Ramon said. "That's where I grip my two-seamer. That's my out pitch, man."

"What the fuck did you do to make him bite you?"

"I didn't do nothing. We had his little army men set up on top of the box. I went after his bazooka guy with my bayonet man, and he chomped down on me. Violation of the fucking Geneva Convention, if you ask me."

Joy came in and got the hot sauce. It was parked in the same cabinet as the hydrogen peroxide, as if the two went hand in hand. She left the peroxide and a Band-Aid with me and Ramon, then headed through the door to take care of little Gene.

Ramon had a concerned look on his face. "Oh, man," he said. "That was Texas Pete with habaneros. She's gonna light that kid up."

"You shouldn't have made such a big deal out of it," I said. "Joy's a big believer in this corporal punishment shit. She listens to that guy Dobson on the radio every day."

Ramon was looking like he regretted the commotion he'd stirred up with his screaming; although now that I'd gotten a glance at the puncture wounds, I couldn't blame him. Little Gene had some serious fangs on him.

Ramon flexed his index finger. "You got any more of those Vikes?"

I lied and told him I was out. Truth was, I'd broken into Gene's bat-bag stash that morning. This was, after I'd spent half the night with a bag of frozen peas pressed against my bad knee.

"Quit worrying about your two-seamer for a minute," I said. "You and me, we're gonna be pallbearers at Gene's funeral."

"Oh, yeah?"

"Yeah, and Joy wants me to get the rest of the pallbearers from work. Do you know how many they usually have at these things?"

Ramon thought it over. "Nine?"

"No, that's a jury."

"Well, it's gotta be at least eight for Gene. He was pushing a deuce-fifty when he went down."

"I think you can have honorary pallbearers, too. Not everyone has to carry. Maybe I'll just ask everybody on the team. We'll have some honoraries."

"I think they'll be down with that," Ramon said. "We'll do it as a team. Gene would've wanted that."

"Gene would've wanted a hand job from an unlicensed masseuse," I said. "Trust me, he never gave this kind of thing any thought."

Ramon took a moment to consider my summation of Gene's true wants. It made him frown.

We could hear little Gene crying and screaming *"No, no, no!"* out in the living room.

"That poor fucking kid," Ramon said. "Losing his father like that, it's gotta suck."

I didn't say anything. As cold as it sounds, I couldn't help thinking that maybe little Gene had caught a break in all this by not having to grow up with the bat man for a father. A man like Geno carried the kinds of burdens that could stunt a kid's growth. Now little Gene was free of all that: the weight and the clouds. He'd never have to put those things down in the future, never have to climb out of his box and run from it all. Rest in peace: that was a nice thought for big Gene. But truth be told, little Gene could now live in peace.

CHAPTER 6

Me and Ramon were the first to arrive at the church for the funeral. We sat in my car with the AC running and some old De La Soul coming through the speakers from Ramon's iPod, drinking vanilla lattes and reading the *New York Post* (we always went with two copies so we could discuss the sports pages as we read them).

Ramon was the only one I'd told about the ambush in the parking lot. We'd been trying to figure things out for the past few days.

"Maybe the guy was speaking code," Ramon said. "Maybe the word *bat* meant something else."

I let the paper rest against the steering wheel, grabbed my aviators off the dash, and slid them over my eyes. "I think where Gene was concerned, a bat meant a bat. He was a pretty literal guy."

"You're probably right," Ramon said. "What was the fucking deal with him and those bats, anyway?"

"Joy had this theory," I said. "It involved the size of a certain appendage. She floated it one night when she and Gene were fighting. Needless to say, he didn't like it much."

Ramon nodded.

"Whatever shit he might have been involved in, all I know is that he paid his end of the rent every month. It was usually two weeks late, but nevertheless. Now that he's gone, we're all fucked. The businesses. The team. The whole empire, as it is. Unless . . ."

Ramon took off his thick Dolce & Gabbana wraparound frames. "Unless what?"

"Unless Joy keeps the limo business going."

"You think she'd do it?"

"I floated the idea. I told her I'd handle the day-to-day operations."

"Did she go for it?"

"She never said. That's when she asked me about the pallbearer thing."

Ramon sighed, shook his head, and looked out the side window, up at the stone facing of the Ridge Front Bible Church. The place was huge, like a government compound. They even had a parking deck and an on-site coffee shop. That's where we'd bought the lattes.

"Fucking Gene," Ramon said. "I liked the guy and all, but he could really be a pain in the ass."

"He still can be," I said.

As funerals go, it was not a stellar affair. The trouble started before the service with the whole pallbearer thing. Some of the honoraries felt slighted. One of Gene's drivers, Artie, got right in my face about it in the church parking lot.

"I've been driving longer than that cocksucker Jerry Burns. You should hear some of the shit he used to say behind Gene's back. He's a fucking backstabber."

Jerry was only two cars down from us, standing amid a pool of Gene's drivers. He turned his head like he'd caught a scent of trouble, and then he marched over to join the fray, already wagging his finger at Artie.

"Fuck you, Arthur, you fucking boozehound."

He gave Artie a shove, sending him against the backside of a Mercedes SUV. I stepped between the two, grabbing the front of Jerry's no-wrinkle dress shirt. He was really proud of those shirts, a Lands' End Internet exclusive, as he liked to point out.

Artie straightened himself, tugged at his lapels. He was a blocky guy, probably a 46 short. He loved barreling into second basemen and shortstops, even when there was no need to break up a double play.

I told the two of them to ease up. "This is a goddamn funeral. Show some fucking respect."

Jerry was nodding his head, gazing over my shoulder at Artie. "You just wait, motherfucker. This ain't over between us. We've had some shit to shore up for a long fucking time. And the account is coming due."

"I ain't going nowhere," Artie said. "And I can tell you another thing. Geno's gonna be spinning in that fucking box when he realizes you got your mitts on him, you backstabbing cocksucker."

Jerry made a lunge, but I already had my feet set. I squatted down, picked him up at the waist, and moved him back into the midst of the other drivers, who, by now, had migrated toward the trouble.

"You'd probably drop the fucking casket," Jerry said. "That's why Rice never plays you, you dumb shit. You got a glove like a fucking pizza pan."

I set Jerry down and backed away. Ramon and Benny, another of Gene's guys, started massaging Jerry's shoulders like he was resting between rounds of a bout.

"Listen the fuck up," I said, "all of you. We got twenty minutes to get our shit together. Now, whatever problems you got between yourselves, it's time to forget about them."

Ramon and Benny looked at one another. Benny nodded, granting Ramon the floor.

"Here's the thing," Ramon said. "It's got to do with the Roto league. Jerry, here, has a grievance he wants to take up with Artie."

"Fuck you," Artie said. He was standing on my flank as if he expected me to be his chief ally. "Jerry's got no beef, and you got no beef. You're just looking in the rearview mirror, waiting for my Roto Ferrari to plow its way up your ass."

Jerry went after Artie again, but Ramon and Benny held him back. At that point, Jerry resorted to taking a kick at Arthur. In the process, his shoe flew off and landed on the trunk of a Lexus, setting off the car alarm. Artie was smiling through the whole thing, which wasn't helping matters.

"This is not the place," I shouted. "But let's hear it out. I'll make the ruling."

Considering the fifteen-hundred-dollar pool and my status as league commissioner, I decided it was best to vet the matter and put it behind us. I pointed to Ramon. "Give me the details."

Ramon stepped forward and clasped his hands in front of his chest in a thoughtful way. "Okay, Commish, here goes. Artie was in the garage two days ago, when his sports beeper informs him that the Sox had put Pedro on the DL with shoulder stiffness."

"Jerry offered the fucking trade," Artie said. "Not me. Let's just put that on the table from the start."

"That was a month ago," Jerry said. "I didn't know Pedro was going down."

Mercifully, the car alarm stopped blaring. The only thing left to give me a headache was all the yelling. As best I could piece things together, Jerry had previously offered to trade Jim Edmonds to Artie's team in exchange for Pedro. Artie's response was, "Go fuck yourself, you dumb shit." But then Artie got the fresh information about Pedro on his beeper, at which point he called Jerry on his cell phone. Jerry, who was on his run to Dulles Airport, was not privy to the information about Pedro's sore wing. Artie told Jerry he had reconsidered the trade and wanted to accept. Jerry, of course, closed the deal.

"And now," Ramon said, "Jerry believes he was misled and dealt damaged goods. His request is that you overturn the trade and issue a stern rebuke to Artie."

"Rebuke this," Artie said, grabbing his cock. "He offered the fucking trade, not me."

"You better watch your mouth," Ramon said. "This kind of shit is no good for the league. It's sneaky."

"So get a fucking sports pager." Artie pulled back his suit jacket and patted the little device hooked to his belt. "Hundred fifty bucks, you cheap shit. I'm running a first-class organization, and you two are like the fucking Kansas City Royals."

"I was on a fucking pickup at Dulles," Jerry said. "There's gotta be a grace period. ESPN didn't even have the news yet."

The church bells started up, momentarily drowning out the argument. The September sun was flashing its big, hopeful face over everything, and a bead of sweat was working its way down my back. Everybody was looking at me. I could see Artie's point. He'd gone to the trouble of investing in the beeper, unlike the others. Then again, the deal was sneaky as hell, and it was Artie to boot. Artie, who'd smacked up one of Gene's Town Cars when he was drunk and then busted out of the rehab place Gene had gotten him into. Artie, who was always looking for an advance on his paycheck and who'd been the prime suspect when money and valuables had gone missing from the lockers at work. Artie, who'd been so coked up two seasons ago that he tried to tag up and score from third on a pop-up to the fucking shortstop.

"Arthur," I said. "You gotta give him Edmonds back."

Artie gyrated like he'd been shot. "Oh, that is so fucking ridiculous. So, I get penalized for being informed, for being competent and trying too hard. Well, if that's my only crime, then let me be guilty."

"Look it," I said, "I appreciate the effort with the pager. You just can't use it to deal damaged goods. And you better turn that fucking thing off before we go into the church. We don't need to know about Barry Bonds's knees during the eulogy."

Now that we had the Roto matter straightened out, at least for the moment, I tried to turn everyone's attention to the funeral and our few simple tasks.

"Who's got the hat?"

Ramon and Benny exchanged glances again.

"Fuck," I said. "What happened?"

Benny shrugged. "I'm sorry, Skip. I couldn't find it. I looked through the equipment bag, went back to the field, called the hospital, the ambulance service. It's gone, vanished."

The hat in question was Gene's, his beloved Yankees cap, autographed under the bill by his hero Graig Nettles. Joy thought it would be a nice touch to lay it beside Gene in his casket.

"Maybe we could bury him with Big Red," Artie said. "He loved that fucking bat."

Ramon snorted. "The fuck you say. I've hit five dingers with that bat. That thing is team property. Gene would have wanted it that way."

"I think I may have a solution," Benny said. He reached into the backseat of the Town Car and brought out a Sports Authority bag. Therein lay a brand-new Yankees cap. Benny had taken it upon himself to sign Graig Nettles's name under the bill with a Sharpie.

"I don't think anyone would notice," Benny said.

Artie took the cap and looked at the signature. "You misspelled his fucking name, you imbecile. It's Graig with a *G*, not a *C*."

Benny frowned but didn't say a word. In his heyday, he would have kicked Artie's ass. It would have been "motherfucker" this and "cocksucker" that. But after Benny's marriage broke up over several dalliances with female limo customers, he went scooters for a while and subsequently into counseling. Counseling led to 50 milligrams of Paxil daily, which led to a calmer, not to mention fatter, Benny. Seeing how he was our left-handed closer, I sort of missed the old angry and lean Benny.

"We got no choice," I said. "The hat goes in. At this point, we're doing it as much for Joy as Gene."

"God bless his soul," Benny said.

My solution to the pallbearer problem did not please Joy. We had fourteen guys carrying that box down the steps of the church. They were stepping all over each other's feet. Artie almost took a header into the minister. I was trailing the casket, and Joy was standing at the bottom of the steps among the other mourners. She looked up at me and mouthed the words "What the fuck?"

Gene's guys handled the driving duties, ferrying Joy and the rest of the family to the grave site. I put Benny in charge of Gene's mother, and I assigned Willie to drive Joy, little Gene, and Joy's parents. I figured Willie was the least likely of Gene's guys to say something inappropriate. He was polite, respectful, and always impeccably dressed. The ladies loved him.

We all stopped by the house after the graveside business, paid our respects to the family, and went back to the garage to have our own little farewell to Gene. Ramon and Jerry picked up the beer, and me and Benny grabbed the rotisserie chicken. We all sat around the big, messy desk, eating and drinking and watching the Yankees pound the Orioles.

"That funeral was a fucking travesty," Jerry said.

I raised my Heineken and agreed. "The minister didn't even know Gene. He just talked that shit about fathers and husbands and then he started making his sales pitch. 'Are you saved? Do you know God on a personal level?' Nobody wants to hear that shit at a time like this. These ministers, all they care about is their building fund. Did anybody see the fucking gymnasium in that place? That parquet floor was plush."

Jerry noted Gene's appearance. "I don't even think that was Gene. It didn't look like him. The skin and all gave me the creeps."

Artie agreed. "I don't want people staring at me. And no ministers. You guys have a party and bring in some hookers and a cover band."

"Yeah, we'll call your bookie," Jerry said. "Get him to foot the bill. He'll be crying louder than any of us."

"I don't have a fucking bookie," Artie said. "I use an offshore place. Bookies are a thing of the past. They're like fucking shoe cobblers."

I asked Artie what kind of juice he was paying the offshore place.

"Ten percent."

"Yeah, well, I can find you some cobblers who'll give a better fucking deal than that."

"My father used to bet hunches," Benny said. "Played a dime on the Raiders for six straight weeks in 1980. Rode them all the way through the playoffs to the Super Bowl. Scored twelve grand."

"So, what'd he blow it on?" Artie asked.

Benny smiled. "A stripper named Sylvie."

"Must have been a helluva lap dance," Artie said.

"He ran off with her," Benny said. "Left the family. Not a good hunch, though. They only stayed married for three years."

"Thirty-six months," I said. "That's the fucking Mendoza line of marriages."

"Where'd you hear that?" Jerry asked.

"It's Theresa's theory."

"You mean that sexy redhead with the southern accent?" Artie said. "That voice of hers, it does something to me."

Benny set his beer on the floor, leaned forward in his seat. "I'm gonna tell all of you something. It might change the way you look at me, but I think I've got some wisdom to share here. It's no secret I had some problems for a while after my marriage went to shit. But I got into therapy and started taking this medication. One of the side effects has been that I just don't have the same kind of drive anymore."

"Yeah, we've been watching your fastball," Ramon said.

Ramon was still pissed about a couple of saves Benny had blown back in the spring. True to his new form, the hefty lefty didn't give a shit about Ramon's comment. In the old days, they would have gone round and round about who had the better stuff and who had gotten more breaks or been squeezed by a shitty ump.

"This ain't about baseball," Benny said. "It's sex. I'm talking about sex. I just don't have that drive anymore. I don't want to go sticking my cock everywhere."

"Holy shit," Artie said. "I'm sorry."

"Yeah," I said. "Maybe you need to lower the dosage on that stuff."

Benny just laughed. "I don't mind. In fact, it's the best thing that ever happened to me. Before, all I ever thought about was getting laid. I wanted to screw every woman I met. Now it's different. I'm enjoying life. I can take a trip to the beach and enjoy the sunset because I'm not trying to bang the woman on the sand next to me. I can enjoy a meal because I'm not thinking about how to get in the waitress's pants."

He'd been enjoying his share of meals, all right. He was pushing Gene territory in the girth department. I'd been worried he was going to snap a hammy on the pitcher's mound.

"Get this," he said. "I even got on the Internet and tracked down my old man. He's still up in Philly. He's got prostate cancer, living at the VA hospital. I went to see him last weekend."

This made us all go quiet for a moment. The only sound was Jim Palmer on the television, analyzing a pitching situation and then comparing it to something that had happened when he played twenty-five years ago.

I asked Benny about his father's prognosis, and he said it wasn't good. Benny was planning to move his father down from Philly and put him up in his apartment. He'd drive him to his chemo treatments at the local VA. "I want my kids to meet their grandfather," he said.

"Honey." Willie spoke the word with certainty. "You should give him honey from the local bees."

"Is that what they do in El Salvador?" Benny asked.

"No, my massage instructor told me. There are no documented cases of cancer among beekeepers. The bee pollen is a highly concentrated source of vitamins and minerals."

Willie was studying to become a massage therapist, though he seemed also to be learning quite a bit about natural remedies for a variety of ailments. At various times, he had counseled coworkers on issues ranging from sinus infections to irregular bowel movements. He'd also brought in his table on a few occasions and worked on some of the drivers. Lower-back issues were the bane of the limo business.

Willie wrote down a whole list of vitamins, minerals, and other natural supplements for Benny to feed his father. "If he won't take it," he said, "crush it and stir it in his beer."

I gathered up the chicken carcasses and empty beer bottles and tossed everything in the big metal trash can. Gene's bat bag, along with Big Red, was still sitting beside the desk. His bottle of Vicodin was in my pocket, seven pills to be exact. I'd planned on slipping the bottle back in the bat bag and taking the bag to Joy. But maybe it wasn't such a violation of the dead to take a few pills. My knee wasn't all that bad, but I needed to slow my brain down for a little while, sort through all of these problems concerning the business. After all, it concerned Joy and little Gene as well.

"One last thing," Ramon said.

We were all standing now, moving toward the door. Everyone stopped and waited to hear what Ramon had to say.

"We gotta get some black armbands for our jerseys," he said. "We gotta dedicate this season to Gene."

As much time as I wasted playing, watching, talking, and reading about sports, I'd never been too big on the notion of dedicating a game, or a season, to someone who'd checked out prematurely. I thought it reflected the basest instincts of a competitor. It was, after all, just a game. And to trivialize someone's life in that manner seemed more a dishonor than a distinction. More than that, it was a selfish act to use someone else's misfortune to motivate yourself in a meaningless competition.

Having said all of that, it's necessary to point out that I was the first one to second Ramon's suggestion. I suppose I was caught up in the moment.

"Fuckin' A," I said. "We're gonna win this trophy for the bat man."

Fueled with beer, chicken, shock, and loss, we gathered in a circle and put our hands together. For one time, at least, we were all on the same page, perfect teammates. Ramon led the call, just as he had on the one occasion that Gene had hit a walk-off home run.

What time is it?!
Gene time!
What time is it?!
Gene time!
Who's the man?!
The bat man!
Who's the man?!
The bat man!

I screwed around until everyone had left, making sure that I was the last one in the place, and then I sat down in the office chair with a Heineken. I washed down a few painkillers, switched off the television, and enjoyed the quiet, only the quivering fluorescent lights humming above me.

One thing about Gene is that he didn't want to die. The thought of it scared the shit out of him. A couple years back, when the Beltway snipers were running around the area picking off people as they pumped gas and shopped for groceries, Gene refused to go out by himself to fuel up the limos. I had to ride with him and perform the honors. While I was outside pumping the gas, he'd be slumped down as far as he could go in the driver's seat, telling me to hurry the fuck up. He even rolled down the window this one time and advised me to walk in circles while the tank was filling up.

"Jesus Christ," he said, "at least make 'em hit a moving target."

I was smoking a cigarette and shaking my head, enjoying the touch of a warm October sun. We were actually in first place that season until the league canceled the fall playoffs because of the sniper threat.

"If it's my time," I told Gene, "then it's my time. I mean, what the fuck can I do?"

He turned down the radio, glanced over his shoulder, checking the Target parking lot across the street. "I'm glad you recognize your mortality," he said, "but I plan on taking all precautions necessary. And you remember that, too. If I'm ever hooked up to any machines at the hospital and Joy starts talking about unplugging them, you better fucking stop her. I don't care if I gotta breathe with a machine or can't wipe my own ass. I'm hanging on until the bitter fucking end."

"That's very unselfish of you," I told him. "I'll bring you a box of baby wipes to the hospital."

He wagged his finger at me. "Just make sure they got aloe."

Gene could never recognize his own end in that of others. It was something that I'd come to understand long ago, back when I found my uncle's Mets jacket lying in the back room of the bar, his blood splattered on the floor around it. I could get shot, beat in the head with a baseball bat, or go crazy like my mother. That kind of shit happened every day. Anything and everything could be taken away from you. It was an understanding you carried with you at all times, just like a wallet. Of course, Geno had always kept his money wrapped with a rubber band.

CHAPTER 7

I kept my word to Joy, overseeing things with the limo business for the next few days. There was an outpouring of sympathy from the community at large, flowers and cards rolling into the garage from customers, the chamber of commerce, the Kiwanis Little League where Gene and I had sponsored the double-A Yankees, and even from the Thai Touch Spa. All the girls on the staff had signed a greeting card. They even included a 10 percent discount coupon for massage services, which Artie quickly slipped into his suit pocket.

With Gene gone, there was a little more juggling to do in terms of handling phone calls and staying on top of drivers' logs and whatnot. But I found the added responsibility was pretty manageable. After all, Gene had never exactly been a workhorse. I'd always spent a good deal of time covering the phones for him when he was out roaming around.

Ramon showed up late in the day, after his computer class at the community college. He had his laptop satchel slung over his shoulder and an Armani Exchange shopping bag clutched in his hand. He set his stuff beside the desk and dropped an envelope in front of me.

"Those the tickets?" I asked.

Ramon shrugged. "Not as good as we wanted. Section one-twenty-two."

"That's on the side."

"Yeah, but second row. I think Celine Dion moves around a lot, anyway."

"I'll have to eat some shit for this. The man wanted floor seats. It's his wife's birthday."

"It's a tough ticket this late," Ramon said. "I had to deal with the godless to get these things."

"Fuck it. I'll have to throw in the limo for free."

We had the garage door open, sun pouring in. A couple of my detailing guys were vacuuming a red Mercedes. They had a Beny Moré tape playing on the boom box. "The Cuban Sinatra," they called him. Moré was singing a bolero in that smooth voice of his. He was one suave motherfucker. I would have paid my own good money to see Moré had he not been dead for the past forty years.

Willie, who'd just gotten back from a downtown run, was rummaging through Ramon's shopping bag. He held up a silky plum-colored shirt.

"I have this in black."

Ramon asked him what size he'd gotten.

"Large," he said. "It's a close fit. I put Band-Aids on my nipples with this one."

"Check out the pinstripe pants," Ramon said. "Nice and slim, keeps it all in proportion."

Ramon turned back in my direction, giving Willie some time to contemplate the new ensemble.

"You heard from Joy?" he asked.

I told him she'd had a meeting with a lawyer. "She said she'd call tomorrow and fill me in on things."

"She still pissed about the pallbearer thing?"

"Yeah, she ripped me a new one. She says we're all gonna burn in hell."

"So, what do you think she'll do about the business?"

"Hard to say. She agreed to let me handle things here, at least until she decides what she wants to do."

"You think you could come up with the dough to buy the limo service?"

"Not in the short term. I've got a criminal record. Banks don't like that sort of thing."

Not that it mattered. Joy called me that night around nine o'clock, crying and scared shitless. I drove out to the house. She met me at the front door with a butcher knife in her hand. She was wearing gym shorts and her pale blue Italia '82 soccer T-shirt. It was very tight and very distracting.

"The only thing they took was one of Gene's bats," she said.

"Who?"

"These two guys. They came into the garage behind me. I didn't see them. I'd just picked up little Gene from his tae kwon do class."

I asked what they looked like. And then I had another thought.

"Little Gene's taking tae kwon do?"

"It's a self-discipline thing," she said. "But these guys, they were wearing jerseys and caps like rapper wannabes. One of them had a pistol and the other had some kind of stun gun."

"It's a Scorpion Six hundred," I said. "We've been introduced."

While we walked to the kitchen, I told Joy about my own encounter with the pair.

"They kept asking about a bat," she said. "I told them Gene kept a closetful in the back bedroom."

"Did they hurt you, or little Gene?"

"No, the big one sat in the living room with me and little Gene while the other one went back there. Apparently, he found what he was looking for."

"Just one bat?" I asked.

"That's all they left with."

I sat down at the breakfast table while Joy mixed a bowl of Frosted Rice Krispies and Honey Nut Cheerios for little Gene. He was in the living room watching a *Veggie Tales* DVD.

"Could I have a bowl of that?" I asked.

"Sure. You want bananas?"

"If it's not too much trouble, that sounds good."

She brought me the bowl of cereal and carried little Gene's out to the living room. When she came back, she went right to the thermostat and throttled up the AC. It was already like a meat locker in the house, condensation forming on the windows just like the freezer at Baskin-Robbins. She sat down across from me.

"A fucking baseball bat," I said. "What kind of bat could be that important?"

Joy lit a Marlboro Light and crossed her legs. "It was one of those old wooden ones that he collected. It was in a frame."

"It must be worth some money," I said.

Joy shrugged. "Yeah, well, that's something I could use right now."

As she went on to explain, the attorney had informed her that Gene had no will and no plan whatsoever for his estate, as it were.

"But you inherit the business, right?"

"Oh, yeah," she said. "I get the whole kingdom, leveraged to the fucking eyeballs."

She turned her chair to the side and crossed her legs. Her Adidas shorts were thigh-length and red. They showed off her legs nicely. God knows Gene focused too much on breasts. Joy's legs were almost perfect.

I tried to look away, to focus on the task at hand. This was important stuff. My businesses were at stake.

"He took out a second loan last year," she said, "unbeknownst to me. Lumped in the house *and* the business."

"Can you manage the payments?"

She laughed, clearly dismissing the thought. "Gene couldn't even fucking manage it. He hadn't made a payment in six months. And you know who inherits that? Me, goddammit. I inherit his fucking shit. Plus, I gotta pay estate taxes on it. Estate taxes on what? There is no fucking estate. Apparently, the most valuable thing he owned was a baseball bat that I didn't even know anything about."

I finished the bowl of cereal. The Cheerios and Rice Krispies textures were perfect together. I couldn't believe I'd never thought of mixing the two. To top it off, she'd drizzled a little honey on top. Fucking outstanding.

"He fucked me over when he was alive, and now he's doing it from the fucking grave," Joy said.

We sat there for a moment, no sound but the AC humming along.

"Fuck, it's hot." She fanned her face. "I fucking hate September. Are you hot?"

I told her I was fine, even though I could have used a sweatshirt.

"You wanna know how much is in our checking account?" she asked. "Exactly three hundred dollars. That's it. That's the extent of our liquidity. And it's all owed to about six different people."

I asked her about bills, if she needed any money for those.

"My father's gonna cover some stuff for me. That's his fucking guilt money. He oughta feel guilty, the sonuvabitch."

The bank account didn't surprise me. Gene had always been a cash guy. He liked customers who paid in paper, and he often compensated his drivers in the same fashion. He was a firm believer in unreported income. His accountant was a guy named Witherspoon who spot started for the Devil Rays. The Spork, as we called him, threw a knuckleball and drove a beat-to-shit Geo Metro. He and Gene thought *Walker, Texas Ranger* was the greatest television series ever made. They owned the first and last seasons on DVD and had taped every other episode off the daily reruns on USA Network. Naturally, I'd resisted the Spork's pitch to manage my own taxes.

"So, what kind of advice did your attorney offer?"

Joy sighed, took a long drag on her cigarette. "You're not gonna like this, but here's the thing. He says my best move is to forget the business. It's a hopeless cause. If I let the bank foreclose, that's one less thing I gotta pay estate taxes on. Are you with me?"

I was with her, all right. Gene had fucked us both, not to mention Ramon, Willie, Benny, and all the other guys who worked for us.

"Well, what if I wanted to buy the limos? What kind of numbers are we looking at?"

She waved her hand through the air. "Forget it, Joe. I'd have to rape you from here to Monday to get what I need out of those fucking cars. It's not worth it. I'm shutting the business down."

My thoughts wandered the maze of possibilities. I could borrow money from a nontraditional lender and buy my own cars, but that would take a while. I couldn't afford to pay rent on the garage in the meantime, and all the employees would scatter. I could see the garage sitting empty, the dugout vacant at the ball field, a string of forfeits by our team name, the season of Gene a complete bust.

"Let me ask you something, Joy. Did Gene ever say anything to you about moving to Nevada?"

"Fucking Nevada," she said. "I told him there was no fucking way

I was moving there. He had some kind of hard-on for the desert, he and that retard cousin of his."

"Do you think this Nevada talk had anything to do with the bat these guys took?"

She walked over and opened the drawer beside the refrigerator. "Check these out." She tossed me a set of keys.

"What about them?"

"Gene rented a storage space about a year ago. He moved a bunch of his baseball shit over there. Tommy Pumpkin is really interested in getting his hands on these keys. He says he's got some memorabilia he'd like to retrieve."

"I'll drive over there tomorrow and check it out," I said.

"See if there's anything valuable," she said. "I could care less about that shit. But if there's anything with monetary value, I'd like to have it before that douchebag gets his paws on it."

Joy walked me out the front door and stood there, apologizing for the way things had turned out.

"I know your business means a lot to you," she said. "That and your stupid baseball team. But maybe you need a kick in the ass like this. Maybe you need to make some changes."

"I'm not big on change."

"Is this what you wanna do with the rest of your life? Manage a bunch of shitheads at a car wash?"

"I'm happy."

"Bullshit. You're fucking lazy. That's what I think. How old are you, anyway?"

I told her I was thirty-four, and she shook her head. "Why don't you fucking get married already? Be fruitful and multiply."

"I *was* married."

Joy laughed. "Yeah, when you were what, like twenty-one? Gene told me all about that. He told me about all these girls you string along, too." She raised her eyebrows. "The married woman?"

Goddamn Gene. Couldn't keep a fucking story straight to save his life.

"She's not married. She's got a kid. And *she* says I'm lazy, too. So maybe the two of you would get along."

I wasn't even certain that Joy had heard me. She was looking over my shoulder at a man who was pushing a big green trash can out to the curb.

"That fucking bastard," she said. "He won't let little Gene play with his precious Jennifer because he bit her."

She watched the guy for a long time. She was standing in the doorway, and I was on the porch. And when her eyes finally settled onto my face again, her chin quivered and all of the anger vanished.

"Oh God, Joe. What am I gonna do?"

She put her hands over her face and sobbed. I started to reach for her, but then I remembered the father on the other side of the street. Here I was out in the open, under a pair of 60-watt porch lights, no trees around, about to embrace a woman whose husband had only been dead for a week. I figured she had enough problems around the neighborhood with Gene's biting, so I led her back inside the house, shut the door, and pulled her against my chest.

CHAPTER 8

The situation with the so-called married woman was a little more complicated than I could have explained to Joy at the time. As I'd told Gene earlier, and as I'm sure he would have told Joy if he hadn't dropped dead before he'd gotten the chance, Theresa had put the brakes on the thing we had going.

Of course, we still had the arrangement for me to keep Theresa's kid, Louis, when she worked late. So, it wasn't like she'd terminated all contact with me. It felt more like being on the inactive list pending Theresa changing her mind about a few things, which she was more than capable of doing.

I was sitting in my 'Vette beneath the big American flag in the parking lot of the Chick-fil-A, eating my chicken sandwich after the talk with Joy. The car was dark except for the dash lights. I turned off the radio and hit the speed dial on my cell. Theresa picked up on the third ring.

"I just got in from work."

She never said hello when she answered. Either she ignored the caller ID, or she picked back up like I'd just walked out of the room for a few minutes.

I told her I was at Chick-fil-A.

"Let me guess. You're eating in the car."

"Fucking delicious sandwich," I said.

That's when I remembered why I called her. The chicken had gotten me sidetracked. And so I started in with the whole story about Gene, explaining how he'd died and how I'd been jacked up by the guys who were looking for him and how the whole business operation was on the ropes. I was laying all the details on Theresa. I'd been talking for a good three or four minutes, when the call waiting clicked in. "Hold on," I said. "I got another call."

I checked the incoming number and saw that it was Theresa's. I'd lost the call.

"Goddamn this fucking piece-of-shit phone."

"You know," she said, "you should think about changing services."

"I can't. I got four months left on my contract. I'm fucked."

"So, what were you saying about your friend Gene?"

"Oh, yeah. He died. Had a heart attack while we were playing ball."

"Are you serious?"

"Yeah. Can you believe it?"

"Of course I can believe it. The man was a walking heart attack."

"You got a point," I said. "Too fat to live, too young to die."

"Bye, bye," she said.

"Still, it's not like you expect this sort of thing to happen. You know what I'm saying? He was only thirty-five."

"Well," she said, "people earn what they get sometimes."

I filled her in again on the situation regarding the business and this mysterious bat that somebody seemed to want really bad. I asked her to respond with some *yeah*s or *okay*s just to let me know we still had a connection going.

Once the Gene business was out of the way, Theresa told me she was working five to midnight the following day. She was a bartender at Chili's, had been there for a couple months after quitting her gig at Ruby Tuesday's when she couldn't get along with her manager. It was a familiar pattern for her. She made the rounds of the chain restaurants: Chili's, Applebee's, T.G.I. Friday's. She called them "the apostrophes." Despite her work in the service industry, she was not exactly a people person. She told me once that she'd never relied on anyone else to make her happy. I admired that type of thinking.

"You sound good," I said. "Are you still taking those Ambien pills?"

"Don't start with me," she said.

"I'm just saying. You must be sleeping good."

"Fuck off, Rice."

"You like pickles?" I asked.

"What?"

"Pickles. Do you like them?"

"I guess so." She sounded bewildered.

"That's what gives the sandwich the good flavor, because it's got no mayonnaise or nothing."

"Rice?"

"Yeah."

"I'm really not that hungry. And besides, I have to take Louis to his doctor's appointment in the morning. I have to fill out a bunch of paperwork before I go to bed."

"Oh, yeah. So, do you still want me to keep Louis tomorrow night when you're working?"

"If it's still okay with you," she said.

"I already told you, it's nothing."

"Well, he's got this school project," she said. "He needs to work on it. Would you mind helping him?"

"No sweat. What's it on?"

"Blue crabs."

"Jesus, is he already taking sex-ed?"

"It's not for sex-ed, you idiot. It's civics class. Blue crabs are the ones they grow in the Chesapeake—the ones they make the crab cakes out of. The population is going down, and it affects the ecology of the bay."

"Oh, fuck. I'm already getting sleepy."

"I'm serious, now. He's gotta work on this thing, so don't you two spend all night playing video games and watching that stupid Maury Povich DVD."

"Hey, I'm on it. We'll play one quick game of *Madden*, and then it's all business."

"And no Cokes with supper. He doesn't need caffeine after six o'clock."

"I got you."

"And take him out for some eggs in the morning. The doctor says he needs protein, it's good for his brain. I'll leave you some money and his multivitamin. Don't forget that either. It's important."

"Yeah, yeah."

"And don't be late for school. He'll stall, if you let him."

"It's covered. Just fucking relax."

She went quiet for a moment. I heard her light a cigarette.

"I appreciate you doing this," she said. "You know, all things considered."

I resisted the urge to talk about us. And I'd already said enough about the chicken.

"It ain't nothing," I said.

CHAPTER 9

I had actually met Theresa on account of Gene. Or I should say on account of Gene's hard-on for baseball bats. One of his goals as a collector had been to own a personal bat from every member of the '78 Yankees. Surprisingly, the last and most difficult piece of lumber to procure had been that of utility infielder Brian Doyle. Gene had eventually found a guy on the Internet, a memorabilia dealer by the name of Walt Belder, who had promised to deliver the Doyle lumber. According to Gene, the man also had some other interesting artifacts from the Bombers.

Geno called me from the garage at two in the morning bragging about this X ray of Tommy John's elbow that he'd bought.

"What the fuck is your problem?" I asked. "Do you know what time it is? I don't give a shit about Tommy John's fucking X ray."

The bat man was shit-faced, wanting me to come by the garage, pick up this guy Belder, and drive him to his hotel.

"I promised him a limo," Gene said. "I can't drive. I think I'd blow a .08 if I got pulled over."

"Yeah, well, you can blow *me*. I ain't driving this fucker to a hotel in the middle of the night."

"Come on, Rice. This guy completed the bat collection. It's the '78 Yankees, man. You know how I feel about that team. I was ten years old and my old man was dying of cancer. We used to watch the games in his bed on Channel 11, and every night they won, every game they made up on the Sox, he got a little better. I'm convinced he survived because of them."

"Your old man had a raging case of gonorrhea. Joy told me all about it. I believe her exact words were, 'The fruit, it don't fall far from the tree.'"

I ended up making the run for Gene. I knew that if I didn't, he'd probably go out and crash a limo and get himself and the other guy killed. That would be the end of his business, the team, and probably my own business. I suppose I was seeing into the future to some degree.

It took both of us to get this Belder character into the back of a Town Car. The man was drunk off his ass and didn't look like anybody to be trusted. His hair was gray and pulled back into a ponytail. He was wearing cowboy boots, a little diamond earring, and a Harley-Davidson of Reno T-shirt.

Gene handed me a piece of paper. "This is where he's staying."

I took a look at the address. "This street runs behind my apartment building. There ain't no hotel back there."

Gene chomped down on his cigar, patted my shoulder, and staggered backward a little. "What can I tell you? That's where the man says he's staying."

Belder was slumped down in the backseat, talking almost incomprehensibly. He mentioned something about stopping for a six-pack, and then he said he had to take a squirt.

"Pull over, shithead."

"Fuck you," I said. "You piss in this car, I'm gonna fucking wipe your face in it like a schnauzer."

He didn't say anything else. By the time I'd pulled up to the house where I was supposed to deliver him, he had completely passed out. His pants were unzipped and wet with piss.

"Fucking asshole," I said.

The house was small, a Cape Cod with a scratchy front lawn. All the lights were off, even on the porch. I had no idea if anyone inside was expecting, or even knew, Belder. For all I knew, I was about to get my fucking head blown off.

I rang the bell twice, and Theresa opened the door. She was peering around the corner of it, wearing blue pajama pants and a white tank top. I could tell that I'd frightened her.

"I have a man in my limo who says that you're expecting him."

"Excuse me?"

"A man. He says his name is Belder."

"Oh, shit. What did he do?"

"Nothing too bad, but I think he may have pissed in my car. And he's passed-out drunk."

She rested her head against the door and closed her eyes like she wanted to go back to sleep. I asked if she knew the guy.

"His name's not Belder," she said. "It's Walter Phillips. And if he gave you a credit card, it's probably stolen."

"What about baseball bats?"

"What?"

"Well, he hasn't flashed any plastic. But he just sold my business partner some high-end baseball memorabilia."

I suspected Gene had just drunkenly purchased some fakes, but I wasn't looking to get involved in the stupidity.

She let out a big sigh before stepping onto the stoop. "Good Lord. Let's just get him inside."

It wasn't until we opened the car door that I understood he was her father. "Daddy," she said. "What the hell are you doing here?"

He roused a little. "I've got your money, bitch."

"I don't need the money. I told you to stay the fuck away from here."

"I want to see my grandbaby."

"He's not a baby anymore. He's in the fifth grade, you asshole."

"Well, fuck it all," he said. He groaned a little, and that's the last we heard from him.

I hauled him inside, dragging him under the arms, doing some serious mouth breathing because of the piss smell. I had his nearly empty duffel bag slung over my shoulder. Theresa told me to dump him in the hallway bathroom.

"At least he'll be close when he starts puking," she said.

She had the same accent as Belder, at least the pitch and flow of it.

"You're not from around here, huh?"

"Is anybody?" she asked.

I made the turn into the bathroom, my eyes following Theresa. I ended up banging Belder's head against the doorjamb.

"I just meant that I detected a bit of an accent. It's nice, though."

"I'm from North Carolina," she said. "Raleigh."

"Oh, yeah? I drove down there once. Picked up some cigarettes for my uncle."

She watched me as if I was mildly interesting, dragging her old man across the floor in my Adidas warm-up pants and Whip Spa Car Detailing T-shirt.

"Where did you drive from?"

"New Jersey," I said. "It was sort of a wholesale run."

I laid Belder's head on the bath mat. He let out a pained sigh, like I'd just slipped a knife out of his gut.

Theresa kicked him in the kidney with a bare foot. "You better hit the toilet if you throw up, you sonuvabitch. I'll make you clean up every drop if you don't." Then she flipped off the bathroom light like she couldn't stand the sight of him.

We walked back out to the foyer. "I'm only letting him stay here so you don't have to fool with him anymore. I'm sorry he pissed in your car."

"It happens," I said.

"No, it doesn't. Normal, considerate people don't piss in the back of somebody's car."

"You'd be surprised what you see in the limo business."

"Is that what you do?" she asked.

"No, but I share a warehouse with a limo service. I'm in the car detailing and ticket brokerage business."

"Ticket brokerage?"

"Yeah, like when people want good seats, or don't feel like standing in line."

"A scalper."

"That's actually an unflattering word," I said. "It's a legitimate business. I even belong to a trade association."

We finally told each other our names. She smiled a little, and then she pushed back a strand of hair. It was this dark, unnatural red color, most of it gathered in a ponytail. She wasn't exactly beautiful, but I liked the expectancy in her green eyes. I felt like she wanted me to talk to her, forget the hour or the circumstances.

I asked Theresa if her old man was a gambler.

"How much does he owe you?" she asked.

"Nothing. I was just wondering. I grew up around a lot of gamblers."

"One is enough," she said.

I handed her the duffel bag. It was light, almost empty except for a wad of Gene's cash with a rubber band around it.

"What's this?" she asked.

"I think that's the money he was talking about."

She appeared skeptical of its origins. "Where'd he get it?"

"It's cool," I said. "Don't worry about it."

She walked me to the door. For the first time, I noticed that the house was out of hand: dusty, despondent, piles of clothes, piles of mail, stacks of newspapers. It reminded me of somewhere I'd stayed for a few days back when me and my mother were moving around. I just couldn't remember where it had been. It may have actually been several places, to tell the truth.

I could see this street where Theresa lived, all of these little houses, from my living room window, and this was the first time I'd ever been inside one of them. I had seen the Latino man two doors down who always played soccer in the backyard with his kid, and the man directly behind Theresa's house who had the pickup truck that never ran. The cops came to his house one night and hauled him away. A woman was standing in the doorway with a garden hoe, and he was limping around pointing at her and screaming. I felt connected to all these people even though I didn't know them, felt like we were all happy in our own way, settled into our lives, living moment to moment, waiting for whatever came next.

"You got a nice house," I said.

She explained that she was just renting. "It's a mess. It's gotten away from me lately."

I told her how everybody kept telling me I needed to quit renting and buy a place. She asked where I lived.

"Over at Bridgewood. The high-rise behind the strip center."

"Isn't that where people live when they're in between moves?"

"Well, some of us live there long-term."

She smiled, nodded. Her eyes caught the overhead light and shined a little. She appeared to be waking up.

There was a big mirror hanging in the foyer, a coatrack nailed above it. I pointed to a small Philadelphia Eagles parka hanging there. "How old is your son?" I asked.

"He's ten," she said. "His name is Louis."

"That's nice," I said. "What's he like?"

"Well," Theresa said, "I'm starting to see a lot of myself in him: the lies, the deceit, the impulsive behavior. The doctor says he's got oppositional defiance disorder."

"Maybe he'll grow out of it," I said, even though I didn't know what the hell she was talking about. "Besides, you don't seem that way to me. I mean, if you weren't a nice person, you wouldn't have let me bring your old man inside."

She didn't say anything to that, but I could tell that she liked what I'd told her. Never mind that I knew less than shit about kids or fathers. I guess she just needed to hear something like that.

I gave her my card before I left, and she brought her Saturn in a few weeks later to be detailed. The thing was beat all to shit, like she'd been driving around with her eyes closed. She told me she'd had a few accidents.

"Sometimes, my mind wanders," she said. "I like to think when I drive."

"Maybe you should think about taking the bus."

We picked back up pretty easy. I gave her the full Whip Spa deluxe package for free (rims, carpet shampoo, upholstery conditioner). I noticed a CD wallet on the front seat and took a peek inside. Aerosmith, Mötley Crüe, Bon Jovi. I recalled that there was a Bon Jovi concert slated for the end of the month, so I quickly procured a pair of floor seats. They had never been a favorite of mine. In fact, on more than one occasion, I may have said they sucked. But I figured, what the hell. Everybody's got different tastes.

Theresa got a babysitter so we could go to the concert. We ate Peruvian chicken beforehand, went out for drinks afterward, wound up back at my place, just past 1 a.m., standing at the living room window, looking down at the houses and strip centers.

"You didn't like the show, did you?" she asked.

I was standing behind her, my hands on her shoulders. She'd gotten back into her bra and panties. I was wearing my Adidas basketball shorts.

"What makes you say that?"

"You said, 'Oh, shit,' when they came out for a second encore."

"I had to pee, that's all."

She smiled. "So, what kind of music do you like?"

"I like salsa, hip-hop, Johnny Cash."

"That's an odd combination."

"I guess it is."

She took her finger and dragged it along the window. "Look," she said, "there's my house."

She noticed the light still shining in Louis's room. "That little shit. I told him to be in bed by midnight."

"At least you know where he is," I said.

She placed her hand flat on the window. "I can't get away from him."

A moment passed. And then she turned around, looked up at me. "I'm sorry. That was a mean thing to say."

"It's okay. Everybody says mean things. It doesn't matter. It's just words."

She was looking past me, at her drink on the end table. Our clothes were still piled on the floor in front of the sofa. The only light in the room was the flicker of the television. YES was replaying the Yankees-Rangers game from earlier.

She slipped into her jeans and sweater, sat on the sofa, took a drink of her Jack and Coke. "You should be careful with words," she said. "You never know."

I sat down beside her, lit a Marlboro Light, offered her one. She smoked and drank, and her eyes turned glassy.

She started telling me about her family and how her father had left when she was seven. She had a little brother named Paul with cerebral palsy, a high-maintenance case of it. Her mother drank, dated, left the bulk of the brother's care to Theresa. She went through high school like that, stayed at home and attended community college, thought she wanted to be a nurse before realizing the last thing she really wanted to do with her life was take care of any more sick people.

"Not to mention, I failed chemistry," she said.

She was twenty-two, tending bar, still living with her mother and

Paul. She went to a guy's apartment one night. They were lying in bed drunk, and she realized she needed to get home. She told the guy about the situation with her brother. She said, "I just wish he'd fucking die already."

Two months later the kid quit breathing. He was home with the mother, watching TV in his wheelchair. Theresa's mother didn't even notice. Theresa found him when she got home from work. A *Golden Girls* rerun was playing on the television.

"I've got this aunt," she said, "from my mother's side. And at the funeral, she comes up to me and says that God took Paul's life so I could have one."

She ground her cigarette into my ashtray. "Do you think I wanted to hear that?" she asked. "After what I'd said."

"That's kind of like what happened to Joe Pep," I said.

She stared at me. "Who?"

"Pepitone," I said. "I read his autobiography when I was in the ninth grade. It's my favorite book. My uncle gave it to me. But the thing is Joe Pepitone's father had a heart attack when Joe was in high school. So two days later, Joe got shot at his high school. And the way things worked out, Joe got better but his father ended up dying. So his aunt told him that God took his father so that he could have his life back because he was the one who was supposed to die when he got shot. It made him feel terrible."

"But that's not what my aunt meant," she said.

"I know that. But I'm sure it must have made you feel really bad."

She just sat there staring at my face. "So, that's your favorite book?" she asked.

"It's a good book," I said. "And we've got the same first name."

This was not a great response from a thirty-one-year-old man. And besides, there was something about the way she had posed the question that embarrassed me. I couldn't look her in the eye for a moment.

"There was also this yoga book that I read once," I said. "It was really good. It was about breathing. You'd be surprised how important it is to breathe the right way."

I went out to the elevator with her, asked if she wanted me to walk her home.

"I'll be fine," she said. "I walk around here all the time."

"After midnight?" I asked.

"I don't sleep very well," she said.

The elevator dinged. She walked inside, and I held back the door.

"I'm sorry. I didn't mean to compare what you went through to a baseball book."

"It's okay," she said. "At least you were listening to me."

I went back to the window after she'd left. I watched her walk up the street toward her house, taking the two-block detour to the 7-Eleven for cigarettes. She came back the long way, smoking and circling an extra block before going into the house.

CHAPTER 10

Ramon was loitering at the Barnes & Noble, kicked back in an easy chair, vente vanilla latte in hand, pile of *Fantasy Football* magazines beside him. I walked up and kicked one of his gold Pumas.

"You moved in here, or what?"

He gazed over the top of his magazine. Mike Vick was on the cover, eluding a tackler. The cover posed a crucial question: FANTASY POINT MACHINE, OR INJURY WAITING TO HAPPEN?

"Man, I wish I could live here," Ramon said. "It's an oasis. I got peace and quiet—pastries, coffee, magazines, good-looking women. I came here the other day to take a nap. No fucking lie."

"The baby?" I asked.

Ramon sat up straight, wiped his hand across his face. "That baby's got a motor like a fucking Weed Eater. I don't understand it. My mother said I was a good baby, slept through the night from day one. I'm telling you, he gets it from Estelle."

"Don't go putting it all at her feet," I said. "You're in fifty-fifty on this thing."

He looked up and shook his head. "This *thing* is killing me. Look at me, I got circles under my eyes. And I haven't got a true nut in three months."

"So, where's your friend?" I asked.

Ramon stood up, stretched, and yawned. "I told her to meet us in the self-help section. She oughta be here soon."

"It's a she?"

Ramon led the way back through the maze of shelves. "I want you to check out the ass on this girl," he said. "I'm telling you, I just wanna slap it one good time. You know, grab a handful."

The girl in question worked at the Best Buy on the other end of the shopping center. According to Ramon, they'd met when he went in to buy a baby monitor. The sole purpose of our meeting her at Barnes & Noble was to pick up an advance copy of the new *Madden* football game. The official release was still a week off, but Ramon's new friend had procured a copy from a box in the Best Buy warehouse. Ramon thought we could get a jump on the rest of our Madden league compatriots by starting our own training camp a week early. It might make a big difference in getting off to a fast start in league play, where the weekly pots could eclipse $200. Like a pair of veteran quarterbacks, we needed our reps.

I told Ramon about Gene's storage space and asked if he wanted to go check it out with me.

"What the fuck's with you and this bat thing? You're starting to sound like Gene."

"Hey, I took six hundred volts because of this bat. I want to find out why these guys had such a hard-on for it."

"It's a fucking bat. What do you care?"

"It's gotta be valuable for somebody to want it that bad. Who knows, maybe Gene was sitting on a gold mine of wood."

Ramon waved his hand through the air. "Forget it, man. The memorabilia market ain't what it used to be. It's gotta be something real special to bring in any serious cash. And considering all the times Gene got taken to the cleaners by these memorabilia guys, I wouldn't get my hopes up on finding anything that's gonna bring you some cash."

Ramon's friend, Deandra, showed up in tight, dark jeans and a blue Best Buy shirt, smiling at Ramon and shaking her head. The first thing she did was ask Ramon about his nephew.

"He's good," Ramon said. "Handsome like his uncle."

He gave me this guilty look. "You remember my sister's kid," he said. "The cute one."

"Yeah, the one that cries all night."

Ramon shrugged. "He gets the colic sometimes."

The girl pulled a little plastic bag from her purse and reached out like she was going to hand it to Ramon. Right at the last second, she pulled it back and smiled.

"Wait a minute." She cocked her head to the side. "Are you still taking me dancing Saturday night?"

Ramon smiled. "I'm all over it, girl."

"Club Touché?" she asked.

"None other."

"And I wanna eat at the Cheesecake Factory. I want some of those popcorn shrimp."

Ramon sighed. "They always have a fucking two-hour wait there. How about Chili's?"

The girl frowned, exaggerated, like a little girl. She looked about nineteen, had long brown hair, permed down at the ends. One hand on her hip, the other braced against the bookshelf.

"All right," he conceded. "We'll get some popcorn shrimp."

When it came to being a player, Ramon had never been in the same league as Gene. Gene was indiscriminate, insatiable in his urges. His tales of debauchery were the equivalent of watching a man eat until he threw up—a "reversal of fortune," as Gene called it. Ramon, on the other hand, was merely young and stupid. I couldn't give him much grief, not with my own past. Plus, he'd already burned himself in a bad way by getting Estelle pregnant. Estelle had been his high school sweetheart, whom he'd dumped after meeting a girl named Brooke when she brought her Audi TT in for a detail job. Brooke's father was a lobbyist for the oil companies, worth millions, and Brooke fell in love with Ramon, even talked about marriage. But Ramon was still carrying on with Estelle from time to time, and when he got her pregnant, it appeared to be over between him and Brooke.

Ramon watched Deandra walk away, followed her to the end of the self-help aisle, and then he turned around and slapped his hand up against a row of book spines. "I don't even take Estelle to the Cheesecake Factory. Now she's gonna eat those fucking popcorn shrimp and run up a fifty-dollar bill. That ain't even counting those fucking Kir Royales she's gonna drink. And there's no guarantee she's even gonna let me lick that lollipop."

"Fuck you," I said. "You quit drinking those four-dollar coffees, maybe you can afford some popcorn shrimp. Besides, I didn't need to see that shit. What do you think's gonna be in my head next time I see Estelle? You wanna play, then play. But don't go getting me involved."

Ramon looked away, eyed the cluster of books on the shelves. "All right, I should have said something to you."

"No, you shouldn't have said a fucking thing to me. I don't wanna know."

"Know what?"

"About your extra particulars. Gene used to tell me about all that shit, and I still don't feel comfortable around Joy."

"Hey, man. Gene was a freak. Don't go putting me in the same boat with Gene. You know, you need to remember what you said about five minutes ago. It's fifty-fifty when you're with someone, and Estelle hasn't been pulling her fifty. Besides all that, she knows me. She knows I roll like that. And I don't let it interfere with family. I keep this shit separate. And I need it, too. It helps me deal with all the other shit. School, baby, work. I need a release. I've got a lot of fucking pressure on me. And Estelle, she fucking wanted this baby but now she's mad all the time. Pissed off and acting like everything's my fault, not giving it up for nothing. She's got this low-blood-sugar thing, it turns her into a fucking hatin' machine. I don't even know her sometimes. It's scary. I fear for my safety when I'm at home. That's no lie."

"Maybe you need to give Estelle a break," I said. "She just had a baby. Besides, it might not be the low blood sugar making her feel bad. She might have that post-party depression, or something."

Ramon sighed, dropped his head. "You got an answer for everything," he said.

I looked away from him, up at the shelves, and spotted a book I'd seen on Theresa's coffee table: *The Purpose-Driven Life*. It was about the time this book showed up that she decided I'd mistaken contentment for laziness.

Ramon had his eye on a different book. *"Five Steps to Financial Freedom,"* he said. "Here's one I need to buy."

Every conversation with Ramon lately had seemed to work its way around to the subject of cash, namely his lack of it and how his grandfather, who'd raised him, had refused to help him out. The old man, Hector, was pushing eighty, and Ramon was part of the family he had started after leaving Cuba in 1946. Hector had been a star in his home country for Club Almendares. A center fielder with power and speed, he also played some ball for the New York Cubans in the Negro League. That's where he met Ramon's grandmother Flora, who persuaded him to stay in the States.

I asked Ramon if he needed to borrow some money again.

He acted annoyed. "What do you mean, again?"

"I'm just asking."

He set his book on the checkout counter, turned away, and looked across the store at the people working their way up and down the aisles.

"Me and Brooke have been talking again."

"Talking, or getting busy?"

He gave a little shrug. "Well, you know . . ."

Ramon said that Brooke was going to set him up with a Pollo Campero chicken franchise. He'd already been in touch with their headquarters in Guatemala. They wanted to expand to certain areas in the States and had already opened a franchise in Los Angeles.

"They did seven million in sales the first month," Ramon said.

"What about Estelle?" I asked.

"I figure it'll be best for her *and* little Ramon. No offense, but I ain't going nowhere working for you. And even if you wanted to sell out one day, it's not like I want to do what you do."

"You make it sound like a fucking prison sentence or something."

"Whatever makes you happy," Ramon said. "But your life ain't gonna make *me* happy."

"What the fuck is so wrong with my life?" I asked. "People are never satisfied. They want this, and they want that, and they want to be famous and have everybody love them. And all they end up leaving behind is a big fucking mess. Look at Gene. Prime example. Man, when I go, I'm leaving no messes for anybody else to clean up. No piles of shit lying around. That takes a lot more effort than anyone seems to realize."

Ramon signed his credit card receipt, and we headed out to the parking lot.

"All I want is a fucking Pollo Campero franchise," Ramon said. "If that leads to other business ventures, then so be it. I like to stay on the move. Not everybody is like you, Rice. It takes all kinds of personalities. You think we'd have ever gotten to the moon if everybody was like you?"

"I'll grant you this," I said. "It's good fucking chicken. I'll be first in line."

"You're like fucking Wade Boggs with the chicken," he said.

CHAPTER 11

We headed out to Gene's storage space to check the bats. The facility was called EZ Plus, and it was one of those modular structures dressed up to look like permanent housing of some sort: fake windows with flower boxes and plastic daisies, and a rental office with a pitched roof and a chimney. They even had a Big Wheel parked in front of the office. I couldn't tell if it was a prop, or if a family actually lived there.

As storage spaces go, Gene's was an upscale nest. He had opted for the twelve-by-twenty, climate-controlled unit, and then he'd laid down a Persian rug and a leather sofa, along with some scented candles and a coffee table. A portable DVD player sat on the coffee table with porn titles scattered around it. A bottle of Rémy was sitting there, too, along with a pair of crystal shot glasses. The only storage materials in evidence were a few cardboard boxes stacked up behind the lounge area—not enough to warrant a space like this.

"Looks like the fucking Pottery Barn in here," I said.

Ramon whistled. "No shit. This is nicer than my apartment. Cleaner, too."

The place still smelled like a cinnamon candle. The ventilation was good. The sofa looked inviting. Despite dipping into the pill pocket of Gene's bat bag, I still hadn't gotten much sleep. I'd spent the last few nights lying on the sofa, watching old college football games on ESPN Classic and running through all the shit concerning Gene and the business and this stupid bat that had gotten me zapped with the stun gun.

"I guess this was Gene's hideout," I said. "The fucking bat man cave."

"Well, he was never at work," Ramon said. "I knew he couldn't be spending all that time getting hand jobs."

I went around behind the sofa and ripped open one of the cardboard boxes. Ramon flopped down on the sofa and evaluated Gene's porn collection.

"This is old-school shit," he said. "*Nympho Nurses 4* with Connie Lingonberry. That's like from '75. My uncle used to have it on Betamax."

The first cardboard box was mostly autographed game jerseys. Gene had a yellow Tony Gwynn, a Jim Abbott Yankees road jersey, a Dale Murphy in powder blue, and four Rob Deers. The old Tommy John X ray, real or fake, lay at the bottom of the box, along with a signed eight-by-ten of Chuck Norris in his Walker getup. There was also a bumper sticker that said ON THE 8TH DAY, GOD CREATED CHUCK NORRIS. Gene and that fucking accountant with their *Walker* reruns.

The second box housed a bundle of bats, but there was nothing spectacular among the bunch. No slight intended to the wood of Sheffield and Thome, but you don't need to pack heat and a stun gun to retrieve one of their bats.

By now Ramon had the DVD player going. "It's still got some battery left," he said.

Soon, the wah-wah guitar started, followed by a woman's voice.

"Dr. Cummings, what's the status of the patient in room 69?"

"There's a good bit of swelling, Nurse. You'll have to take care of that."

"What do you recommend?"

"Well, it's been my experience that manual stimulation is always effective."

"You mean like this?"

"Nurse, what are you doing? We can't. Not here in the supply closet."

So far, the memorabilia had been less than impressive. I was beginning to wonder why Tommy Pumpkin had such a hard-on to get at the goods in the storage space. That was before I opened the last box.

"Holy shit. Look at this."

"I know it," Ramon said. "She's got a nice ass, huh?"

"Forget the fucking movie and get back here. Check out this box."

The last box contained no memorabilia. It was packed instead with white pharmaceutical bottles, had to be hundreds of them, the kind you see behind the counter at the drugstore. I picked one up and read the label: Oxycodone HCl. And then in larger letters: OxyContin.

"Oh, man," Ramon said. "Bat man's got himself a box of hillbilly heroin."

"Did you know about this?" I asked.

Ramon didn't answer. He was staring down into the box, stroking his chin in a thoughtful sort of way, like he was trying to add up two large and complicated numbers.

"Hey, did you hear me?"

Ramon looked up. "Huh? No. I mean hell, no. Why would I know about this shit?"

"You knew about the Nevada thing and kept a lid on it. Why wouldn't you do the same about something like this?"

"I swear to God," he said. "I don't know anything about this shit. Gene used to hook me up with Vicodin for my shoulder, but that's it."

I tossed the bottle back in the box and taped it shut again. "Now we know why Tommy wants to get in here."

"No lie," Ramon said. "That dude's a walking pharmacy. Steroids, painkillers, you name it."

I sat on the back of the sofa and tried to figure things out. This was more than a personal stash. This was inventory.

Ramon stepped over the bats and jerseys to get at the ice cooler, a red Igloo with a New York Giants bumper sticker on top. Gene had used it for tailgating when he drove up to the Meadowlands for games.

"Goddamn," Ramon said. "Look at this."

The cooler held another unexpected find: money, mostly twenty-dollar bills, banded and laid out in rows that stacked almost halfway to the top. A twenty-gallon cooler.

"There's gotta be at least fifty large in there," Ramon said. "Easy."

"That's a lot of baseball bats," I said.

I told Ramon to close it up. I walked over to the door and looked up and down the hallway to make sure nobody was around to witness any of this.

Ramon asked what we were going to do with the pills and the money.

"We leave the pills and take the money," I said.

"Are you wacked? Tommy Pumpkin's gonna come in here and haul this shit away. Trust me, those pills are worth more than what's in that cooler."

"I'm not putting that shit in my car. What if we get pulled over?"

"We get pulled over, we play dumb," Ramon said. "We're just running an errand for a widow."

"Forget the pills, Ramon. We take the cash, and that's it."

Ramon shook his head, just like when I came to the mound to tell him to quit trying to challenge everyone with his fastball. But I knew I could trust him. He bitched and moaned, but he always threw the right pitch in a tight spot.

"This is too fucking crazy," he said.

The DVD was still playing, the moaning and the guitars going on and on. But there was another sound, too: footsteps coming down the concrete hallway. I hoped they might be headed for another unit, but I quickly realized we had guests.

"What the fuck?" Tommy Pumpkin asked. "The door's open."

He was startled to see us, even looked a little scared. He took a step back like he thought we might rush him.

I was surprised by the company that followed him into the room. It was Funderburk and Gene's fucking accountant, Gordon "The Spork" Witherspoon. They stopped in their tracks and looked a little uneasy as well. Nobody said a word.

Funderburk was dressed in his usual getup, like he'd just come from the golf course: khakis, a sweater vest with a patch from some charity disease tournament, and a white Ashworth baseball cap. This wouldn't have been odd if he actually played golf. But he didn't. He just liked the look.

The Spork, on the other hand, at least looked halfway professional: suit pants, dress shirt, tie. The only thing giving him away as a complete shit were the ostrich cowboy boots and scraggly beard.

"Well, look at this," I said. "It's Walker, Texas accountant, and Dr. Freddy Couples. You boys must be headed out to play eighteen with Ranger Cord."

"That's real cute," Funderburk said. "By the way, I like those warm-up pants you're wearing. I didn't know they had a clothing department at CVS."

"They're fucking Adidas, you moron. If you're gonna bust my balls, at least put some thought into it."

"Here's a thought," Funderburk said. "I think you've got a bit of an inferiority complex."

"Inferior to what? You don't even practice anymore, you jerk-off. Gene told me all about how you butchered that woman's nose job."

Funderburk clenched his fists. "You don't know what the fuck you're talking about. Washing cars and scalping tickets for a living. You're nothing but a fucking hustler. I've been to India. I was operating on deformed children while you were out scalping Menudo tickets."

"Yeah, and then you bragged about your charity work so a bunch of rich women would let you blow up their tits for three grand each. You're a real Albert fuckin' Schweitzer."

"At least I can go to sleep at night knowing I've helped people."

"You didn't help anybody. In fact, I got a hunch you never even went to India. You ask me, I think you were in Vegas, and all those photos were frauds."

Funderburk laughed. "You've been sniffing too much Simoniz, Rice. Maybe you should get out of the garage for a while, take a walk in the park."

"I heard all about the little seminars you gave, showing photos of all the poor children you helped. It's a good business approach: appeal to the heart, reshape the body. Joy went in for a boob job, and then you start talking about her nose and her eyes and her chin being out of proportion. You're a fucking car salesman with an MD."

"You're a fucking . . ."

Funderburk was seething, beyond words. The Spork peeled off his sunglasses and started massaging Doc's shoulders. "Rise above it," he said. "Be the bigger man, okay?"

Funderburk eased up, appearing to think twice about the possible outcomes. He was still eyeing me, though, so mad he'd actually turned pale. "If you start saying shit about me, I'll sue your ass for slander. I've worked on the wives of at least seven personal damage attorneys, and they were all extremely pleased with the results."

Tommy Pumpkin was looking past me and Ramon, to the boxes behind the sofa. When I leaned into his field of vision, he smiled and tried to act all friendly.

"You looking for something?" I asked. "A certain bat, maybe?"

Tommy ignored the question and continued the innocent routine. He'd had a lot of practice over the past two years with the workman's comp scam.

"So, what are you guys doing here?" Tommy asked. "Scared the shit out of me when I saw the door open."

"Yeah, I bet," Ramon said. Ramon was still pissed about a couple of errors Tommy had made in the spring playoffs. He had a long memory when it came to unearned runs.

I told Tommy we were there at Joy's request. "She wants Gene's things."

"Things?" Tommy asked.

"You know, his baseball memorabilia. The bats and whatnot."

Tommy nodded his head as if that made sense. "Yeah, well, I was just stopping by because I stored some memorabilia here, too."

"Oh, yeah?" Ramon said. "What kind?"

Tommy shrugged. "The usual. Bats and shit. I got a signed bat that's worth three hundred dollars."

And then he got a concerned look on his face. "Did you see that piece?"

He was obviously trying to figure out whether or not we'd gone through all of the boxes.

"Depends," I said. "Who the fuck signed it?"

About that time, Tommy noticed the DVD. He tilted his head to get a better look at the action on the screen. "What the fuck is she doing with that hot water bottle?"

Tommy looked up from the movie. He must have decided we hadn't found the stash. He relaxed a bit.

"You must have missed a box," he said as he tried to get past me and Ramon.

We both put our arms out and stopped him. Tommy looked confused, but offered no resistance.

"If it's your stuff," I asked, "then why the company?"

Tommy didn't have an answer. Instead, he turned and looked at Funderburk as if he were legal counsel.

"Not that it's any of your business," Funderburk said, "but we all went in together on this storage space: me, Witherspoon, Tommy, and Gene. I've got some memorabilia here, too, as does Witherspoon."

I walked over and ripped open the box of pharmaceuticals. "We already saw the money and the pills, you morons."

Tommy being Tommy—that is to say, the kind of idiot who'll always try to pull a pitch that's a foot outside—immediately reached into his Serpico jacket and pulled out a piece. It looked like a nine-millimeter Beretta.

"All right," he said. "Cut the cat-and-mouse shit and back off. We're taking those fucking boxes."

Ramon threw his hands up in front of his face. "What the fuck are you doing?" he asked. "Put that gangsta stick down before it goes off."

Despite Tommy's penchant for errant throws from shortstop, the gun made me more than a little nervous. Even Funderburk and the Spork looked scared, and they weren't even the ones in Tommy's sites.

Funderburk finally stepped up and placed his hand on Tommy's shoulder. "How about we put down the cannon, okay? Geez, there's no need to get nuts."

But Tommy told Funderburk to shut up. "You and Spork get the cooler and the pills," he said. "We're taking our shit, and I'm not answering any more fucking questions."

Tommy leveled the gun at my chest. "Fuck you," he said, "batting me sixth in the lineup. For your information, you don't know shit about managing a baseball team. I got drafted by the fucking Pirates."

Had he not been brandishing a nine-millimeter, semiautomatic weapon, I would have reminded Tommy that he never made it out of the Florida instructional league and hadn't even hit .300 in two seasons in a Friday-night beer league. After that, I might have recounted a number of plays that he had butchered at short. Hell, he shouldn't have even been in the starting lineup. Even Funderburk would have agreed with me on that point.

Funderburk reluctantly lifted the cooler, grunting against its heft.

He paused and looked at me as if he wanted to explain something, but then seemed to give up on the idea. "He's *your* fucking teammate," he muttered before walking out the door and down the hallway.

The Spork was a little slower in corralling the box of pills. I could see that he also wanted to haul away the bats. He tried stacking the bat box on top of the OxyContin and carrying them both out that way, but he couldn't see over the load.

"Put the fucking bats down," Tommy said. "I'll bring those when I'm done here."

"Fuck you," the Spork said. "You're not getting your hands on that bat. Gene would have wanted me to have it. We were the only ones with a vested interest."

"What kind of fucking bat are we talking about?" I asked.

Tommy looked at me—"You, shut up"—then back at the Spork. "I told you already. I don't give a shit about that bat."

I felt it was time to share some information.

"Two guys showed up at Gene's house the other night," I said. "One of them held a gun on Joy while the other one ransacked the place. All they took was a bat."

Tommy smiled and shook his head. "Well, I'll be damned. He had it at the house all along."

Witherspoon's gaze was bouncing between me and Tommy like a Ping-Pong ball. "Fuck the both of you. You're probably in on this together. I'm taking these bats."

The Spork had barely gotten the words out of his mouth when a Louisville Slugger fell out of the top box. Taking his first step toward the door, he tripped over the bat—I think it was the Tony Gwynn—and fell right into Tommy. They both went down on the Persian rug, bats and pill bottles scattered all around them. Tommy dropped the nine on his way to the floor, and it bounced under the table.

While they were tangled up on the ground, I hopped over the sofa and grabbed the pistol. Instead of pointing it at them, I popped out the clip and stuck it in the back of my pants. Ramon quickly headed for the door to try to chase down Doc and the money.

Tommy slapped the Spork upside the head. "Get off me, you asshole. You and Gene and your fucking bats . . ."

When Tommy looked up and saw that I had the gun, he kicked

the table, half mad and half resigned. The Spork had already scrambled to his feet and run out the door with two bats under each arm.

"What the fuck's gotten into you?" I asked. I tossed the empty Beretta at Tommy. He flinched and covered his face. "You could've killed somebody with that thing."

The place was quiet now. Even the DVD had shut down during the melee. Tommy sat up. He appeared relieved that I wasn't going to shoot him.

"First of all," I said, "you should have been batting eighth, not sixth. I kept you up in the order as a favor to Gene. If you would just hit the fucking ball to right field sometimes, they'd quit feeding you all that outside junk. Then you could fucking pull something."

Tommy lay his hand on his forehead and looked down at the rug. "That's how my dad taught me to hit," he said. "So, just give me a fucking break. I got a lot on my mind right now."

"You and me both."

Tommy lit up an American Spirit. I took the pack and the lighter and lit one for myself. And then Tommy started talking. He said that Gene and Funderburk had taken on a business venture together about ten months back. The product was online pharmaceuticals, namely painkillers. Gene was the pharmacist, and Funderburk was the prescribing physician. Despite being kicked out of his practice, Funderburk still had a medical license in West Virginia. They sold the pills through a website Gene had started: pillacommunity.com.

"Get it?" Tommy asked. "Like pillar of the community."

"It's a stretch," I said, "but I get it."

Customers would contact Gene through the website, and he'd refer them to Funderburk. After a five-minute conversation about their supposed ailments, Funderburk would prescribe the medication, which Gene would fill. They split the profits.

"When the hell did Gene go to pharmacy school?" I asked.

Tommy took a drag off his cigarette. "He didn't. All you need is a pharmacy license. Geno got one in Nevada. Took less time than I spent at the DMV last week getting my new plates."

"You mean the bat man already had a place in Nevada?" By then nothing would have surprised me. Separate house, separate family. He might have been the real fucking Batman for all I knew.

"Don't need one," Tommy said. "All you gotta do is prove you have a corporation and a P.O. box. They don't check you out, or nothing. State board makes you fill out a two-page application. Boom, that's it. You're in business."

"And let me guess: you make money on the markup."

Tommy laughed. "Bat man was getting that OxyContin for fifteen cents a tablet, turning it out for two-fifty, sometimes three dollars. People eat that shit up with a spoon."

"Where do you fit in?" I asked.

"I'm the one who gave him the idea. I was buying Vike and some other stuff online, for my back, you know. Anyway, my ex-wife had this idea of doing an intervention for me. A fucking ambush is more like it. So Geno shows up for this intervention thing, and he becomes interested in how I was getting hold of all these pills. You know how he was: a man of many interests. So after I get out of rehab, I tell him what I know, and he does the rest. Being an honorable man, not to mention a relative, he helped me out with a business venture of my own. You know, a chance to wet my beak."

"What kind of business?"

"Nutritional supplements. That's where the money in the ice chest came from. That's my cash, not Doc and Gene's. They get most of theirs from the credit cards."

"Fucking steroids," I said. "You're selling juice, aren't you?"

"Whoa," he said. "You make it sound so vulgar. Steroids today are not what you've been taught to think they are. There's no testicle shriveling, bulging forehead, 'roid rages, or any of that other shit the media talks about. I'm selling clean-burning fuel. You supplement with a little HGH, maybe some red beans, and you're good to go. I got literature from a doctor in my car."

"I don't have a lot of faith in doctors right now."

He looked me up and down, like I needed some kind of evaluation. "I could take somebody like you," he said. "One-ninety, already got a nice cut, a good *V*-shape to the body, and with a little work, we'd get you up to about 220 with some serious shredding going on. Get you some of those nipple shirts and a buzz cut, and you'd be sexy as hell—like Vin fuckin' Diesel. And all those singles you're slapping to right field, we're talking opposite-field dingers from here on out. And your knees wouldn't be hurting from all that squatting you do behind the plate. It's all about recovery, Rice-Dawg, helping the body heal. And there ain't no side effects. We'll get those guns so pumped you won't even be able to reach around and wipe your ass."

"So, what size hat are you wearing these days?" I asked. "About eight and a half?"

Tommy sighed, shook his big dome. "I'm not even wasting my breath on you. You've been brainwashed by the fucking media."

Ramon walked in empty-handed, no money and no doctor. "Almost ran me over with that fucking Lexus," he said. "Then he gives me the finger out of his sunroof. I'm drilling his ass next time we play. You better have Benny warming up, because I'm sticking one right in his fucking ear. I don't give a fuck."

After Ramon had calmed down, I asked Tommy what he planned to do about his ice chest.

Tommy looked at the pill bottles. "I got what Funderburk wants, and he's got what I want. We'll hook up and make a trade."

"What about the accountant? What's his stake in this?"

Tommy shook his head. "He was keeping the books for Gene and Doc. But all he gives a shit about is that fucking bat. It's the one Babe Ruth hit the called shot with in the '32 World Series."

Ramon and I looked at each other. It didn't take a serious collector to understand a bat like that must be worth a pile of cash. We were talking about one of the most famous home runs of all time. Fifth inning. Game three. The 1932 World Series. Ruth stepped in against the Cubs' Charlie Root. Players in the Cubs dugout were talking shit, so Ruth talked back. And then, with two strikes on him, he extended his arm and index finger. I've seen the grainy film. To me, at least, the evidence is inconclusive. Maybe he pointed to center field, maybe not. Whatever he intended, Ruth launched the next pitch, a curve, into the center field bleachers, and the legend of the called shot was born. Seventy years later, all hell was breaking loose around me because of this bat.

Ramon asked if the bat was the real thing. Like me, he was aware that Gene had been taken to the cleaners a few times by memorabilia dealers.

"It's legit," Tommy said. "Ruth gave it to the little daughter of an old friend from the orphanage he grew up in, signed it for her and everything. And she held on to it for years, never said a word about it until she got cancer. She lived up in Baltimore her whole life, and the bat man read an article about her in the *Sun*. Heard she was sick, so he called her, offered to help out with the medical care. She had all these collectors bugging the shit out of her, and Gene shielded her from all that."

"What's a bat like that worth?" I asked.

"The article said between two and three million at auction. But Geno got it for a lot less than that."

"You mean he bought it from her?" I asked.

"He became this old lady's best friend," Tommy said. "She had thyroid cancer, didn't want to do chemo or anything, had refused all treatments. She just wanted to be comfortable. So Gene gets Funderburk to prescribe all her pain medication, which Gene provided for free, of course. Medicaid don't cover shit anymore. But Gene was going up there a couple times a week to visit with her. She didn't have a husband or any kids. He'd bring a bunch of videos, and they'd watch TV together."

Ramon smiled. "*Nympho Nurses.*"

"I think she liked those old *Columbo* movies," Tommy said. "But when she died last year, she left the bat to Gene. Had it in her will and everything. The deal was that Gene had to make a $250,000 donation to her church in her name."

I told Tommy 250K sounded skimpy considering the value of the bat.

"This old lady had no idea what the bat was worth. She thought Gene was a fucking saint."

I asked if Geno made that kind of cash from the pharmacy setup.

"Not at the time," Tommy said. "He borrowed the two-fifty from a guy up in Jersey."

"A shark?"

"Not a shark, but he's a connected man. Used to be a Jersey street boss for some New York family. Anyway, he went legit about ten years ago, got into commercial real estate, and made a fortune. Moved to Westport, built a big house. He's a huge fucking Yankees fan. Got four season tickets behind the Yanks dugout, six rows back from where Giuliani sits."

"The assholes with the stun gun must have been working for him," I said.

"Apparently, there was some sort of dispute over repayment of the loan," Tommy said. "Gene swears he paid it back, plus interest. But there was a disagreement. So this guy somehow finds out about the bat and sends muscle down here to take it from Gene."

"That explains the broken nose," Ramon said.

"Yeah, but me and Geno fought the guys off," Tommy said.

"Two guys?" I asked.

Tommy nodded, flicked his ashes on the rug.

"What'd they look like?"

"I don't know," Tommy said. "They were wearing those orange ski masks, like hunters. One of them had a rifle. He was shaking Gene down in the parking lot. I come out of the warehouse, see him busting Gene in the face with the butt of the gun, so I charge him, get him around the neck, and give him the old *shimewaza*."

"What the fuck is that?" Ramon asked.

"Sleeper hold," he said. "I put a little pressure on the carotid artery and laid the cocksucker on the ground. Gene kicked the other guy in the balls."

I asked what kind of car they were driving.

"A big white conversion van. It had Maryland plates. I remember that."

"And neither of them had a stun gun?" I asked.

Tommy shook his head. "Nah, I would have remembered that."

Didn't sound like either of the guys who came after me, or who'd rousted Joy for the bat.

"Must be a different crew," I said. "The guys I'm talking about were wearing throwback jerseys, and the chatty one was driving an NSX."

This got Tommy's attention. "Throwbacks?"

"Yeah, the old-school threads. Dr. J and Namath."

"This former mob guy," Tommy said, "has a son who's into that shit. The old man set him up with a sweatshop making counterfeit throwback jerseys. Good stuff, too. They look just like the Mitchell &

Ness, only the kid's turning this shit out for like six dollars a pop with Mexican illegals, then selling them on eBay for a hundred fifty."

"Selling the Mexicans?" Ramon asked.

"No, you nitwit. The fucking throwback jerseys."

Tommy was going on about this Harold Carmichael jersey he'd bought from the kid, describing the shade of green.

I had to interrupt again to get him back on track. "How do you know so much about these people?"

Tommy hedged. "Me and this kid, we're from the same neighborhood. I used to be in collections."

"So, tell me about the old man. What's his name?"

"Fuck that," Tommy said. "It's time for me to shut the fuck up."

"Don't screw around," I said. "I could tell the cops about your little vitamin shop."

Tommy looked up, sighed. "Look, this kid's father did ten years on RICO charges, took the fall for some bigger guys. They owed him when he got out, set him up with money for a legit business, basically let him do his own thing. But he still lives by the code, you know. And this kid of his, he's a real jackoff. Not to mention very unpredictable. So you can threaten all you want. I ain't saying no more than that."

CHAPTER 12

After all the fakes and bullshit memorabilia Gene had poured his money into, it turned out he'd actually acquired one of the most coveted items in sports. It felt just about right, too, seeing how Ruth likely never intended to call any shot. This bat, no matter how much it was worth, carried its share of deception.

Gene had brought a tape of the home run into the warehouse a couple years back and insisted that I watch it with him. He popped the tape into the VCR, and grainy black-and-white images appeared on the screen.

"Where the hell did you get this?" I asked.

"You don't want to know."

Ruth, the original hefty lefty, stepped to the plate. According to Gene, the Cubs fans and players had been riding his ass all day.

There was shit being talked. That much was evident, even though the film had no sound. Ruth appeared to be paying as much attention to the Cubs dugout as he was to the pitcher. It looked like a contest between us and Funderburk's D-Rays. Bad vibes all around. Ruth took a strike, and held up his index finger, staring at the Cubs bench and acknowledging the count. He took a couple of balls, then another strike. Looking at a 2-2 count, he made another gesture, an extended arm, the index finger raised again. Gene and I disagreed on where he was pointing and just what he meant.

"He's pointing to the Cubs dugout," I said. "Look at those guys waving their arms at him. They're busting his balls."

Gene paused and rewound the tape. "Bullshit. He's pointing to fucking center field."

"Maybe he's pointing to the pitcher," I said.

Gene rewound again and froze the image. It was just too hard to tell what Ruth had meant with the gesture, and I didn't care enough to debate Gene on the matter.

"Look," I said. "Either way, it's a helluva thing. They rode his ass, he talked back and then backed up his words."

That wasn't enough for Gene. He rewound and watched the moment over and over again until I got bored and walked out of the office.

I invited Joy to dinner in order to tell her about the Babe Ruth bat. My thinking was that if I could get hold of the bat and give it to her, she could auction it off and come away with enough cash to live comfortably *and* to buy the limo business out of hock. My only remuneration—a small finder's fee—would be an opportunity to buy the limo outfit from her over a designated period of time. If everything fell into place, I could save my business, Gene's business, and the Whip Spa Yankees, which is all I wanted to begin with and which wasn't, to my mind, greedy at all. Exactly how I'd reacquire this bat without being subjected to gunshot wounds and/or the wrong end of a stun gun was the part I hadn't figured out just yet.

I suggested Chick-fil-A for dinner, but Joy countered with the Cheesecake Factory. Fair enough, I said. "I hear they got good popcorn shrimp."

She was giving me shit when we sat down in the booth, wanting to know why I'd insisted we take my car instead of Gene's Navigator.

"I'm accustomed to my own car. Besides, that Navigator sucks down the gas."

"Bullshit," she said. "I know why you won't ride in it. Gene told me. It's because of his flag."

"What are you talking about?"

"You're embarrassed by his American flag."

I dismissed that idea, even though it couldn't have been truer. That flag took up the whole rear quarter panel. I'd seen flags in car lots that weren't that big. Gene had gone a little overboard with the flag stuff after 9/11, even put them on his limos and tried to plaster one to my 'Vette. It didn't help that Joy had also stuck her PRAY FOR AMERICA sticker on the Navigator's rear window.

"Are you ashamed to be an American?" she asked.

"I'm not ashamed. I'm just not into making statements, you know. Not with my car, anyway. I like a clean look."

"Do you have any allegiance at all?" She motioned to my warm-up pants. "I mean to anything except Adidas. You go around dressing like you're in fuckin' Run-D.M.C."

"I'm a loyal consumer. Besides, they make good shit. It's the brand with the three stripes."

"I actually like the black T-shirt," she said. "I can live with that. A good fit, no logos. But for Christ sake, wear some pants with fucking belt loops once in a while."

Thankfully, the waitress came over to take our drink order. Joy ordered a Kir Royale, and I got a Jack and Coke. After the waitress left, Joy went right back at me. It was the same way she used to go after Gene. I wondered if it was therapeutic for her. If so, then I was willing to take the shitstorm—for a little while at least.

"Gene said you didn't even have a favorite baseball team. You're this big fan, and you don't give a shit about any particular team. I don't get it."

Truth was, I'd been a Yankees fan ever since I read Joe Pepitone's book. But I had to keep quiet about it around my uncle Phil because he'd always hated the Yanks so much. For some reason, it had become more difficult, rather than easier, to express my loyalty to the Bombers after Phil was murdered. I would have felt like I was double-crossing him.

Joy leaned forward and waited, as if she'd just asked a question. She was wearing this white sweater, and it looked like she'd had something done to her hair. It was still long, but she'd had bangs cut straight across her forehead. It looked good, and I told her.

"You think so?" she asked. "I'm trying this new hairdresser. The other girl wasn't working out, always breaking up with her boyfriends, and then she'd fucking take it out on my hair. These hairdressers, none of them are consistent. They're flighty, artistic types."

Her hair problems made me think of this business idea Gene once had. He'd wanted to send strippers to tonsorial school and open a barbershop for men, a gentlemen's establishment. Shave, haircut, and a hand job. All for one price. He went so far as to copyright the name: The Trim Palace.

I finally steered Joy toward the subject of the storage space. I'd decided not to tell her about Gene's foray into pharmaceuticals. She'd find out from someone else, but I wanted to spare her one more troubling secret of Gene for the time being. The Babe Ruth bat, though, was something I felt she should know about.

"Are you sure it's worth two million?" she asked.

"Maybe even three," I said.

The waitress dropped off our drinks. Joy took a sip of hers, made a face, and leaned back in her chair.

I laid out my plan in its simplest form: I fetched the bat, she put it up for auction, then I managed the limo operation while slowly purchasing the cars from her.

She laughed. "So you're saying I keep all the money? All you want is the stupid limo business?"

"Correction," I said. "An opportunity to purchase the limo business. I'm asking for no gifts, just an opportunity."

She took another sip of the drink and shook her head. "If it was anybody else, I'd suspect he was working an angle. But you don't even want the aggravation of having money. Do you realize how stupid that is?"

"Joy, I had a good thing going before all this started. I just want to ease back into the old routine. No problems. Lots of peace and quiet. Besides, the bat belongs to you."

"These guys who came to the house," she said, "I don't think they'd hesitate to kill you over something like this."

I drained my Jack and Coke, which was mostly Coke in the first place. It wasn't doing much for my nerves.

"That's why you go public as soon as you have the bat in hand," I said. "Hire an attorney, a PR guy, somebody to put your face out there. Once we get Gene's story out in the open and how he came to acquire the bat, I think these morons will back off."

"So, just how *did* he get the bat?"

I told her the story Tommy had told me, about Gene befriending the elderly woman whose father had known the Babe at St. Mary's

Industrial School for Boys, and how Gene had promised to give $250 thousand to the woman's church after she died. Joy's response wasn't what I expected.

"He probably fucked her, the sonuvabitch. I wouldn't have put it past him."

"I think this woman was in her seventies."

Joy just laughed. "Trust me, Gene was into some weird shit. Sick, twisted shit. He used to defile me, Joe. He would take a carrot and make me—"

I slapped my hands over my ears. "I don't want to know about this, Joy."

She leaned forward and fixed me with a softer look. "I'm just saying it hasn't been easy for me. Gene provided the material goods when he was alive. I can't deny that. But there were too many strings attached. Do you think I ever knew intimacy from him?"

Joy looked around, checked the booth behind us, and then whispered, "I slept with someone last year. I don't feel good about it, but it was something I did to survive."

She let out a weary breath, turned her gaze from me to her drink, and then back.

"I guess you think I'm a slut."

"No, not at all."

"I'm sure Gene told you about how I used to dance at that club in Philadelphia. But even then, I never slept around. There were a couple of guys in high school, a boss I had at IHOP, a neighbor who was really more of a father figure, maybe a couple other people here and there. But that was it when I met Gene. I thought I'd be true to him for the rest of my life."

"It's not easy," I said. "I mean, who could blame you under those circumstances, the thing with the carrot and all, whatever that was, not that I'm asking."

I looked around for the waitress, hoping she'd come back and interrupt the conversation.

"This woman I was seeing," I said, "she thinks you got three years, tops, in a relationship. So, I had this idea that maybe marriages should be like professional sports contracts, you know. You ink a three-year deal, maybe four with an option for the fifth. You lower the pressure that way. That and the expectations."

That's when Joy asked about my marriage. "Gene told me you didn't like to talk about it."

"Not much to say. I made some mistakes. I was an asshole back then."

She took a drink of her Kir Royale, shivered a little at the alcohol. "I can't believe you were ever an asshole."

"Yeah, well, it's true."

"What did you do? Tell me. Gene said you weren't even together a year."

"I slept with another woman."

"Just one?"

"One was enough in my case."

"How did you meet her?"

"Who?"

"The woman you slept with."

"She had this kid," I said. "I was coaching Little League baseball. I was just off paper from my probation, living up in Cliffside. Me and this girl, Pam, had gotten married. I wasn't one of those holy rollers, or anything like that, but I was going to church back then, and that's where I met Pam. I was trying to get involved in the community, do something good, like coaching Little League. So, this woman had a son who was kind of peculiar. He was on my team, and I felt bad for him. They were new to town, and he couldn't hit for shit. Was kind of cross-eyed, couldn't catch the ball. All the kids made fun of him, but I tried to encourage him. Anyway, his mother was divorced, and she thanked me for reaching out to her son in a difficult time."

Joy shook her head. "And you fucked her?"

"I told you I was an asshole."

She didn't disagree this time.

What I didn't bother explaining to Joy was that I'd never set out to sleep with the woman. I'd truly believed that the mother of this ballplayer was a deep person and that I was a deep person and that there was something worth knowing behind her sad, murky-green eyes, something important we both needed to share with one another.

I'd been dead wrong, of course. All we ended up doing was fucking on her bathroom floor, which I'd offered to retile. We fucked a second time on the passenger side of my Caprice.

My wife, Pam, grew up in a house where phones didn't ring in the middle of the night and steak knives didn't lie around waiting for trouble. She was exotic to me, Episcopalian, and I'd never thought for a moment that I'd fail her. I just assumed that we'd have children and land in a home like her parents': clean, cool, quiet, and void of strife. There was always a calm hum in that house, the air conditioner, or the furnace or a humidifier, or maybe God himself. I could go to sleep there and not wake up for days. Of course, girls who grow up in houses like that don't expect their new husbands to sleep with itinerant waitresses.

Pam was kneeling at the toilet in our apartment, crying and puking and still clutching the hairbrush of the ballplayer's mother. She'd found it on the floorboard of the car.

"Oh, God. This is the worst thing I've ever heard in my life."

"There are a lot worse things to hear, Pam." It wasn't the kindest thing to say, but I was saying it to myself as much as to her.

I squatted and touched her back, pulling the brush out of her hand at the same time. I laid the brush in the trash can, slid it down in there quietly as if she might not notice.

"I think maybe I should get my stuff and leave," I said. "It's probably the best thing."

She let out a sob and a gag at the same time, but nothing came out of her mouth.

"What did I do?" she asked. "Just tell me what I did. I'm so sorry."

At that instant, it became clear to me that the only thing I could ever do is let this poor woman down. That was the only thing. I owed it to her to get the hell out of her life. And then, two years later, after I'd moved to D.C. and gone into business for myself, I got a call from a guy I'd coached Little League with in New Jersey. He said that Pam had died. She'd found out she had ovarian cancer only six months earlier.

I called Pam's older sister, who remembered me with very little fondness. She accused me of stealing time from a woman who only had a limited supply to begin with.

"She might have married somebody decent if it hadn't been for you. She might've had a baby and left behind a part of herself. You took that from her and from her family and from all of her friends, and I hope you ask God to forgive you for that."

When she put it that way, I didn't feel like I even deserved to ask for any kind of forgiveness. I'd found out that her parents were requesting that people make donations to their church in Pam's name. I sat down and wrote a check for $1,783.37, all that was in my savings account, but then I shredded it, thinking the gesture would only upset her family.

Joy asked me to come inside, even though we'd already reached a decision on the bat: if I could track it down and deliver it to her, she'd put the wood up for auction, buy Gene's business out of probate, and give me a chance to purchase it from her. She even wanted to pay me a salary during the period that I would be running things.

While Joy paid the babysitter, I sat down on the sofa and whipped through the Extra Innings package on Gene's plasma Hitachi. The Devil Rays and Mariners were getting cranked up in Seattle, Ichiro leading off the bottom of the first with a slap hit the opposite way, exactly what I wanted Tommy Pumpkin to try at least once in his life.

Joy took off her shoes, these pink Pumas, and picked up a couple of little Gene's toys.

"You want something to drink?" she asked.

"Nah, I'm good."

"Well, I need a glass of water," she said. "Those fucking Kir Royales will give me a headache if I don't."

The house was cold, as usual. Lou Piniella, Devil Rays manager and the greatest slow outfielder in baseball history, looked snug and warm in the Rays' dugout, wearing his black-and-green warm-up jacket. That's what Joy needed for houseguests: warm-up jackets. She went to the kitchen, fixed a glass of water, came back, and sat down at the other end of the sofa. I could feel her staring at me. I figured she was a little lonely, maybe just wanted to talk some more.

I pointed at the TV screen. "Un-fucking-believable picture on this thing."

Joy shook her head. "Yeah, Gene used to come down here in the middle of the night and watch his porn movies. He'd get the surround sound going. I'd wake up thinking I was in the middle of a fucking orgy, walls vibrating and everything. He was so fucking inconsiderate."

I made a conscious effort to look at Joy, and not the game. "I wish I could think of something to say. I know this must be a difficult time, mixed emotions and so forth."

She lifted her legs onto the couch, crossed them beneath her.

"I gotta tell you something," she said.

"Okay." I hit the mute button on the remote, a gesture of sorts.

"I was lying at the restaurant. You know, when I said I slept with someone last year. I didn't. It's just that I thought about it. I thought about it a lot. There was someone I was really attracted to, only they didn't know it."

I took my time coming up with a response, tried to craft it just so. Don't say too much, don't say too little. I settled on this one: "Everybody has those kinds of feelings sometimes."

"This was different," she said. "I used to imagine that I was married to this person, that I had his kid instead of Gene's. I used to think about how things would be different if I was with him."

I was trying to come up with another response. I'd just about decided that maybe the best thing was to recommend she seek some grief counseling—I'd heard about that somewhere—when I noticed the way her hands were shaking on the water glass and the way she was looking at me.

"Oh, shit," I said. "You mean . . ."

She looked down. Neither of us said anything for a moment, and then she set her water glass on the coffee table and moved closer.

"I've seen the way you look at me sometimes," she said. "It's not dirty, and I like that. It's not dirty at all."

"You're a very beautiful woman, but this might not be—"

I never finished that sentence. What did she mean, not dirty? She made it sound honorable, important, like an achievement. It's not that I believed she was a deep person, and I'd realized long ago that I wasn't deep. Truth was, there were empty spots in me, lots of them, cold little hollows that I could mostly ignore. But now they were full and warm, like I'd been the one drinking those Kir Royales, like Lou Piniella had draped his jacket over my shoulders. And instead of finishing that sentence, I reached up and traced the line of Joy's bangs, watched her eyes close and the subtle teenage scars on her cheeks relax. And there we were, on the couch where Gene used to watch his dirty movies.

CHAPTER 13

"You think you're gonna run a motherfucking cover two on me? Ha!"

Theresa's son, Louis, was beating the shit out of me at *Madden*. It was the brand-new version that Ramon and I had picked up, and the skinny little sonuvabitch had already mastered it.

"Just snap the fucking ball." I was perched on the edge of my recliner, hunched over, PS2 controller in hand, trying to save myself from another beatdown at the hands of a twelve-year-old.

Louis was standing, braying and talking shit in his Donovan McNabb jersey. "No. Uh-uh. Here's the thing. I'm gonna fucking *tell* you how I'm gonna burn your ass on this play. And your ass is gonna have to sit there and suck on it."

He went on like this as the play clock wound down, explaining how the audible he'd just called would leave his slot man open over the middle and his tight end uncovered on a post route, and how, if I brought my safeties up, he'd burn my ass deep with both wideouts. "You are seriously fucked, Mr. Riceballs."

I was fucked, all right. I could hardly remember how to call a play. When it was working for me, that controller felt like a glove. Now it looked like a plastic frown in my hands. None of the buttons could erase the image of Joy crying after we'd been together on the sofa. She said she hadn't felt anything in so long that it had just been too much. "It's not a bad thing," she said. "All you did was make me feel good for a change. I think I had given up on that ever happening again." What I should have been feeling at that moment was guilt for disrespecting Gene's memory, for sleeping with his wife while he lay dead in the ground. But what I really experienced was fear that I could make someone feel anything that strong.

The cover-two pinch was my favorite defense. It was also a chickenshit defense, guarding against the big play but allowing Louis to nick me up between the corners and the safeties. Fuck this, I thought, calling an audible and bringing the house at him. I put a spin move on his tackle, charging Ray Lewis right into his backfield for a sack. But I was too late. Louis was already laughing. He released the ball, via David Carr, and lofted a fifty-yard touchdown pass to Corey Bradford.

"*That's* how you run the West Coast offense, motherfucker! Just like that!"

He was in my face, pointing. I swatted his hand away. "Get the fuck outta here, you little shit."

He stepped back but didn't let up. "Dude, this is the fucking Texans doing this to you. You got the Ravens, Ray Ray, and the number one defense in the whole NFL, and I'm going at you like a bitch-ass high school team. It's sad. It really is. I'm not putting you on."

The kid spoke the truth, I couldn't deny it. It was there on the screen: 49–3 in the fourth quarter.

He settled back onto the sofa, shook his head with pity. "This is fucked up. Seriously fucked up."

"Will you just kick off?" I said. "And hush the cussing, while you're at it."

Louis laughed. "I thought you were cool with that. Now that I'm beating your ass, you're gonna play like that, huh?"

"I am cool with it. It's Theresa. She says you come home from my place sounding like a fucking Ludacris CD."

"She's got problems," he said. "It ain't none of my doing."

He kicked off, dropped my return man at the eighteen. I asked if he'd noticed Theresa acting any different lately.

Louis snorted. "Depends on what you mean by different. She's always acting different. Especially since her daddy came around."

He took his eyes off the screen, stared at me. "Why? She been giving you shit about something?"

I didn't go into it with Louis. He was always in my corner when

Theresa was having a bad time of it. We joked how the two of us were constantly one and two on her shit list. It was a confidence we kept, a good thing considering stories Theresa had told me about men she'd seen in the past. Louis went after one of the guys with a fire poker when he came out of his room and saw the guy kissing Theresa. He was only eight at the time. Louis keyed up another guy's car, carved the word *fag* in the driver's-side door. He'd stolen money from their wallets, lifted watches, cell phones. The worst he'd done to me was routinely whip my ass at video games. And so I felt a responsibility—to do what, I wasn't sure.

I asked Louis about Theresa's old man. I hadn't heard of him coming around since the night I met Theresa. She didn't have much to say about the man, and what she did say was all bad; about his gambling and how he'd disappear for weeks at a time when she was little and how he finally just went away for good when she was seven. He'd resurfaced when she graduated from high school, had tried to make amends, but ended up stealing $600 of graduation money she'd gotten from various relatives. The next time he came around, Theresa got herself arrested for assaulting him with a butcher knife. She said he called her a "cold bitch." He told her a normal girl would have cried or tried to understand why he took the money. Theresa wasn't cold, but she didn't cry either. She'd never let anybody get to her like that.

Louis said that Theresa's father had something wrong with his liver. "Must be bad," he said. "Talking about he needs a new one."

"A transplant?"

Louis shrugged. "Snap the ball, man."

He smothered Jamal Lewis in the backfield.

"I'm telling you," he said, "the draw play simply *does not* work on *Madden*. It's something that fat ass needs to work out."

"Is he in town?"

"Who? Madden?"

"Theresa's old man."

"He came by last week," Louis said. "Middle of the night, saying he's dying. I don't blame Theresa, throwing his ass out. I don't like the way the man looked at me."

"You never met him before that?"

Louis shook his head. "You may as well go for it," he said. "Down forty-six in the fourth. You got nothing to lose. Maybe some more pride."

"What'd Theresa say?"

"Told him to take his redneck ass back down to Raleigh. Said he didn't deserve a new liver, and she hoped he died slow and painful just like her brother."

I went ahead and punted, feeling more comfortable on defense. It was better than being stopped cold at every turn. Louis went right back to work through the air, moving across midfield. And then my cell phone rang. Louis had downloaded Biggie's "Notorious Thugs" for me as the ringtone. I was real happy with the way it sounded and always let it go on a few extra seconds before answering.

It was Ramon calling. He said he had some information on the Babe Ruth bat.

"Remember that Joe Montana throwback jersey I bought?" he said.

"The Niners, or the Chiefs jersey?"

"Chiefs," he said. "Home model from '94. It was red, but it faded to pink the one time I washed it. Piece of shit. Thing is, I bought it on eBay, thought it was a Mitchell & Ness but turned out it was a counterfeit."

"What's this got to do with the bat?"

"I think I bought it from the dude in Jersey, the kid that took Geno's Babe Ruth bat. He's got an eBay store called Lansing Throwback Originals."

"What makes you think this is the same kid?"

"I was pissed about the jersey, so I tried contacting the seller. Never got a reply to my e-mails, so I took another avenue for contacting this Lansing prick. I write him an e-mail from a different address, tell him I'm directing a Nelly video and I need some throwbacks for the shoot."

"Nice tactic," I said.

"Damn right, it was. Next thing I know, Lansing e-mails me his cell number, and I call him up and threaten to beat his ass and turn him in to Mitchell & Ness's lawyers. And he tells me if I want a war, he'll bring a fucking war, and that he's got my number on caller ID and I better back the fuck off if I know what's good for me."

"What'd you do?"

Ramon took a deep breath. I could hear the baby crying in the background. "I didn't have time to get involved in any shit. But I just did a People Search on this Lansing motherfucker and got his address. It turns out he lives in Edgewater, New Jersey."

Louis had switched over to DVD. He was lying on the sofa, watching my uncensored Maury Povich disc and drinking a Coke. I stood up and walked over to the kitchenette.

"This has gotta be the mob guy's son," I said. "The shithead who rousted me that night at the warehouse said the same thing about bringing a war."

"So, what do you wanna do?" Ramon asked.

"How do you feel about going to New Jersey after our game Friday night?"

Ramon went quiet, but the baby was still going strong in the background.

"I'm going fucking crazy over here," he said. "Sometimes, I don't think I even like this kid. Check that. Most of the time I *know* I don't like him. I'm the biggest asshole in the world. You don't even have to say it. I wanna feel something, but I don't."

"That's probably normal," I said. "It's a stressful time. Maybe it'll get better once the kid starts sleeping through the night."

"I tell you," he said, "I can't wait until he's like twelve, or thirteen, and all calm. Then we can do some shit together. It'll be a lot better then."

"I'm sure it will," I said.

Glancing at Louis, who was sprawled across the sofa, made me feel like a liar.

"All right," Ramon said. "I'm in. What are we gonna do up there, steal it back?"

"We'll see what this little prick has got cooking for starters. Maybe talk to him, see what we can work out."

"Won't he recognize you?"

"I doubt it. It was dark that night in the parking lot. Plus, I was wearing a cap and my uniform. Let's wear suits Friday night. We can say we're attorneys representing the Dellorso estate."

CHAPTER 14

Louis and I never got around to working on the blue crab project. Nickelodeon was running the *SpongeBob* episode where he had the rancid breath, and then Comedy Central had the *South Park* where Jimmy takes steroids. We figured what are the chances of two great episodes like that airing back to back, and so we bagged the report, which would have been a pain in the ass anyway, because Louis would have sat there not doing shit while I Googled everything.

I took the last couple of Vikes from Gene's stash, drank a Jack and Coke in a Solo cup, and fell asleep in my recliner. Louis slept on the couch. I'd found this to be the best arrangement when he stayed with me, seeing how he was afraid to sleep in a room by himself. The first time he came over, I set him up on the sofa and went to bed. I got up to take a leak in the middle of the night and nearly stepped on Louis's head. He'd snuck in my bedroom and made a pallet on the floor beside me. Theresa only told me later that he did this every night at home.

Neither of us remembered to set the alarm, so we overslept. There were no eggs in the refrigerator, and I was out of cereal, so I stopped at 7-Eleven and let Louis buy a box of Froot Loops and a Dr Pepper for breakfast. I grabbed a Red Bull for myself, and we dined in the car.

"If Theresa asks, I cooked eggs."

Louis nodded. He was a different kid when I took him to school in the mornings. Never said a word, just wore this long expression like he was being hauled off to do a ten-year stint at Rikers.

"And you took your vitamin, too," I said.

By the time we got to the middle school, Louis was thirty minutes late, so I had to walk him into the office and sign him in. He stayed about ten yards behind me the whole way, delaying the prospect of entry, like maybe if he hung back a chunk of space debris might fall out of the sky and kill him so he wouldn't have to go in the building. I hated school enough in my own day, skipped enough classes when I was working with my uncle Phil that I ended up not graduating. But I'd never seen anything like Louis. His feelings for this place ran right down to the bone.

The office had that school smell going on, like dust and yeast rolls and desperation, the smell that reminds you of shit you don't want to remember. I picked up a late slip for Louis and handed it to him. He just stood there, silent, backpack weighing him down. When he wasn't running his mouth, I realized how skinny he was and how young he looked, young even for his age.

School is a good prep course for incarceration: the feeling and the hope that you don't belong there, that there's something better on the outside, the fact that you can read six pages of a book and not know what the fuck you just read, that even when you try you don't get the point or the metaphor the lazy-ass teacher wants you to get. All of that shit has gotta mean something, that everybody else there is fucked up and you're not, or maybe it's just that you can't wait until 3:10 to get the fuck out of there for another seventeen hours, get out in the real world where important things are happening, and there *are* more meaningful lessons for a lot of kids, whether by choice or not. Most educators don't take this into account.

I told Louis I had to go to one of his favorite places, Sports Authority, that afternoon to pick up some game balls for the Whip Spa Yankees. It was a bullshit story, but I liked going there myself, so I thought maybe it'd give him something to look forward to while he did his time. We always had fun at the Authority, throwing footballs around and playing street hockey in the aisles until some asshole told us to knock it off.

Louis nodded, looked at the big clock on the wall, and rolled his eyes. It was still a long time until three o'clock. I watched him walk down the hallway and go into a classroom. As I stepped out into the sunshine, a woman called to me.

"Are you Louis's father?"

She was young, dark hair pulled back, carrying files under her arm. Her eyes looked a little tired behind her tiny red horn-rims, and it put me at ease. Despite the Red Bull, I felt tired myself.

I told her I was a good friend of Louis's mother. I didn't want her to think that Theresa would dump him with just anybody.

"I'm sorry he was late. It was my fault. I forgot to set the alarm, and then I wanted to make sure he had breakfast, so I cooked him some eggs. Protein, you know. Theresa says it's good for his brain."

She smiled, and I realized I'd tried too hard to sound competent.

"Is there a problem?" I asked.

"No, it's just that I've been trying to call her. I've left some messages but haven't heard back from her."

Theresa was probably screening her calls and didn't want to talk to the woman. She wasn't a big fan of the public school system. She said it was only there to serve "the little genius fuckers, and nobody gives a shit about a kid like Louis. They'd just as soon he drop out than bring down their fucking standardized-test scores."

"She's having a tough time right now," I said. "Her father's sick, and she's been working a lot. You know how it is, single mother and all."

The morning sun felt warm on my back. My head was starting to pound, and my knees ached. I was actually thinking about making a call to Tommy Pumpkin, asking him where I could get some more Vike.

The woman told me she was the school's vice principal.

"I just wanted to talk to her about Louis's IEP."

I didn't know what that was, but I told her I'd pass along the message.

"Just out of curiosity," she said, "do you spend much time with Louis?"

"Well, it's not like she just abandons him, you know. We have an arrangement. I help her out when she works. This child-care thing can be expensive. Plus, she doesn't want him to stay at home by himself all the time."

"I think that's good," she said. "Or what I meant to say is that I think it's good that he's spending time with someone. It can be important with a child like Louis to spend time with a pro-social adult, especially if the adult encourages him."

I couldn't be sure, but it felt like I'd just received a compliment. Either way, the fog in my head was beginning to burn off.

She moved the files to her other arm and smiled. "Louis is probably never going to be a great student. As I'm sure you know, he takes medication for his ADHD. But sometimes people who have these problems are very gifted in other areas. It's just important that he's encouraged in areas in which he excels."

I knew about ADHD. I hadn't been in a hole or anything. But all Theresa ever mentioned was the oppositional defiance thing, and she never said anything about medicine. The vice principal was throwing a lot of stuff at me. I needed to step out of the box and think it over.

"He's really good at *Madden*," I said.

"*Madden*?"

"Yeah, the game. He's like a—what do you call it?—a progeny."

"Prodigy," she said.

"Either way, it's amazing. He doesn't read the instructions, or nothing. He just starts playing, and he gets it. Every little detail."

"It can be as simple as that," she said. "Make him feel good about it. Who knows, maybe he'll be a game designer one day."

She smiled and waited for me to say something. I felt like I was on the spot, a teacher calling on me to cough up something useful.

"That'd be cool," I said. "I could get advance copies."

CHAPTER 15

I thought I had a better feel for Theresa's situation than she might have imagined. After all, my own mother had been tied down because of me. She must have felt like Theresa, that she couldn't get away from her kid. But she managed it in her own way. When she heard those sounds in the distance—cars, trains, people laughing and drinking—she didn't resist, not like Theresa. She'd find a place to leave me, usually with good people, and then she'd go out and try to live a life. It wasn't so bad for me, not always. I understood that my mother had this life away from me. And when she'd come back from wherever she'd been, it was okay. We didn't fight too much, not like Louis and Theresa, and my mother never let things like schoolteachers and bosses get to her. Granted, she was too busy stealing from most of her bosses to hate them, so maybe she wasn't the best comparison, but still.

I tried to talk Theresa into lifting the communication blackout with the school, but she wasn't having it.

"You just don't know," she said. "You have no idea what I put up with from that school. It's like they expect me to—"

She shook her head like there was no use talking to me, like I didn't have enough sense to understand. A strong argument could have been made.

"It's like they expect you to what?" I asked. "You're talking in circles again. You know, it's very frustrating when you do that. You start telling me something, and then you don't finish."

She was pounding ice cubes on the kitchen counter with a ball-peen hammer, had them wrapped up in a dishrag. She'd just gotten in from her Thursday-afternoon shift. Me and Louis had been waiting with pupusas, fresh off our Sports Authority sojourn. We were in a good mood, had the pupusas plated, the aroma swelling, and Louis was wearing the Randy Moss road jersey I'd bought him at the Authority. For my part, I'd taken a stroll through Theresa's medicine chest. She took Ambien to help her sleep. I pocketed three for later. I was in serious need of some shut-eye.

Thing was, Theresa could suck the joy right out of a room when she was off her game. You could tell it before she even spoke a word. She had this way of looking at you, like she was sizing you up, measuring your stupidity. Louis got up and went back to his room the minute she walked in, shut the door and cranked up his T.I. CD. *"You can look me in my eyes, see I'm ready for whatever. Anything don't kill me, make me better."*

"This woman seemed nice," I said. "She said something about Louis taking medication for ADHD."

Theresa looked up from the ice she was cracking. She had a strand of hair hanging in front of her face, and she looked tired, like the Ambien wasn't helping.

"She's got no fucking right to be telling you that."

"What? You don't want me to know?"

"For all she knows, you could be anybody. Besides, you're not related to Louis. You're not his father."

"She said he could have hidden talents. The important thing is to encourage him."

I had my throwing hand resting on the counter. Theresa raised the hammer and slammed it down on my hand. Right away, I knew something was broken. She was very athletic and could hit the shit out of a ball at the batting cages, even against the fast machine.

"What the fuck?" I said.

She raised the hammer again, like she was coming after my head this time. Her eyes had that crazy look to them, like Nicholson in *The Shining*.

"You don't think I fucking encourage him?" she screamed. "You don't think I've tried everything I know to do? Well, you don't know shit. Do you hear me, you motherfucker? You don't know shit about me and him. You don't know shit about anything, you *or* that fucking vice principal."

I backpedaled and leaned against the refrigerator, feeling nauseous, trying not to clutch my injured paw. The evening sun beamed through the kitchen window, dropping those heavy September shadows across the dusty counter and the bottle of brandy Theresa had set out. This kitchen wasn't nearly as sunny as Gene and Joy's. Theresa only had one box of cereal on top of the refrigerator: Louis's Cocoa Pebbles.

She gritted her teeth and stepped toward me. There must have been a reason that she decided not to go after my skull. It certainly appeared that all my body parts were in play. But she brought the hammer down on the counter—slammed it down with intent—then dropped it on the dirty linoleum floor. She slid down right behind it and sat back against the cabinets.

The nausea passed, and the pain in my hand turned to a steady throb. I'd taken enough foul balls off my limbs to get through it, although I knew I'd need an X ray later. In a way, I was thankful. At least I could procure some pain medication out of this.

Theresa had her knees up, arms resting across the knees and her head atop her arms. She wasn't crying. I'd never seen her cry. But she looked as dejected as I'd ever seen her, like a whole bunch of shit had caught up to her at once.

I took a piece of ice and held it to my hand, and then I sat down on the floor beside her.

"You're right," I said. "It's none of my fucking business."

She didn't answer for a long time. In that moment, I realized the music from Louis's room had gotten quieter.

"I always thought that when I had a kid, it would be different," she said. "I always imagined that I'd be the kind of parent my mother never was to me. But the thing about Louis is that he's never let me be that way. He's always been difficult, right from the start, like he was just put here to push my buttons."

"It's gotta be tough," I said, "being with him by yourself. You always have to be the boss lady, keeping him in line, making him do homework and all that shit. It's not like the two of you ever get to enjoy being with one another, you know, like without some kind of pressure built up."

"One day, he's going to leave," she said, "and I'll probably never see him again. Or if I do, it won't be very often. He won't give a shit about me. And what scares me is that I might not give a shit about him either."

"I don't think that's gonna happen," I said. "I haven't seen my mother in years, but I still give a shit. I still wonder how it's going for her."

She reached up on the counter and grabbed her Camels. She lit one, took a long drag, and leaned back against the cabinets. I borrowed her lighter and lit one of my Marlboro Lights.

"I'm kind of lucky," I said. "I'll be the first to admit that I'd never be a good father. I don't think I could administer the discipline or maintain any sense of order. But the thing is, because I suck at that kind of thing, I think Louis is kind of relaxed when he's at my place. He cusses like hell, but so what? He's funny. I like having him around."

She finally smiled, a hint at some brightness inside, something I could tend for her. It was the kind of thing that stayed with me when she wasn't around, when she took weeks, here and there, to be by herself.

"There was this one time," she said, "when Louis was little—maybe three or four—and I had some extra money from this guy I was seeing. He had family money, didn't work, just hung out at the bar I was working in, leaving me big tips. A fucking asshole, like a child. He had this thing where—"

She shook her head, stopped talking.

"Fuck this guy," I said. "What were you gonna tell me about you and Louis?"

She sighed. "So I took Louis to Myrtle Beach, just me and him. I had all these ideas of how fun it would be: reading a magazine while he dug in the sand, splashing in the waves, even going out to restaurants together. I figured, you know, that I could make it work, being a woman alone with a kid. I thought it would be good. No, I fucking thought it would be great. But then he was just such a little shit, even then. He threw sand on this little girl who tried to play with him, wouldn't go in the ocean because he was scared. And restaurants, forget about that. All he wanted was Chicken McNuggets. Just laid his head on the table at this one place and cried. Wouldn't pick his head up, and then he starts kicking me under the table. I totally lost it, jerked him up by the arm, and people were looking at me like I'm some kind of fucking bitch monster, like poor Louis got stuck with this crazy woman for a mother."

She took another drag off the Camel, tilted her head back, and blew the smoke up toward the ceiling.

"I took him to McDonald's, and then I went to 7-Eleven and bought two packs of cigarettes and a forty-ounce Budweiser. And that's where I got some peace and quiet. That's where I fucking finally got some peace and quiet. So, maybe I am a bitch."

She looked at my hand. The back of it was already swollen, a red circle at the point of impact. "Is it broken?" she asked.

I couldn't bend my first two fingers, which was a bad sign, but I didn't want to make her feel bad. "It's cool," I said. "No harm, no foul."

We both stood up. She stubbed out her cigarette in the sink and went back to the ice, emptying it into a couple of glasses, going back to work on the Brandy Alexanders. That was her favorite drink.

"I told you we were moving, right?"

She said it in a casual way, like she didn't want me to act surprised, even though we both knew she hadn't said a word to me about any plans to move. Not that I hadn't wondered. She was like a lot of people who'd landed here, each with a different reason, none of them ever really taking up residence, at least not like I had. Thing is, she'd just go off and find a similar place. She'd told me how she had done it before: Atlanta, where Louis was born, and then Charlotte, and Richmond. But there wasn't any place different from the last. She'd find a Chili's, an Applebee's, a Macaroni Grill.

I asked her what was the point.

"I've just been thinking," she said, "that I need some plans. And not something mediocre either. I need something significant."

She poured milk over a glass of brandy. A cloud spread through the dark liquor, around the crushed ice, slowly making its way to the bottom of the glass. She took a drink, a long one, not a savor-and-make-it-last kind of drink.

"I was online a few weeks back," she said, "and this guy I used to work with in Charlotte IM'd me. He just opened his second restaurant down in Florida; somewhere around Fort Myers. He needs a manager. Not a bartender but a manager. It's exactly what I need, what Louis needs. Get away from these schools and the cold weather before it starts up. Plus, my father's been driving me crazy lately. I want to go somewhere he can't find us."

"What about his liver?"

"I can't take care of him," she said. "I'm not saying, 'Fuck him.' It's not like that, but I can't do it. I gave up a lot with my brother. I gave up years to take care of him. Never finished college. And that's another thing I'm going to do—take management classes."

I didn't ask about the man in Fort Myers, didn't need to. You don't go popping yourself onto somebody's computer screen unless there's been something between you in the past.

I did ask when they were leaving. She said her rent was paid through the end of October, and she wanted to take a trip down to Fort Myers in late September to find a new place.

"You think you could keep Louis for a few days while I'm out of town?"

"Yeah, no problem."

I felt that catch of the breath that always happened when I called the wrong pitch during a game, and just as I reached out to snag the ball from the air, a streak of aluminum took it from me, sending the ball out into the distance, where it shrank and then disappeared over some rusted chain-link fence.

Theresa was holding the bottle of brandy over a fresh glass of ice, smiling in a detached way. "Hey," she said. "You want a drink, or not?"

CHAPTER 16

About six months before he disappeared for good, my uncle Phil had to go away for a couple of weeks. He was in trouble again with the numbers guys he worked for. A deal had to be negotiated so he could come back to the bar. The eventual settlement involved giving up his controlling ownership, but that was to come later. For the time being, Phil needed me to bring supplies to the place where he was staying in Pennsylvania.

I drove out to the mountains in the green Porsche 914 he'd given me when I turned sixteen. The scrawled directions sat on my lap, and Phil's shit was piled up on the passenger seat: fresh copies of the *New York Post, Sports Illustrated,* and the *Sporting News,* a couple of Mets T-shirts, Adidas warm-ups, and a Dopp kit, which held toothbrush, paste, Bic shavers, and a half-ounce of coke.

He was staying in this rickety little cabin, halfway up a mountain, just off a dirt road. I stepped out of the car and looked up. The sky behind me was enormous and blue, and a little farther up the incline some sharp-winged birds were flying sleepy circles. I'd only seen this sort of thing on television. They circled and circled but never dove. I wondered if something was already dead or merely dying.

"How the fuck did you find this place?" I asked Phil.

He took the stuff out of my arms, leaned his head out the front door, looked both ways, then waved me inside and latched the deadbolt.

"I own it."

He tossed the clothes on a dirty sofa and headed back to the bathroom, already checking the contents of the Dopp kit. He emerged a moment later: face wet, dark hair slicked back, nose red.

"What do you mean you own it? This is a fucking dump."

"Actually, me and Lily own it together. We inherited it."

"From who? The Clampetts?"

I looked around for at least one creature comfort. It was an exercise in futility. The television was small and worked off rabbit ears. Aluminum-foil vines stretched up to the mantel and across the floor to the coffee table. The reception still sucked. *The Game of the Week* was on, and I couldn't even identify the team uniforms through the snow. A big box fan was whirring in the corner, blowing dust but little else. The air smelled like stale tobacco and beer.

A refrigerator was plugged into the back wall of the main room. There was a metal sink and a woodstove nearby. That's what passed for a kitchen. Phil pulled a couple of Tuborgs from the fridge and walked over to the sofa.

"We inherited it from our parents."

He sat on the sofa, put the beers on the coffee table, then reached forward and slid the aluminum foil a little to the right.

"Have a seat," he said. "At least drink a beer with me."

I eased myself into the upholstery, not wanting to wake the bugs in case there was an infestation.

"So, what do you think?" Phil asked.

I took a sip of beer. "It ain't the fucking St. Regis."

He laughed, raised a skinny arm to drink. He'd been dropping a lot of weight and looked vulnerable in his white tank, like a guy who'd have a hard time fighting back if the situation called for it.

"This is it," he said. "Our fucking inheritance. A good place to hide. That's about all it is."

He stared up at the maze of webs on the pitched ceiling, his tube-socked feet resting on the coffee table. He was wearing a pair of Islanders boxer shorts.

I tried watching the game on the snowy screen. All I wanted was to finish the beer and get the hell out of there, get back to Cliffside and the bar. We had a softball game the following morning. I'd been running the team and helping out in the bar's kitchen while Phil was gone.

"We won our last two games," I said. "I juggled the lineup a little bit, tried to space out our speed guys so we don't have all the rally killers bunched together at the bottom of the order. It's been working out pretty good."

He turned and studied me, tap-tap-tapping his fingers on the beer bottle. The quick beat betrayed the sad look on his face, the circles under his eyes.

"Things are starting to snowball," he said. "You might want to look at some options."

"Options?" I honestly didn't know what he meant.

"Yeah," he said. "Get the hell out while the getting is good."

"Come on," I said. "You'll work this out. How mobbed up are these guys, anyway?"

"You don't need to know that shit."

"Why not?" I said. "I could start taking a bigger role in things. I mean, if you want me to."

"Look," he said, "things end. Every dynasty collapses under its own weight. You got your honeymoon period, and then . . ."

He appeared to lose his train of thought. He sat there with his jaw clenched.

"Every good run comes to an end," he said. "You gotta learn that. You're no different from anybody else. If you accept it, then it's not so bad. You can see it coming, and then you can make plans for the inevitable."

"You need to get outside," I said. "I think you got cabin fever or something."

He pulled his feet off the table, leaned forward, and slammed his beer bottle down. "I'm not fucking with you," he said. "I'm trying to tell you something important here."

He'd never been a screamer. Even at the bar, when he'd rip somebody a new one for fucking up, he immediately felt guilty about it. It was no different in that cabin. He let out a tired sigh, lay his face in his hands, and shook his head.

"I'm sorry," I said. "I hear what you're saying. I understand."

And I must have understood on some level, because I remember that day with Phil, and the things he told me, as clearly as I remember anything about him. I remember that cabin and the thin, bitter air inside of it, so thin it was hard to draw a breath. All I wanted was to get out of there, to drive down that mountain as fast I could, to get back home and make sure everything was still intact.

It's true. Sometimes, things snowball for a team. It doesn't matter if you're a dynasty, or the Whip Spa Yankees. One injury leads to another, and then another, and then you got guys pressing and slumping and everything goes to hell on a rock. It was turning into that kind of season at the warehouse. Artie hadn't shown up for work in three days, a strong indication he was doing coke again, or maybe even crystal meth, as Ramon had guessed. Meanwhile, my hand was fractured, Ramon's finger was infected from where little Gene had bitten him, and now Benny was calling from home to tell me he had the gout.

"You gotta be shittin' me."

"I wish I was, but Doc says I gotta stay off my feet for a while."

I heard him inhaling.

"Are you smoking?"

"Yeah."

"Well, that can't be good for the gout, can it?"

"These cigarettes are the only thing keeping me sane right now."

I was sitting in the warehouse office, smoking a Marlboro Light. Willie had commandeered the computer to order a shirt from J.Crew. Meanwhile, Joaquin and a couple of his guys were detailing an SLK and listening to a Willie Bobo CD.

"Can't you give me two innings tomorrow night? That's all I'm asking. Ramon's finger is swelled up like a fucking plantain."

"Look, man. I can hardly walk right now. Besides, with everything going on, with Gene dying and my old man coming down here, I don't have my mind on baseball. I mean, shit, it just doesn't seem that important."

Ramon was sitting nearby in a folding chair, watching the '84 Rose Bowl on ESPN Classic. I remembered Phil holding out some bets on that game, thinking Illinois would have no trouble covering the spread. Instead, they got clobbered by UCLA, 45–9. Phil had to go deep into his pockets and then some on that game.

I turned my head so Ramon and Willie couldn't hear me. "Maybe you're right," I said. "I been thinking I should've forfeited the rest of the season. You know, Ramon got me going with all of that 'season of Gene' bullshit."

Benny sighed. "I don't know what to tell you. I'm forty-seven. I got three hundred dollars in the bank, twelve hundred owed in child support. Me and my old man got into it last night, and now he's caught a cab back to the VA hospital in Philly. I just don't need the frustration. I don't need to go out on that mound and get rung up like a fucking bell by a bunch of assholes."

"You don't sound too good," I said. "What about that medication you've been taking?"

Benny went quiet for a moment, even stopped puffing the cig.

"I quit taking that shit."

"When?"

"Last week. Right after I talked all that shit to you guys. Right after Gene's funeral. I just got to thinking how that wasn't the real me."

"Well, I have to say you were pretty fucking convincing."

"No shit. I had myself convinced. But then I start feeling sick, and I got these pains inside me, and I realize I've gained thirty pounds. The doctor says I got an inflamed prostate."

"From what?"

"What do you think? From not getting a nut every once in a while. Turns out, you ain't supposed to go without sex. It's not good for you physically."

"So, you're off the meds for good?"

"Completely off."

"Well, aren't you supposed to consult your doctor before you do something like that?"

"Fuck him," Benny said.

I told him he might want to reconsider that position, but he turned the tables and started asking me questions.

"Are you still seeing Theresa?"

"Nah, she told me she was moving to Florida."

"What about Joy?" he asked.

"What do you mean?"

"I just mean how is she holding up? What did you think I meant?"

"Nothing," I said. "I mean, I don't know. She's doing okay, I guess. I'm supposed to go over there in a little while. She asked me to cut the grass."

Benny laughed. "Hey, look at you: George fuckin' Toma."

CHAPTER 17

Little Gene was scampering around the living room, sucking his pacifier and whacking a Nerf ball with a little wooden bat Gene had bought for him up at Yankee Stadium. As soon as I walked in the door, he ran over to me and whacked the shit out of my shin.

"Goddammit."

Joy turned around. She'd been sitting on the sofa watching the Channel 8 news. "Gene Dellorso, you put that bat down right now."

Little Gene spit out his pappy and smiled, but it wasn't a funny kind of smile. "No, Mommy. You're stupid. I play bat ball."

And then he turned and took a swing at my other shin. Out of instinct, I tried to block the bat with my right hand, not thinking about the cast and the fractured metacarpal. The pain went through my broken hand like a tuning fork.

Joy hopped off the sofa and grabbed the little bolo paddle she kept on the coffee table. She used the paddle because James Dobson had said not to use the hand because kids should relate a parent's hand to love, or some bullshit like that. I'd seen her wear little Gene's ass out once before, and it was not something I wanted to see again, so I snatched the bat away from little Gene and shooed him out of the room. With the paddle in play, he didn't even think about trying to retrieve the bat. He grabbed his pacifier and beat feet for the kitchen.

"I'm gonna blister your ass, mister."

"Let him go," I said. "I'm fine."

Joy took a step toward the kitchen but stopped like she didn't really have the energy for a rundown. "Are you okay, for real?" she asked.

Her expression softened as she walked over to me, paddle still in hand. She pointed at my cast. "What the fuck happened?"

"Foul tip," I said. "I didn't even realize it was broken."

"Well, are you okay?"

"Yeah, it's a removable cast. See?"

I thought it best to change the subject, so I told her about my plans to visit this Lansing character in Edgewater.

"Are you going by yourself?" she asked.

"Ramon's coming with me. I had to promise I'd pay him for the hours, but at least it'll give us numbers if the guy is alone."

"Well, what's your plan? Are you even sure this is the right guy?"

"I'm pretty sure it's the right guy. How many counterfeit jersey makers can there be in one state?"

Seeing how I didn't have an exact plan for getting the Babe Ruth bat from this little shit, I changed gears again. I asked Joy if there was any gas in the lawn mower.

"There's a can in the garage. It's a mix, gas and oil."

I turned to head outside, but she reached for my arm.

"Wait."

I stopped, turned around slowly.

"It's awkward," she said. "I know. I'm sorry if I put you in an uncomfortable position the other night."

I'd been hoping maybe we could get through this encounter without mentioning the tangle on the sofa. It seemed like a natural way to handle the situation: pretend it didn't happen and never speak of it again.

Then again, she was looking really good: jeans and a white T-shirt, those pink Pumas that I liked, her hair pulled back, the new bangs still in place.

"You know, Joy, I feel really bad about the other night. I feel like I may have betrayed Gene."

"Fuck him," she said. "I loved him, and I miss him. Don't get me wrong. But he never treated me like a wife. He never showed love, or compassion. He never showed anyone respect, not even himself. That doesn't mean he deserved to die like that, and it doesn't mean I'm happy. But what the fuck am I supposed to do? I lost time being with him. Six years. Am I supposed to lose more of it now worrying about what's right and wrong?"

"Well, what would James Dobson say about this?"

Joy stepped back, fixed me with a hard stare. "Don't you fucking make fun of me," she said. "And don't you belittle what I believe in."

"That's not how I meant it."

"The fuck it's not," she said. "Do you think anybody ever helped me figure out how to do all of this? My lousy father? My mother? Gene? I've had no one for thirty-four fucking years. Where the hell am I gonna go for guidance? Tell me. You think you got all the fucking answers. Well, you don't. I like you a lot, but you don't know shit. You don't know any more than me."

She threw the paddle across the room, flung it sidearm so it twirled through the air and bounced off the wall. And then she started crying. She buried her face in her hands and started crying. And I felt like shit about it.

"Joy, I'm really sorry. I didn't mean anything. I've just been thinking a lot about what we did, and the woman I'd been seeing says she's moving to Florida, and then she's got a son I've been watching, and I'm supposed to go to Jersey tonight to see what I can learn about this bat. It's just been some crazy shit lately."

Next thing I knew, I was pulling her into my chest, rubbing my hand across her back, and telling her everything was okay. I can't say it felt wrong. It hadn't felt wrong on the sofa either, at least not until afterward. Across the room, the kitchen door opened a crack, and I could see little Gene. He was lying on his stomach, looking through the sight of a toy rifle. I couldn't tell if the orange tip was pointed at me or Joy.

CHAPTER 18

We had to forfeit our Friday-night game against the Phillies, on account of only having six players fit for duty. The Phils were a weak-ass crew, usually good for a notch in the win column, and we needed to take advantage of those opportunities. But instead of playing ball, me and Ramon put on our suits and headed to New Jersey in the 'Vette. We were planning to pay this Lansing prick a visit to discuss Gene's bat. I was paying Ramon time and a half for his assistance, plus coffee.

We loaded up at a Starbucks in Edgewater and parked across the street from Lansing's brick townhouse. There was a line of brand-new attached homes parked a few blocks from the river, surrounded by restaurants and shops.

It was a little after eight when we got there, dark except for the streetlights. A cool, mid-September evening. Nobody was home, so I parked at the curb. We sat there with John Sterling on the radio, calling the Yankees-Indians game.

Ramon sipped his vente. "This is a nice area. Lots of new things."

"Yeah, I hardly recognized the place."

I couldn't say the same about my old neighborhood, which I'd driven through on the way in. It had shown some scars, though maybe I was the only one who noticed.

Ramon asked how long we were going to wait for this guy.

I told him all night, if it came to that. "We made the drive. We might as well accomplish something."

"So, what's your tactic here?" he asked. "Hard-ass, or what?"

"We talk," I said. "We make him think we're lawyers representing

Gene's estate. The main thing we want to learn is the location of the bat. We can't do anything until we know that."

Ramon asked if Gene had a legitimate claim to the bat.

"If Gene held up his end of the deal," I said, "giving the $250K to the old lady's church, and if all of this was in her will, then I guess—"

"Yeah, but where is this woman's will?" Ramon asked.

"I don't even know if she had a fucking will," I said. "I'm going on what Tommy Pumpkin told us. So, consider the source."

"We need documentation," Ramon said. "Paper."

"You're taking this attorney role pretty serious," I said.

Ramon rolled down the window, lit a cigarette, and tossed the pack on the dashboard. "My old man is an attorney. Can you believe that?"

"You never talk about your father."

Ramon shrugged, blew smoke out into the cool air. "This People Search thing is pretty crazy. You ever get to wondering about somebody, you just type in the name. You can search their background, criminal record, hotels close to their house."

I grabbed the cigarettes, lit one myself. "So I've heard."

"I think he's an ambulance chaser," Ramon said. "Personal damages."

"You get in touch with him?"

Ramon shook his head. "I thought about it. Almost did it. But the thing I realized is that you gotta forget some things if you're gonna move on. I mean, fuck him. My grandfather raised me. He's got his own problems. I know that. But I can't have my head fucked up with any more shit. I gotta worry about the here and now."

He settled back into the seat, drank his coffee, stared out over the hood of the old Corvette. The hum of the crowd noise was coming up from the dashboard.

"You gotta wonder," I said, "what he's doing and all. Right?"

Ramon took his time with that one. "I'm forgetting I ever looked him up."

"My mother's writing a book," I said. "About yoga."

Ramon flipped his cigarette onto the street and rolled up the window. He turned and gave me a puzzled look.

"What?"

The day Phil and I visited her in the hospital, the day she kept apologizing about making me pee in a chicken bucket, I wouldn't have laid very good odds on her writing a book.

Ramon sat up straight, pointed to Lansing's townhouse. A red Acura NSX was pulling into the short driveway.

"That's him," I said. "That's the asshole who jumped me in the parking lot."

The kid was alone. It looked like he'd been to the gym. He was wearing shorts, an Earl Monroe throwback, and carrying a gym bag. He was drinking out of a Smoothie King cup.

I sipped my latte. It was just now cooling off enough to drink. "Let's give him a second to get inside. We don't want to scare him right away."

I could tell I was going to have problems with the kid as soon as he opened the door.

"Who the fuck are you?" he asked.

He'd already changed out of the Monroe jersey, was wearing a Houston Rockets hoodie in the old red-and-yellow colors. A Slayer CD was playing loud inside the house.

"We're representatives of Gene Dellorso's estate," I said.

Lansing shrugged. "What'd I inherit?"

"We understand you have a collectible that belongs to Mr. Dellorso."

"Oh, yeah. What kind of collectible?"

"A baseball bat."

The kid laughed. "I don't handle no fucking bats, just jerseys. You can check my eBay store."

"I already checked your eBay store," Ramon said. "You got a satisfaction rating of shit, my friend."

"Hey, it's from one guy," he said. "Bought a bunch of jerseys and fucked up my rating because I stole his girl from him. I talked to eBay, and they're straightening the whole thing out."

Lansing had a look in his eyes that I recognized: a hitter who didn't think beyond the next pitch. Probably had a good swing, could jump all over a straight fastball, but had no brain to handle the junk. And that's what I should have fed him: changeups and breaking balls all day and all night.

"First of all," he said, "I don't know any Dellorso. And secondly, as I have already stated, I got no bats. So, if that's all you're here for, then I'll kindly ask you to get the fuck off my property."

I threw my forearm into the big wood-and-glass door as he was closing it. I pushed it back and him along with it. Sometimes, my impulses won out, and I called a fastball when logic dictated junk. It kept the game interesting.

"The fuck is your problem?" Lansing asked.

He grabbed the front of my dress shirt, and I took the opportunity to smack him in the nose with the heel of my good hand. It was a clean shot, very little pain on my end, and Lansing went down and started bleeding.

"You fucking cocksucker," he said. "I'm gonna kill you. You don't know who the fuck you're messing with."

He was still on his knees, holding his nose and trying not to bleed on his Rockets sweatshirt.

"Where's the fucking bat?"

I pulled him up by the back of his shirt and punched him in the stomach. When I let go, Lansing went back down to his knees, gasping.

Ramon grabbed my shoulder, leaned in close to my ear.

"What the fuck are you doing?" he asked. "I thought we were gonna talk."

"Relax. I know what I'm doing."

I told Ramon to keep an eye on Lansing while I checked the house. Ramon appeared uneasy. "You're paying me double time now," he said.

I pulled my Marlboro Lights out of my suit jacket, shook one out of the pack, and lit it. The kid's home furnishings were sparse and pale as an egg. The carpet was wheat, the walls white, the living-room sofa tan. No pictures on the walls, but a framed eight-by-ten of Lansing with Derek Jeter sat on the mantel. They were both wearing suits at a nightclub. Jeter looked like he wanted to hurry up and get the fuck away from Lansing.

A 65-inch Panasonic plasma was nesting in an entertainment cabinet. Very nice. I glanced at his DVD collection: *Scarface, The Godfather I* and *II,* the first three seasons of *Boy Meets World,* and a bunch of porn.

The Yankees game was playing on the TV with the sound muted. I stopped and watched Jeter plate a couple of runs with a base hit to right. Beautiful piece of hitting on a 1-2 pitch.

I strolled through the kitchen. Nothing in the fridge but Heinekens and a box of Popeye's. I tossed my cigarette into the sink, grabbed a beer, then popped a couple of Vikes that I had in my jacket pocket. I'd run through my supply of pills and had to phone Tommy Pumpkin for a refill. The Popeye's was calling my name, too. I took a leg and went back to searching for the bat.

Lansing had converted a bedroom into a tight workout area: treadmill, stationary bike, one of those rowers with water in the flywheel, free weights, a Smith machine, and a flat-screen television.

The walls were mirrored. I noticed a lump on the floor behind the rower. It was covered with three white towels. I walked over and pushed the towels away with my shoe. A glass case lay beneath the towels. I knelt for a closer look. The case held the Babe Ruth bat, thick and dark brown, the wood cracked, the writing on the barrel blurred to almost nothing: "To May, Happy Birthday Kid, Babe."

I set the beer and chicken on a weight bench, grabbed a ten-pound dumbbell, and busted the glass case with it. I pulled the bat out of the case and did what I always did with a bat: checked the balance. It had a good feel. Heavy as shit and thick as a telephone pole, but good balance. That was the key.

Lansing was still sitting on the floor in the foyer with Ramon standing over him. He had his shirtsleeve pressed up against his nose. When he saw me walking in with the bat, he stood up. Ramon grabbed his arm and held tight.

"You ain't taking that fucking bat, asshole."

"Oh, yeah? Watch me, you little prick."

I walked right up to him and rammed the butt of the bat into his stomach, doubled him over on the tile floor and shut his trap. I said, "Now *you* get the short end of the cut."

* * *

Ramon was quiet for a long time. There was no sound in the car except the engine and the hum of the ballgame on the radio. It was getting to me, like I'd scared him or something, like he was seeing me in a different light all of a sudden. I kept catching him stealing peeks at me.

"What the fuck?" I said. "We got the bat, didn't we? We're all set."

"I thought you were gonna threaten a lawsuit," Ramon said.

"Listen," I said. "A little shit like that only knows one thing: strength. And that's what we showed him."

"He also threatened to kill you," Ramon said. "And his old man's mobbed up. You heard Tommy say that."

Ramon was making me uneasy. I realized you could sneak a fastball by a guy once. But you always had to face him again later in the game. I never said that I always made the right call.

"Short end of the cut," Ramon said. "What the fuck was that about?"

"My uncle always got the short end when he was running numbers. He took all the chances, did all the work, and all he got was the scraps."

"What's that got to do with this kid and the bat?" he asked.

"It's the same fucking mindset," I said. "People like that, they think they can take whatever they fucking want—just because they got a gun and their old man is somebody."

"This must be the Jersey Rice."

I pulled off the turnpike at the Clara Barton rest area, bought a Dr Pepper, and swallowed a couple more pills in the bathroom. My broken hand was starting to hurt, and my brain had blown a fuse. Driving through the old neighborhood, it made me feel like I'd walked into Phil's bar again, and somebody had shut the doors behind me. I could smell the cigarette smoke. It was choking me, and the room was dark, and I could hear the clank of a softball bat against the old, wooden floor. Outside, large birds circled the sky with patience.

Ramon was right. You gotta forget some things.

CHAPTER 19

We got the bat into the hands of Joy's attorney right away. He had an auction house send its memorabilia expert down from New York to take a look at it. The guy said there were label characteristics that definitively identified it as a 1932 Ruth bat. Considering that the chain of ownership began and ended with one person and that the Babe himself had been documented as giving it to this girl (his handwriting was right on the cock of the bat), it looked like we were close to having rock-solid provenance.

Me, Joy, the attorney, and the bat guy were sitting around a table outside the safety deposit boxes at Wachovia. The bat lay on the table between us, now covered in a plastic tube thanks to the memorabilia expert. It looked like a giant suppository.

"So, let's go public with this," I said.

The attorney said it wasn't that easy.

"While Mrs. Dellorso does have possession of the bat, we have no proof that the woman actually bequeathed it to Mr. Dellorso."

The memorabilia guy agreed. "We'd never announce the auction until there was undisputed proof of ownership. Otherwise, you'd have supposed relatives of this woman coming out of the woodwork."

The guys in the suits had a point. Still, we needed public knowledge of Joy's legitimate ownership. It was our own best protection.

"There are certain people out there," Joy said, "who have threatened me with bodily harm because they want this bat. I believe they may have broken my husband's nose shortly before his death."

"And they lit me up with a Scorpion Six hundred," I added.

The attorney and the memorabilia guy looked at me like they had no idea what I was talking about.

Joy's attorney assured us that he'd immediately search the public records in Baltimore. As soon as he had the old lady's will in hand, he'd let us know the verdict. My antennae were up, but I had little doubt about the man's motivation, or his name: Roy White, just like the old Yankees outfielder. Joy had agreed to cut White in for ten percent of the bat's auction price.

Joy and I sat in my car outside the bank. My unease put a real damper on the sunny sky above the windshield. Ramon and I had talked about going to the batting cages later in the day. Now I wasn't in the mood.

Joy asked what was wrong.

"I got a bad feeling," I said. "I think maybe you should get out of town for a few days, at least until White clears up the ownership issue."

"I don't have enough money to travel right now."

"I thought your father was giving you money."

"Fuck him," she said. "I told him to stick the check up his ass."

"Don't sweat it. I keep two thousand in cash at my place for just such occasions. It's all yours."

"I could use a break," she said. "Maybe I'll take little Gene and go down to the Outer Banks."

"Don't even tell me where you're going. Don't tell anybody."

I rolled down my window, lit a Marlboro Light. Joy took one out of the pack as well. I'd laid off the Vike that morning. When I was taking those pills, it felt sometimes like things were happening to someone else instead of to me. It wasn't always a bad thing, but I'd started to wonder on the ride back from Edgewater.

On the way to Joy's house, I pulled down a side street to make sure no one was following us.

"What are you doing?" Joy asked. "You're scaring the shit out of me, Joe."

I checked the rearview mirror. There was nothing behind us.

"I just wanted you to know," I said, "that everything's going to be okay. This is all gonna work out."

CHAPTER 20

I had my own plans for getting out of town until White cleared up the matter of bat ownership. I'd read about a *Madden* tournament online—a grand to the winner—at a Ramada Inn up in Philadelphia, so I thought I'd take Louis and see what kind of damage he could do in a high-pressure situation. I got a double room and brought along my PS2 so Louis could take some snaps the night before the competition. We ordered a couple of strip steaks from room service, some Black Forest cake, a half-dozen Heinekens for me, Cokes for Louis.

"Play something besides a cover two," he said. "I'll eat that shit up all day."

"Well, what the fuck do you want me to do?"

"I don't know. Move your linemen around, blitz a fucking linebacker every now and then, maybe a safety. I gotta get my eyes tight checking the defense. You're too damn easy."

We were sitting on the end of the bed, atop the dirty flowered spread. I tossed my controller on the carpet. "Fuck this," I said. "You're ready. Besides, you don't wanna overdo it. Save something for tomorrow."

Louis got up and went to the minibar, grabbed some peanut M&Ms and a Coke.

"How many of those you had?" I asked.

He looked at the Coke label as if it held the answer. "I don't know."

"Well, don't overdo it," I said. "You'll never get to sleep."

Theresa was down in Florida on a preliminary visit, staking out some housing possibilities and visiting her old friend, the restaurant owner. I hadn't exactly informed her about the road trip me and Louis were taking. He and I had agreed to keep this to ourselves.

Louis flopped down on my bed. He smelled like damp laundry and was in need of a shower and fresh threads. Theresa told me to make sure he bathed every day. But he looked happy, so I didn't say anything. He was running through the On Demand movie offerings, mainly the adult titles.

"Let's order this one," he said. *"Teachers Lounge Gang Bang."*

"Forget it," I said. "That shit's not good for you."

Louis snorted. "Yeah, like you don't watch this shit."

"I'm not kidding," I said. "It's not good for you. You watch that all the time, you get desensitized. You forget what being with a woman is all about. You gotta be respectful of girls."

He lay back on the big pile of pillows and laughed like I'd just told a joke. I took the remote control from him and pointed to the book on the nightstand. It was my old copy of Joe Pepitone's autobiography, *Joe, You Coulda Made Us Proud.* Louis had a book report project due in a week, and he could write about the book of his choice. Seeing how he was having trouble coming up with a selection, I'd given him my old favorite.

I pulled the easy chair around to where I could see the TV and sat back in it. I lowered the volume so Louis could concentrate, and then I ran through the channels until I landed on the Phillies-Cardinals game.

Louis kept sneaking peeks at the game over the top of the paperback.

"Say, Rice. How much would it cost to live in a hotel like this?"

"More than you're gonna make in that tournament tomorrow."

"This is the way to roll," he said. "I think I'm gonna live in a hotel."

"It's the way to go," I said. "You got the room service, clean towels, laundry service, current-run movies, and no regular neighbors getting into your business."

I told him about how my uncle Phil used to book a room at the St. Regis every year for the Super Bowl, how me and him would go into the city and order room service and watch the game. We'd have littleneck clams and steaks, and he'd get me an ice bucket full of

Cokes to go with his Heinekens, kind of like Louis and I were doing. We'd even bring along the Intellivision and hook it up to the hotel TV, play our own Super Bowl.

"Is that who you lived with?" he asked. "Your uncle?"

"Pretty much, yeah."

"Sounds like you had the life," he said.

It was the shit, all right. At least I'd thought so at the time. It took me years to understand that Phil never was able to enjoy any of it. Always worrying, looking over his shoulder. Kind of like me at the moment.

I went down to the lobby after Louis had fallen asleep. I was still trying to quit the pills, but my knee and my hand were hurting like shit, and my thoughts were going round and round with possibilities. Lansing might not have recognized me that night at his place, but I knew that things weren't finished between me and him. They might even have just been getting started with his old man, who I hadn't even met but who seemed to scare the shit out of Tommy Pumpkin, so much that he wouldn't even speak his name. Something was coming, I just couldn't figure out what.

I bought some Tylenol PM in the hotel gift shop, wandered into the bar, and ordered a Jack and ginger ale. The place was crowded with the video game crowd. They were easy to spot in their jerseys. McNabb was well represented, along with Vick and Manning. Everybody wanted to be a fucking quarterback. Louis had brought along his Ray Lewis, D-Mac, and Randy Moss jerseys. I was thinking the Lewis jersey might be appropriate. Defense wins championships.

The *Madden* guys were carrying their drinks over to the dartboards and pool table, hanging out there, playing games and watching *SportsCenter.*

There were two women sitting beside me who looked like they were in town on business, still wearing skirts and blouses. I respected their space, took a couple of Tylenols and drank my Jack and G. My intention all along had been to drive over to the clinic where my mother taught the yoga classes. Just drive by, that's all. I still felt a responsibility to make sure she was okay. Of course, I also wanted to see what it was that she saw every day, to try to understand her perspective on things.

And then this businesswoman kind of caught my eye as she and her friend were leaving, so I gave her a friendly smile, nothing more. She looked about my age, dark hair and green eyes. A friendly face, too. Open and honest.

I ordered another Jack and ginger ale and thought it'd be the last one. My head was getting quiet, and I was thinking that going to sleep was probably a better idea than taking a drive.

"Do you think you could spare one of those?"

I turned around, and the woman I'd smiled at was back. She was pointing to my Tylenol.

"The gift shop's closed," she said. "I've got a bad headache."

"Sure, I'm done with them."

I handed her the box, and she sat down beside me, ordered a gin and tonic, and lit a cigarette. She swallowed a couple of Tylenols, knocked back half the drink.

"So, what's with all these guys wearing jerseys?" She looked back over her shoulder.

"Gamers," I said.

She gave me a blank stare.

"Video games. They're having a tournament in the ballroom tomorrow."

She nodded. "Are you playing?"

"My son's playing."

She smiled. "How old is your son?"

I drew a blank. All I could do was sit there and stare at her, wondering why the hell I'd said that Louis was my son.

"Twelve," I said, finally.

She finished her drink, held it up to her lips for a while and let the last drops of alcohol drain from the ice. I could tell that she knew her way around a gin and tonic.

I kept on lying, told her that me and Louis's mother were separated, that she was taking Louis to Florida against my wishes. And then I told her my own mother lived here in Philadelphia, that she was coming to watch Louis in the tournament tomorrow and then we were all going out for dinner.

It turned out the woman was a schoolteacher in Moorestown. Her friend was in town for an accounting conference, and they'd met for drinks. I asked her a lot of questions to keep myself from lying more. She drove a Jetta, played tennis, had seen Prince eleven times in concert, and hated the parents of the kids she taught. She believed they were raising "a bunch of egocentric, overmedicated assholes." I learned a lot about her over the next two hours.

I went to the front desk and reserved another room. We watched *Teachers Lounge Gang Bang* and laughed and did our own thing until about three. When I got back to the other room, Louis was standing by the window talking on my cell phone.

"What the fuck are you doing?"

Louis turned around. "That's him," he said. "He just came in."

He held out the phone for me to take it.

"Who are you talking to?"

He made a face and said it was Theresa. I knew what I was in for.

"What the hell are you doing at a Marriott in Philadelphia?"

"It's a Ramada, actually."

"I don't give a fuck. Louis calls me at two-thirty saying he's in a hotel in Philadelphia and you've disappeared. Do you think I need this?"

"I know, I—"

"Fuck you," she said. "Let me talk to Louis."

I handed him the phone, sat on the edge of the bed. Once he'd finished talking to her, I asked him what she'd said.

"Don't worry. She said I could stay and play in the tournament."

I nodded, flexed my fingers. My hand was hurting again.

"I thought you'd left." Louis sounded like he was sorry he'd called Theresa.

"It's all right," I said.

"So, where'd you go?"

I was working the remote. I went through a few more stations, landed on ESPN Classic. They were running a *SportsCentury* about Reggie Jackson, showing him and Billy Martin going at it in the visitors' dugout at Fenway.

"I drove out to see my mother."

He accepted the explanation like it made sense, like anybody might do the same thing at 2 a.m. He sat in the chair and fell asleep, and I lay back on the bed and closed my eyes. The flickering of the TV was like little explosions inside my eyelids, and I thought for a long time about this one place I'd stayed as a kid, this neighbor's apartment, and how it smelled like the hotel room, and how my mother said I wouldn't have to spend the night there. And then, about two in the morning, when the woman was asleep, I got on the phone and called the operator and tried to get the number of the guy my mother was with: something Tolliver. The operator wanted to help me. I could tell that she wanted to get me home, but I couldn't remember the guy's first name.

Louis took a serious beatdown in the first round at the hands of a grown man from Hartford. He was a tall guy with a throwback Doug Williams jersey from his Tampa days. It was hard to watch, just a serious ass whipping. By the second half, the guy was giving Louis pointers, trying to mentor him as a fellow *Madden* player. At 42–3, the man could afford to be charitable.

"When I got eight in the box, keep a running back in to pass block," he said.

To which Louis replied: "Why don't you shut the fuck up, dickweed?"

The guy in the Williams jersey looked at me. All I could do was shrug. And then he proceeded to beat the ever-living shit out of Louis. Final score: 63–3. Needless to say, my attempt at boosting Louis's confidence had not gone according to plan.

To make everything worse, I'd talked Louis into wearing the Ray Lewis jersey when he'd wanted to stick with the D-Mac. Now he was pissed.

"I should have killed that guy. You took me off my game, got me out of my comfort zone. I gotta have my Donny Mac."

"That shirt's too fucking small. Besides, it wasn't the fucking jersey. You got your ass handed to you."

We were riding the elevator down to the lobby, making our early exit. I had my duffel slung over my shoulder, and Louis was holding his PS2 controller.

"That motherfucker was good," Louis said.

"Well, why didn't you throw the fucking ball? That's what you do against me."

"That's the fucking problem right there. It wasn't you. He knew how to play defense."

"Hey, I won the fucking *Madden* league at the garage last year. And I had to deal with a low draft choice, too. Had to play the whole fucking season as the Lions. They call it adversity. You gotta learn how to overcome it."

"And sometimes you just gotta suck on it," Louis said. He'd already changed back into his McNabb jersey. He charged out of the elevator and walked way ahead of me.

CHAPTER 21

Things continued to slide back in Virginia. Ramon gave me his two weeks' notice when I got back from Philly, saying that he was moving in with Brooke and taking a trip to Guatemala to talk with the Pollo Campero people about a franchise. He said his life was too busy with shit to worry about baseball, as if everybody in the world sat around with nothing to do. I've never understood why ten percent of the people have to bitch and moan like they're the only ones with anything on their fucking minds. Not that it made any difference for the baseball team, since two-thirds of my outfield had been hauled away by INS over the weekend. They were Joaquin's friends, brought to the operation after I started sponsoring him for his green card. I had a feeling Funderburk tipped somebody off. Meantime, Benny had gone to Philly to be with his father, and Artie was still MIA and presumably cranked out of his fucking mind. And so it looked like we'd have to forfeit our next two games. One more and we risked expulsion from the league. The season of Gene was going to hell in a baseball-shaped golf cart.

Joy phoned me as soon as she and little Gene got back from the beach. She hadn't heard anything from White about the bat. I took her and little Gene to an Orioles-Yankees game up at Camden Yards a couple nights later. I abandoned my uncle Phil's hatred of the Yanks and openly rooted for the pinstripers. Seeing how Joy didn't think I believed in anything, I felt I was making a bit of a point, not to mention giving myself the opportunity to forget some things, as Ramon had suggested. Not that I really gave a shit when Bernie hit a two-run jack in the eighth to provide the winning margin. Really, I didn't feel anything at all.

I made the mistake of buying little Gene a minibat in the souvenir store, and while Joy and I were talking, he disappeared from the seats. When I finally looked up, he was at the top of the steps, taking BP on an usher's shins.

When we got back to Joy's house, I lay on the sofa while she put the bat boy to bed. I was starting to feel comfortable in the house, especially on the sofa. I liked the red on the walls, which gave the room a warm feeling even when Joy had the AC set on sub-Arctic. I liked knowing the cereal boxes were lined up in the kitchen, and I'd even come to appreciate the lack of trees, all the open space and how you never saw the neighbors, never had to talk to anybody or listen to their problems: neighbors, teammates, employees, or otherwise. Despite all my hesitations about getting involved with Joy, I really didn't want to go back to my place that night.

We were lying in bed when Joy asked if I prayed. The ceiling fan was spinning lazy circles, and the moon was shining on the pale blue walls. Prince was on the clock radio, just enough static coming in to break up the beats.

"What the fuck are you talking about?"

"I mean, do you ever talk to God?"

I looked her in the eye. She was propped up on an elbow.

"Is that important to you?"

"Of course it's important. I care about you."

"What about Gene?" I asked. "Did he pray?"

"Believe it or not, Gene went to Mass twice a week."

All I could do was shake my head. "He was a busy fucking man."

Joy laughed a little. "Can you imagine taking his confession? You'd need a fucking intermission."

We let that thought settle. It took a moment, and then I felt a need to tell her something. It was like a balloon swelling up in my head.

"When I was in prison, I used to go to chapel. And the thing is, when you're locked up, you keep trying to tell yourself that you're different from a lot of the other people. Some of them, it's like they got no good at all in them. And that's what you're trying to convince yourself of, that you got something good in you. So, I had trouble paying attention in chapel, but the chaplain gave me this *Good News New Testament*—a little fucking book—and I started reading it. And I remember this thing Paul said about how nothing good dwelled inside him and that he could will what was good but his flesh just wouldn't let him do it."

"That's not you," she said. "You're a good person."

"So why did I fuck that waitress in Cliffside?" This is what I asked, thinking also, of course, about the teacher in Philly.

"Well," she said, "you were what, twenty-two or something?"

"She wanted to have kids."

"The waitress?"

"No, my wife. Her name was Pam."

I explained the rest of it, how she'd gotten sick about a year after I'd left, how she died without ever having any kids.

"There's fucking consequences," I said. "Fucking dire ones."

She sat up, crossed her legs, looked down on me. She was holding her hands over her breasts. Her face, in that bluish light, was beautifully worn with disappointment.

"Did you love her?"

"Probably not," I said. "She was different, you know. Had good parents, grew up in a quiet house, didn't drink. She was a fucking virgin, for Christ sake. I'd never seen anything like it, never seen it so pure. I wanted to be like that. I wanted to be pure, too."

We stayed there in the quiet for a while, and the song changed. That's when I asked Joy what she thought about reincarnation.

"I don't think there's anything in the Bible about it."

"Aside from that," I said. "What do you think? You think it makes any sense?"

"If it's not in the Bible," she said, "then we shouldn't be talking about it. That kind of shit scares me."

Her face hardened a little, and she was not as beautiful anymore.

"Anyway," I said, "that's what I pray for sometimes, that maybe Pam gets to come back and have some kids."

CHAPTER 22

Joy woke me in the morning, scrambling to get dressed. "Roy White just called. He wants me to meet him at the bank."

I checked the clock. Nine-thirty already. This was the first time I'd slept a full six hours without interruption since Gene died.

"So, what's the rush?" I asked.

Joy was pulling on a pair of dark jeans, eyeing herself in the dresser mirror. "He said he found the will, and it looks good. The guy from the auction house is meeting us at the bank. We're gonna sell this fucking thing and be done with it."

"Slow down," I said. "Something about this doesn't sound right."

Out of habit, I'd already grabbed the remote from the nightstand and turned on the television. Now I sat up and turned it off.

"Look," I said, "do you ever have a siren go off in your head telling you something's not right?"

She was putting on her earrings. The key to the safety deposit box dangled from her wrist on an elastic band.

"Yeah," she said. "It's been going off ever since I met Gene."

I stood up and leaned against the dresser, trying to flex my sore knee.

"Think about it," I said. "How could White unearth the will *and* get this guy down here from New York by nine-thirty in the morning?"

"Maybe he found the will yesterday."

"Then wouldn't he have called you yesterday?"

She sat on the edge of the bed and tied her Pumas. "Look, I just want all of this to be over with."

"It's a setup, Joy. Think about it."

By the time I got dressed, she had already taken little Gene to a neighbor's house and climbed inside the Navigator. I hopped in on the passenger side.

"Stop off at the warehouse," I said. "Let me grab my forty-four."

She was adjusting the AC. It couldn't have been more than 65 degrees outside, and she had the Siberian wind at full throttle in that truck.

"I'm not stopping," she said.

I quit trying to convince her and focused on a white van that was doing a shitty job of following us. The side mirror wasn't giving me the best possible view, so I reached up and adjusted the rearview.

"What are you doing?" she asked.

"Turn down the next street. Turn and hit the gas."

"You are fucking paranoid," she said.

I reached for the wheel myself, but she slapped my arm.

"Stop it."

One downside to the Navigator's girth was that Joy had trouble parking the fucking thing between two other cars. She was always heading to the back edge of parking lots where there was plenty of room to dock.

I pointed to a space right in front of the bank, a busy, safe area. All she had to do was slide between a Saturn and a Honda.

"There's one."

"It's too small," she said.

"Just swing out wide," I said. "You need the right angle."

But she kept going, all the way to the back of the parking lot, beside the Dumpster. There were no other cars back there, just a clump of trees separating the bank's lot from the Chili's next door. And the van was still in the rearview mirror.

I scouted the backseat to see if Gene had left a stray bat lying around. No luck on that front, though a weighted baseball was rolling around on the floorboard. Gene used the heavy pills to strengthen his shoulder in the spring. This was the eleven-ounce model. I palmed it and stuck it in my jacket pocket.

Joy parked, and the white van pulled into the adjacent space on Joy's side of the truck.

"That's the van," I said. "Do you believe me now?"

The barrel of a deer rifle appeared at Joy's window. The owner was wearing an orange ski mask. That's when I remembered Tommy Pumpkin's story about the masked fools who had broken Geno's nose.

"Let me see your hands. Both of you."

The deer hunter made us climb into the back of the van. He hopped in behind us and shut the doors. Inside, there was another guy wearing a ski mask. White was in there as well, bound by duct tape and gagged with a red bandana. His eyes were open, and he appeared none the worse for wear outside of his tie knot being pulled halfway down his shirt.

The back of the van was empty. No seats. No work gear. Nothing. The guy with the rifle slid to the front so that he and his cohort were positioned on either side of White. He leveled the rifle at us. It looked like a .30-30 with a scope.

The unarmed guy turned out to be the talker. "This is all we ask," he said. "Mrs. Dellorso goes inside the bank, takes the bat out of the safety deposit box, and gives it to us. In return, we release Mr. White."

"And if she doesn't?" I asked.

The man looked at his partner and back to the two of us. "Then we kill him."

"Get the fuck out of here." I couldn't help laughing at these two. "This is the worst act I've ever seen. You got a fucking deer rifle with a scope. Don't talk to me like you know what the fuck you're doing."

The talker got a little uptight all of a sudden. "Now, you listen to me," he said. "I mean what I say."

His voice gave him away as the older half of the duo, maybe mid-forties. The one with the rifle sounded like he could have been in high school. He was wearing jeans and a black T-shirt. The older one was in khakis and a Baltimore Ravens fleece jacket.

There we were, all of us squatting down in the back of this van. Considering the company, I didn't feel all that threatened. Nevertheless, the presence of the rifle did leave room for caution.

"I'll do it," Joy said. "I'll get the bat."

"Hold on just a second," I said. "I think we deserve some answers first. Who do you work for? The junior Lansing, or his old man?"

Neither sounded like they were from New Jersey. I figured they could be local connections.

That was before I noticed the air freshener. It was hanging from the van's rearview mirror. Pine scented, if my nose was on its game. But the smell wasn't important. It was the air freshener's message in big green letters: WWJD?

I hadn't given much thought to the van's Maryland plates when we were being shoved inside. But the plates, plus the air freshener, actually added up to something: *What Would Jesus Do?*

"You're from the old lady's church, aren't you?"

They looked at each other, but neither said a thing.

"What's wrong?" I asked. "Was the two hundred fifty K not enough to keep you happy? Did God tell you to kidnap a lawyer and pull a gun on a widow?"

"He never donated the two hundred and fifty thousand dollars," the man said.

White confirmed the news with a slow, sad shake of his head.

"So, what's the problem?" I asked. "Once Mrs. Dellorso auctions the bat, *she'll* pay you the two-fifty."

"It's too late for that," he said. "We've made other arrangements with Mr. Lansing. The senior Lansing, I should say."

"Lansing's got no right to that bat. There's no way he can sell it."

"Mr. Lansing doesn't want to sell it. He wants the bat for his personal collection."

"So, what do you get in return?" Joy asked.

"If we deliver the bat to Mr. Lansing, he's promised to donate twelve acres of property in Glendale to the church. With the money we save, we can get financing for a twelve-hundred-seat sanctuary, child development center, and coffee shop."

"What's with the fucking coffee shops in church?" I asked. "Is it *that* hard to stay awake?"

Joy asked how they could trust a guy like Lansing to keep his word.

"People aren't always what they seem." That's what he told us through his ski mask. "Mr. Lansing paid his debt to society years ago. He's turned his life around and become a successful businessman. Everything he does is aboveboard."

"Do you really think God wants you to hold a gun on people?" Joy asked.

It had been bad enough getting attacked by Lansing Junior and his electric pal. But this was too much to take. I slipped my right hand inside my jacket pocket, whipped out Gene's weighted baseball, and unleashed a snap throw from my knees. It caught the gunman square in the forehead. As soon as he fell back into the corner, I lunged and wrestled the gun away from him. I popped him in the mouth with the butt of the rifle for good measure and started to back away on my knees. Just as I turned to check the older one, he hit me in the face with some sort of spray. It was a helluva thing, torching my eyes and throat. My lids clamped shut, and I started gagging. I couldn't see a thing, couldn't catch my breath. I dropped the rifle and started rubbing at my face. It felt like I'd been hit in the face with a heavy dose of fire and brimstone, assuming brimstone feels like a blowtorch.

I was pretty much useless after that. I heard somebody say something about opening the doors before the pepper spray choked everyone to death. Soon after, Joy agreed to go inside for the bat. I tried to tell her not to do it, but I'd lost my voice along with my vision. All I could do was grab at air with my hands.

By the time I could see again, Joy and I were standing in a 7-Eleven parking lot. I leaned back against the hood of the truck while she poured milk from a gallon jug into my eyes. White was sitting in the Navigator drinking a Smirnoff Ice and appearing shaken by the whole experience. He had already explained to us the legal situation regarding the bat. The club was not mentioned in the old lady's will. Instead, Gene had signed a contract with the woman promising to pay $250,000 to the Lord's servants at her church no later than twelve months after her death. If he held up his end of the deal, he gained ownership of the bat. If not, the bat went to the Babe Ruth Museum in Baltimore, to be permanently displayed. As default distributor of Gene's probate assets, Joy now had six months to cough up the 250K. Only two problems existed: we were no longer in possession of the bat, and the church now viewed Gene's 250K as chump change.

"You know possession is ninety percent of ownership," I said. "It's highly unlikely that we're ever gonna see that lumber again."

A woman walked out of the 7-Eleven carrying a cup of coffee. It was obvious the sight of us made her uneasy: a shirtless man being doused with milk by a woman at eleven in the morning. She turned and tried to walk back inside without my noticing. I felt pretty certain she was planning to say something to the cashier.

"So, we lawyer up," Joy said. "We sue Lansing Senior and let the courts do the work for us."

"Sue him for what?" I said. "He'll just say he doesn't have the bat. You heard the guy in the van. Lansing wants it for his private collection. He'll keep it under wraps."

"Why the fuck wouldn't he want to sell it?" she asked. "What kind of jackass cares that much about a bat collection?"

It only took her a few seconds to realize she already knew the answer to that question.

"Fucking Gene," she said.

"Why the fuck didn't you listen to me?" I asked. "I told you it was a setup."

"I'm sorry," she said. "You could have gotten killed."

"They were Christians," I said. "They can't do that kind of shit."

"How do you know?"

Through the glass, I could see the woman with the coffee talking to the cashier. He was leaning across the counter to get a better look at us.

"I guess you're right," I said. "I haven't been to church in a long time. Which reminds me . . ."

I took the jug of milk and doused my face one last time.

"What's with the fucking coffee shops?"

CHAPTER 23

Theresa didn't know what to make of my red-eyed state.

"Have you been smoking pot?"

"Fucking allergies," I said. "This neighbor asked me to keep her cat while she's out of town. The fucking dander is killing me."

She gave me this look like she knew I was full of shit and went back to getting dressed for work. Despite being pissed off about the Philly trip, she still trusted me to keep Louis for her. She was working a late shift because another bartender had quit. Needless to say, her last-minute child-care options were limited.

"I can't wait to get the hell out of here," she said. "Two more weeks of this bullshit."

I sat down on the corner of her bed. "You find a place to live?"

"Not yet," she said. "All the rentals I looked at were trashed."

I lay back on the mattress. It was old and soft, and the sheets smelled like Theresa's skin: damp wood and faint perfume. Thing was, I'd never actually spent the night here. We thought it was best for Louis. Actually, it was me who thought that. I closed my eyes, and my head swayed and let go of everything it was carrying around. Next thing I knew, Theresa was shaking my leg, telling me to wake up.

"Are you sure you're not stoned?"

I pushed myself upright, sat there and rubbed my eyes. "You should hang on to this mattress. It's got a nice feel."

She stuck a can of Red Bull into the duffel bag she always carried to work. She zipped it up and stood there looking at me like I was the unmade bed, like she was deciding whether it was worth the trouble to straighten the spread, fluff the pillows, make things presentable.

"The crazy thing is," I said, "when it's time to go to bed I just lay there. I can't shut down."

She frowned. "I know. It's hard to turn it off." She took her purse off the dresser. "Do you want a couple of Ambiens?"

Louis and I went to the library and tried to find some books about blue crabs for his school project, which was now two days overdue. We could only have two sources from the Internet, which blew my original plan all to hell.

I was actually looking forward to writing the paper. I needed to give my brain a boot to the ass, let it latch on to something besides this bat affair. I'd already been shocked and pepper-sprayed by a band of half-asses, so I wasn't eager to tangle with a guy like Lansing Senior without a rock-solid plan. I needed to clear my head in preparation of hatching such a plan. I needed the crabs, and then I needed a good night's sleep.

When we got off the elevator, I could see that my apartment door was open a crack.

"What the fuck?" I asked Louis. "You didn't pull it shut?"

"Wasn't me," he said. "You were the last one out, dumbass."

I walked right in on Lansing Junior. Him and the other prick were sitting on the sofa playing *Madden*. He barely turned around to acknowledge me. Just raised his hand and gave me a, "Yo! What's up, home slice?"

I handed the library books to Louis, pulled a ten out of my wallet, and told him to walk down to the Pupusa Mart and start reading about crabs.

"You're supposed to help me," he said.

"Yeah, well, I got some business to take care of first. Now, get the fuck out of here."

I wasn't sure if Lansing had come to talk about the bat, or start some shit. If he'd really wanted paybacks, he could've jumped me instead of taking the bullshit pose with my PS2.

After Louis had gotten on the elevator, I grabbed the remote off the end table and shut down the Sony. Lansing held up his hands like he was Bill Parcells pleading with the ref.

"What the fuck, man. I was driving."

He was wearing baggy cargo shorts, a throwback L.T. Giants jersey, Yankees cap turned around backward, and vintage Jordans XIIs in the Carolina colors. His cohort, Andre, was dressed more or less the same, except he was sporting a Lance Alworth jersey and pale blue Iverson Reeboks. Andre stood up and walked toward me. He feinted with his right, then caught me in the nose with a left. All the while, I'd been looking for the Scorpion.

It felt like somebody had driven a roofing nail into the bridge of my nose. Blood was dripping into my throat. But I hadn't gone down. I snorted, coughed, looked Lansing right in the eye.

"Where's the stun gun, Junior? Did your daddy take it away?"

Lansing smiled. "Nah, we're just kicking it old-school tonight."

Andre stood there shaking his hand and making a face. "Fuck. I think I broke it. Why couldn't I just use the Scorpion?"

Lansing flicked his hand for his pal to sit down, then he leaned back into my sofa and crossed his legs.

"Now that we're half even," Lansing said, "let's talk bats."

"Fuck you."

Lansing laughed a little, stroked his goatee. He was very fond of that thing.

"I was telling a friend of mine about how this lunatic motherfucker busts into my house the other night and robs me," he said. "And after I give him a description of the perp, he points me in your direction."

"Let me guess," I said. "Tommy Pumpkin."

Lansing leaned forward a little like he hadn't heard me clearly. "Who?"

"Tommy Pumpkin," I said. "'Roided up, big head, no fucking concept of the strike zone."

"You mean Tommy Bahama," Andre said.

"Tommy Bahama's a fucking shirt maker," Lansing said.

"Not *that* Tommy Bahama," Andre said. "The bartender. The guy who used to work down in Lauderdale at Don Shula's Steak House."

"When the fuck would I talk to him?" Lansing said. "Besides, it was a doctor friend of mine who told me where to find you. Very well respected. I believe his ballclub has administered a number of ass kickings on your little shit-ass outfit."

"Fucking Thunderturd," I said.

I sat down in my chair, picked up the remote, and went back to TV mode. Classic was showing the '84 Boston College–Miami game with the Flutie Hail Mary. I'd watched that game with Phil at his old apartment; late, cloudy November day. We were eating calzones on the coffee table.

The TV seemed to take Lansing off his game a little. His eyes kept darting over to the Sony. Meantime, Andre was fully enthralled by the twenty-year-old game.

"If you're looking for the bat," I said, "then you better talk to your old man. He sent a couple of his choir boys to confiscate it."

"Yeah, I heard all about that. Fucking pepper spray's a bitch, ain't it?"

"At least I didn't have to sit through a sermon."

Lansing chuckled. "I'm starting to like you, Rice."

"Can you get to the fucking point?" I asked. "I got a blue crab project that's due tomorrow morning."

"Well, outside of the fact that I owed you a little pain, I believe you've been misinformed as to the true situation here."

"So enlighten me," I said.

Lansing started to talk, but then he glanced at the screen again. Kosar was loping to the line of scrimmage, in the hurry-up, driving Miami to their final score.

"Will you turn this shit off?" he said. "Jesus Christ, this is an important matter."

I shut down the Sony. "Spit it out," I said. "What's the matter, you got fucking ADHD or something?"

Lansing slapped Andre on the shoulder. The big guy stood up and produced a dingy little thirty-eight.

"That's cute," I said, "a throwback gun to go with the jersey."

"Jesus," Lansing said. "Will you just shut the fuck up and listen for a second? Are you capable of that? You ask me, I think you're the one with fucking ADD."

I turned on the TV again and jacked up the volume. Brent Musburger's voice was bouncing off the walls like a nasal symphony.

"I ain't listening to shit until he puts away the weapon."

Lansing pondered the situation, gave his sidekick the once-over. "All right, Dre. Belt the thirty-eight."

I hit the mute button, and Andre slid the piece back into his shorts. He was still flexing his hand from where he had hit me.

"You got any ice?" he asked.

"I got a bag of frozen peas in the freezer."

"Thanks," he said.

"Now," Lansing said, "here's the thing . . ."

Whatever angles he might have been working, the little shit told me a very believable story. Apparently, Gene's business with Lansing Senior was no simple loan to pay off the church. Gene had, in fact, used the 250K he'd gotten from Lansing's old man as seed money for the drugstore operation. The deal with Lansing's father was for interest plus a 15 percent slice of profits once the online store was up and running.

"So, it was a part-ownership deal," I said.

Lansing shrugged. "Silent partnership. My old man, he has to be careful about these things, being tied in with paper and all."

Gene's first mistake was running his mouth to Lansing Senior about the Babe Ruth bat. He told him everything, about the old lady and how he had to pay $250,000 to her church. When Gene disappointed Lansing Senior—as was bound to happen when Gene was involved in anything—the old man decided to confiscate the bat and keep it for himself.

"He started getting a hard-on for memorabilia a few years ago," Junior said. "Plus, he's a big fucking Yankees fan from way back."

Lansing Senior went to the church's pastor and cut his own deal. If the church delivered the bat, they'd get the sweetheart land deal in Glendale. Problem was, the pastor and youth minister were new to this sort of thing. They fucked up, broke Gene's nose, but didn't get the bat.

"That's when I get a phone call from my old man," Junior said.

The bat fiasco had coincided with a cash-flow problem in Junior's business. The ultimatum from his father was firm: fetch the bat or no more financing for the throwback jersey business.

"Is there any fucking money in those jerseys, anyway?" I asked.

Lansing laughed. "Did you see the Jay-Z video for 'Girls, Girls, Girls'? The one where he's rocking that tight '82 Padres jersey? Those shirts are three hundred dollars apiece."

"So, you're telling me you made the jersey in the video."

"Not that precise jersey, but I do a replica. I'm working at a different price point, helping the common man get into these fine threads."

"I think what you're talking about is called counterfeiting."

"And I'd call what you do scalping."

"Let's get back to the bat," I said. "So, you terrorize a widow and her three-year-old to steal this thing and save your jersey business."

"And then you bust into my home like fuckin' Walker, Texas Ranger," Lansing said, "and take the bat. I got suppliers to pay, and the old man's not happy. Do you think my business got the shot in the arm he'd promised?"

I stood up, went to the kitchen, got a Heineken out of the fridge, a couple of Vikes from the counter. I was trying to sort out where all this was heading, but so far it just sounded like a different version of the same fucking situation.

"Your old man's got the fucking bat," I said. "I already told you, the church took it back. So, what the fuck are you doing here?"

He walked over, took a beer out of the refrigerator. I snagged the bottle opener before he got to it.

"I see we have some trust issues," he said.

I tossed him the opener. "Fuck you. I don't trust anybody right now."

Lansing opened the Heineken and took a drink. "Maybe I don't think my old man deserves the bat."

"Great. So, you're pissed at Daddy and you want it for your own collection. To be honest with you, I don't get the whole memorabilia thing. Bats, jerseys, X rays—I mean, what the fuck? And then you got Babe Ruth. Great player, don't get me wrong. But from what I hear, Josh Gibson hit a thousand home runs. Why don't you do something unique and track down one of his bats?"

"I could give a fuck about the Ruth bat," Lansing said. "Yeah, I dabble in memorabilia. But this is strictly business. What I'm talking about is cash."

"You have a lot of trouble getting to the point," I said. "It's not a good way to do business. So let me ask you a simple question. What the fuck are you proposing here?"

Lansing looked down, straightened the front of his jersey.

"A partnership," he said. "I'll cut you in on a little something that could make you a wealthy man."

"I'm not looking for wealth. All I want is to save my business. That's the only reason I got involved in this shit."

"There'll be at least a hundred grand in it for you," he said. "Plus, there's something better than money involved here."

He smiled, took a slow drink from his Heineken.

"And what would that be?" I asked.

"How about revenge?" he said.

"I got no need for revenge."

"Oh, yeah. Well, maybe you just forgot. But that's okay, because I can refresh your memory. I know all about you, all about your uncle Phil, the one who went missing when he didn't cover his numbers for like the thousandth time."

I set down the beer. "Don't fuck with me, Lansing. I don't give a shit if your man over there's got a piece. You better watch what you're fucking saying."

He glanced over his shoulder to make sure Andre was still there. In fact, Andre hadn't even noticed us. He'd turned on the TV and started playing *Madden* against the computer, balancing the frozen peas on top of his hand.

"You're an angry guy," Lansing said. "And the thing is, I think your anger is being misdirected. Maybe if you knew exactly who was responsible for taking out your uncle, you could set about working through some of these anger issues."

"And you're telling me you know who did it."

Lansing smiled. "First and last names."

"Don't fuck with me on this," I said.

But Lansing just ignored me. He set down his beer and walked back into the living room. "Yo, Dre. Let's go."

Lansing produced a business card from his shorts. He set it on the end table. "You help me out, and I'll help you out," he said. "I'm gonna be in town for a couple days working on some other business.

Call me after you've thought it over. We'll get together and talk details."

Andre threw an interception, spiked the peas and my PS2 controller into the carpet, and walked to the door. Before the two of them could leave, Louis showed up at the door.

"I thought I told you to go to Pupusa Mart."

Louis walked past the three of us and plopped his ass on the sofa. "*SmackDown* starts in three minutes," he said. "You and your boyfriends can party in the bedroom."

Lansing and Andre laughed.

"Cute kid," Lansing said. "He's got your mouth."

As he backed out the door, he pointed to the card again. "Don't forget to call. I know you're curious."

CHAPTER 24

I stayed up all night trying to write the blue crab paper. Not an easy task with Lansing Junior's proposal occupying a chunk of my brain. That got me to thinking about Phil, and then about Theresa and Louis moving away, and I didn't really give a shit about the blue crab, a bottom dweller and part of the food chain to begin with. Hell, I was trying to avoid that spot myself. I did my best to piece it all together into something comprehensible.

Louis was asleep on the sofa, the TV still running on ESPNEWS. The sun had come up, and I'd just finished the final sentence ("The blue crab is an important player in the Chesapeake Bay's ecology, and we must never take it for granted") when my cell phone rang. It was Jerry Burns, the limo driver.

I asked what he was doing up so early.

"I had to make a run out to Dulles, some cocksucker flying in from L.A. on the red-eye."

"Is that supposed to be big news or something?"

"No, but this is: when I got to the warehouse, all the limos were being loaded onto a fucking truck."

"What are you talking about?"

"They told me the executor to Gene's estate sold the cars. They're gone, Joe—every fucking one of them. The limo service is history."

"They said the executor sold them?"

"Yeah, one of the guys driving the truck told me."

I drove over to Joy's house as soon as I dropped off Louis at school. He was early for a change.

"You sold the fucking limos?"

She was standing in the door wearing her workout gear: knee-length black tights, a baggy Yankees T-shirt that I'd bought her at the game. It had Rivera's name and number on the back. Her hair was in pigtails. She had a way of showing off just enough of herself. She was never tacky about it.

Nevertheless, I was pissed off. I didn't even let myself admire those pink Pumas.

"I was gonna tell you."

"Bullshit. You were a coward. You didn't want to tell me."

I followed her into the house. We went to the kitchen. I sat down at the table and lit a cigarette. Joy grabbed a bottle of Vitamin Water out of the fridge.

"And what about our agreement? The bat, the business. What about that?"

"We don't have the fucking bat anymore," she said.

"I told you it was a setup."

She sighed, wiped at her brow. I couldn't tell if she had already worked out, or if she was just hot. I had to admit the house was even starting to feel warm to me.

She sat down across from me and lit a cigarette from my pack. "I'm sorry, Joe. I had to make a payment on the house. I didn't know what else to do. I've got creditors coming at me from every direction, and White said the probate judge would okay the sale of the cars. They were the only valuable thing I could unload."

I hadn't even considered the house. Here I'd been thinking all along that I was just in this to maintain the status quo. I'd never imagined Joy and little Gene out on the street.

"Jesus," I said. "You were gonna lose the house?"

"I still may. Geno took out two loans on it."

Now I couldn't even look her in the eye. "I'm sorry. I got this fucking tunnel vision about the business, and I didn't even think about your house."

She reached out, lay her open hand in the middle of the table. I couldn't stop myself from laying my own hand on top of hers.

"I've found myself feeling different about some things," she said. "I got to a point where I expected the worst from people. But you've got a good heart. I'm sorry I screwed everything up."

I couldn't look her in the eye. "You didn't screw anything up, Joy. It's just a bad situation."

"I know that," she said. "And I feel guilty for saying this. But there's been times the last few weeks, like the night we went to the ballgame, when I was actually happy. I'd kind of forgotten what that was like."

"You can't rely on me to make you happy, Joy."

She narrowed her eyes. "What are you talking about?"

"You can't rely on anybody to make you happy."

"Who told you that?"

I slowly pulled my hand away from hers, checked my watch, and thought about Lansing's card, which was tucked into the breast pocket of my jacket.

"Lansing Junior came by to see me last night."

She appeared frightened by the mention of him. "What did he want?"

"He said he had a business proposition for me."

"The bat?"

I shook my head. "He was talking about cash."

I asked if Gene had ever told her about my uncle Phil.

"He said your uncle sort of raised you. He told me he got into trouble with some guys, that he disappeared."

"They killed him," I said. "So, Lansing tells me he knows who did it. He says he'll give me a name if I help him with whatever he's scheming. He promised me a hundred grand, too."

"And you trust him?"

"Fuck, no. But the way I see it, this opens a window for getting that bat back. And I am gonna get it back for you. You deserve it."

She sat there slowly turning the bottle of water in her hand, staring at the pale blue liquid.

"Are you doing this out of guilt?" she asked.

"Why would I do it out of guilt?"

"I don't think you want to see me anymore. If you get the bat, you think that'll make it okay."

I stubbed out my cigarette in Geno's New York Yankees ashtray. It had been part of a five-hundred-piece poker set he'd bought. If I hadn't chewed his ass over the first-to-third thing, or if I'd dropped him in the batting order so I wasn't hitting behind him, or even if I hadn't gotten that base hit to right field, the poor sonuvabitch might have lived to play another hand with those stupid chips.

"It was Theresa," I said. "The person who said that thing about not depending on somebody else to make you happy."

Joy looked up. "The woman with the kid?"

"A son," I said. "His name's Louis."

"I thought she ended things."

"She did. She's moving to Florida."

"What about us?" she asked.

"Listen," I said, "I don't want to push you away from whatever it is that you believe in."

She opened her mouth but didn't say anything.

CHAPTER 25

Louis got a fucking F on the blue crab report. The teacher sent a note home to Theresa. In part, it read, "No concept of how to research a paper . . . Footnote format is incomplete. . . . Entire project totally lacking in depth of thought, communication, or creativity."

"But I wrote the whole fucking thing for him," I told Theresa.

"No shit, Merlin. He could've done this bad without your help."

"Give me that fucking letter." I tried to grab it from the kitchen counter, but she picked it up and slipped it into the cutlery drawer. She just stood there staring at me. I could read an abundant supply of pity in that look.

"What the fuck?" I said. "Don't look at me like that."

"What are you going to do with yourself?" she said. "You flunked a seventh-grade project."

"It's a fucking conspiracy," I said. "I researched the shit out of that paper. Don't think this shit doesn't happen. Somebody's got it in for Louis. You were absolutely right about that school."

I'd quit the Vike again; granted, only twelve hours earlier, right after I'd learned about the limos. My head hadn't been agreeing all day, and now my stomach and nerves were joining the revolt. I wobbled a little on my feet, felt my knees and hands begin to shake. I braced myself on the kitchen table, tried to think about measured breaths, good pauses in between; the *abhyantara kumbhaka* and the *bahya kumbhaka*.

"I'm worried about you," she said. "You look like shit."

"I think I ate some bad chicken."

"Bullshit. You're trying to kick those painkillers."

I sat down in a chair, tried to hold back from getting sick. "I fucked up, Theresa. I totally fucked up."

She rinsed out a dishrag in cold water, walked over, and touched it to the back of my neck. "It's okay," she said. "You can't just quit like that."

"I'm not talking about the fucking pills. I'm talking about everything else. Louis's paper. My business. Everything—"

"I never really meant that you were lazy," she said.

The cold rag worked, made the nausea pass. I felt a little stronger, sat up straight.

"Nah, you were right. I've become lackadaisical. A malingerer."

I took a cigarette out of the pack lying on the table. "A much-maligned malingerer," I said. "How's that for a fucking caption?"

She took the rag and lobbed it into the sink. It landed with a splat. She walked back to the counter, lit a cigarette, braced her arm on the edge of the sink.

"I think you should read something besides the *New York Post*," she said.

I'd been driving around all day—ever since the conversation with Joy—thinking about this shit with Lansing Junior. Guilt or not (and maybe Joy had a point there), I still had a lot of things to make right, and I could do it if I made some good calls along the way. For starters, I needed to get the bat back for Joy. Maybe I couldn't make her happy, but $2 to $3 million would open some doors for her. And then there was Phil. It was possible, maybe even likely, that Lansing Junior had been lying about knowing who killed him. But if there was a chance he knew the truth, I needed to find out. I owed it to Phil for looking after me and keeping me at a safe distance from the trouble that was always close to him. And fuck the risks. I should have been at the bar with Phil in the first place.

There was also the money. If I took care of the important things first, then maybe that part would work out, too. I could actually save the Whip Spa, Backstage Pass, Inc., and the Whip Spa Yankees. The key was to read the situation as it developed, to keep Lansing Junior off balance if he was trying to screw me. It was like calling pitches in a game, and Lansing was no Jeter.

I didn't want to tell any of this to Theresa. I was afraid she might not let Louis stay with me anymore. And so, for some reason, I told her that I'd been seeing someone.

"You sound like you're making a confession."

"I just wanted you to know," I said.

"I guess it's really none of my business."

"I know that, but she said something to me, and I wanted to see what you thought."

Theresa held up her hands to stop me. "Does this have anything to do with anal sex?"

"No, it's nothing like that. The thing is she told me the other night that being with me has made her happy."

Theresa shook her head, sighed. "Does this woman make you happy?"

I was looking around the room, my eyes jumping from one thing to the next. They finally landed on the lone box of cereal: Louis's Cocoa Pebbles.

"You make me happy," I said. "I like talking to you. This other woman, she's nice, but it's not the same."

Theresa flicked her ash into the sink, then looked out the window to where everything had been washed pale by the floodlight I'd replaced earlier in the evening.

"How's your hand?" she asked. She wasn't looking at me when she said it.

My hand was throbbing like hell. Everything throbbed when I wasn't taking pills. But I knew I was going to give in later, and the thought alone made me feel a little better.

"It's doing good," I said.

"You know," she said, "we're leaving in a week."

"Yeah, I thought it was getting close."

"It's almost time," she said.

"Were you serious?" I asked.

She turned from the window, gave me a puzzled look. "Serious about what?"

"That you're worried about me."

CHAPTER 26

Lansing Junior had taken a booth at the back of the IHOP, the same one where me and Funderburk had tried to work out our differences back in the spring. I walked over and slid in on the opposite side of the table.

He was talking on his little red cell phone, which matched his Joe Montana Chiefs jersey. "I need a hundred yards of victory blue, goddammit. Now, you tell that little turd I just got a truckful of Mexicans who wanna make some fucking jerseys, and I'm not gonna feed 'em for doing nothing."

He snapped the phone shut, sighed, lit a cigarette, and finally took notice of my presence. The sight of me caused him to wince.

"Jesus, Rice. You look like shit."

"Fucking head cold," I said.

Truth was, I hadn't been able to get in touch with Tommy Pumpkin for more pills. I was running on NyQuil and two Jack and Cokes. A head cold would have been the least of my ailments.

"Listen," he said, "I got some jerseys in the car I want you to check out. I'll give you the Cliffside discount."

"Fuck the jerseys," I said. "Let's talk business."

Lansing smiled. "All right, but I got some silver-dollar pancakes coming up. My only rule is I don't talk business while I eat."

The restaurant was nearly empty after the morning rush. It smelled like coffee and burnt bacon. The odor left a sharp pain in my stomach.

A waitress came over, topped off Lansing's coffee cup, and filled mine. I waved off the menu and settled on a Marlboro Light.

"I don't know how you live down here," Lansing said. "It's kind of depressing."

"Yeah, like Edgewater's a fucking glamour spot."

"It's got a buzz, though," he said. "We're near the city."

"You ever heard of Washington, D.C.?" I asked.

Lansing laughed. "Fucking company town," he said. "And the service at restaurants down here is very unsophisticated."

"So why don't you write a fucking letter to the chamber of commerce?"

Lansing smirked. He took a long drag off his cigarette, let the smoke drift away from his lips. "It was my old man, actually. He remembered when I mentioned your name."

I asked him what he was talking about.

"I'm talking about your uncle. It was my old man who killed him. Or had him killed, I should say. He's never been a hands-on guy."

And there it was, just as casual as that. I didn't really know what to say at first. It was funny, because everything still felt the same. My hand was still hurting, and the busboy up front was still clattering silverware in his tub.

"He had his own crew back then, said your uncle was a hardheaded motherfucker, never learned from his mistakes. Just like you."

I grabbed the knife from Lansing's setting and went across the table after him. I threw my forearm into his chest and pushed the knife against the skin of his neck. He held up his arms, careful with his cigarette, and looked around like I was embarrassing him.

"Why don't you settle down, Rice? It'd take you two hours to saw through my carotid artery with that thing."

I backed off, dropped the knife. I could feel the blood pumping through my head, raking every raw nerve.

"Just leave out the fucking commentary," I said.

"All right, then, that's the story," he said. "Your uncle dug a hole and couldn't get out. They gave him a chance, but he kept going in deeper, looking to bag an elephant, make it all back on one win. And that's not commentary. It's fact."

I asked him why he was willing to share this information with me.

"Maybe I just wanted to take the opportunity to make something right."

"Or maybe you're full of shit and want somebody to kill your old man for you."

Lansing smiled. "Some things are worse than death."

I didn't give him the satisfaction of asking what those things might be. He waited as long as he could.

"Such as taking a person's money," he said. "For some people, that's worse than death."

"So you want to rob your old man. What do you need me for?"

"I need an outside partner, somebody I can trust."

I laughed at that one. "I don't give a fuck about you."

"And that's exactly why I trust you."

The waitress brought Lansing's silver-dollar cakes and a glass of milk. He stuck a finger in the milk. "Do you have anything colder?" he asked.

"What do you want?" she asked. "An iced tea?"

"Never mind," he said.

After she'd walked away, he leaned across the table. "A broad like that'll spit in your food."

"Thanks for the tip. How about getting back on track?"

He stuffed a forkful of pancake in his mouth and smiled. "Now, about your hundred grand . . ."

"I thought you didn't do business while you were eating."

Lansing said his father liked to pretend he'd quit the mob. Of course, anybody knows you don't quit. You either flip to the government's side, or you're retired without compensation. But Lansing Senior had remarried, to a younger woman, a few years earlier, had fathered a son, and invested in some commercial real estate in suburban Connecticut. He had ground leases with big names: Target, Outback Steakhouse, Sports Authority, Lowe's Home and Garden Centers. He drove an Audi wagon, wore Ralph Lauren shirts, went to the son's Little League games, owned the good season tickets at the stadium. "Fucking, phony-ass cocksucker," Junior said. "He likes playing that role: Mr. Suburban Connecticut Dickhead."

Of course, the old man still wet his beak in the old business: namely, sharking and offshore bookmaking. He backed an Internet gambling site based in the Caribbean that brought in about three million dollars on Super Bowl weekend alone. Junior's plan was to blackmail his old man via the Internet; jam up the traffic on a busy football weekend with a blizzard of spam, then send an e-mail to the site demanding that $500,000 be delivered to a drop-off site.

"Protection money?" I asked.

"This is the way it's done these days," Lansing said.

"Why don't you just steal the bat from him, give it to me, and I'll make sure you're handsomely compensated when it's auctioned?"

He was holding the maple syrup in one hand, a cigarette in the other. "You think my old man wouldn't have me killed? Him and his fucking bats. It's sacred shit in his eyes. You'd think Moses had used that Ruth bat to kick the shit out of Pharaoh's army."

"What it sounds like to me is that you're afraid of him."

Lansing raised the milk glass to his mouth, paused, and set the fork back down on his plate.

"This is about independence," he said. "I'm the legitimate businessman in the family. I'm the one who's got a chance to break the cycle of dysfunctionality. But he doesn't really want that, you see. He doesn't want me to succeed. Why do you think I stole the bat back from Dellorso's old lady in the first place? It was because my old man wouldn't give me money to pay for a shipment of fabric. He's got me by the short and curlies just the way he likes it. He's a fucking control freak."

"How do you know I'm not gonna kill your old man now that you've told me this?"

"Straight-up murder doesn't seem like your style," Lansing said. "You may be dumb, but you're a thinker. You can see the benefits in my plan."

I asked if he actually had the technical know-how to pull off this blackmail scheme. He chewed a mouthful of pancake and smiled.

"That's where you come in. I hear you got a guy working for you who's a whiz with a hard drive. Ramon something or other."

"Who the fuck told you that?"

"Funderburk. He said this guy Ramon did some work for his and Dellorso's drugstore operation. He said Ramon was the master of the spam e-mail."

I'd had a feeling Ramon was bullshitting me that day at Geno's storage space, even after he'd sworn to me that he knew nothing about the pills.

"It's not a helluva lot of cash," I said. "Especially split three ways."

"That reminds me," Lansing said, "Funderburk's in for a twenty-five percent cut of the money. He wants to move to Vegas and start his own pharmacy."

"Fuck him," I said. "I'm not doing any deal where that prick's involved."

"You'd be a fucking idiot to pass up this opportunity," he said.

"Yeah, well, I just flunked the seventh grade."

I slid out of the booth and walked away, leaving him sitting there without an answer. I already knew what I was going to do.

He called out one last time. "Don't forget the league championship. With Funderburk in Vegas, it's yours to lose."

CHAPTER 27

The warehouse had never been so quiet on a Wednesday morning. I'd given the detailing guys the day off, and the limo side of things no longer existed. With the cars gone, those fucking vultures at Airport Elite Town Car had snapped up all of Gene's drivers. That finished off the baseball team as well. I'd already gotten an e-mail from the commissioner notifying me of a permanent suspension from the league due to an excess of forfeits. To top it off, this was supposed to be Ramon's last day before his big venture in the Pollo Campero franchise world. He'd already locked down the ticket window a couple days earlier. The whole operation was on the verge of extinction.

I asked Ramon to come in early to discuss a business matter. I didn't go into any details with him. He showed up with breakfast for the two of us: a pair of vente vanilla lattes, raisin bagels with light cream cheese, and *New York Posts*. We sat at the old desk, ate our breakfasts, read the sports, and watched the Ice Bowl highlights on ESPN Classic. It felt good, like something I should savor.

But then I had to get to the point and ask him about his work for Gene and Funderburk.

"You swore to me, Ramon. You said you didn't know anything about it."

"It was true, to a degree," he said. "Tommy P. is the one who hired me. He said he had some associates who were operating this online pharmacy, and they needed a spam guy. I swear to God, I never put two and two together until we saw that box of OxyContin, although

I should've had a clue that Gene was involved, seeing as how I never got paid."

I told Ramon about Lansing Junior's proposed scam while we finished our bagels.

"You'd be in for a hundred twenty-five grand, same as everybody else. That probably sounds like walking-around money now that you're a big man in the franchised restaurant world."

He was about to take a bite of his bagel, but he stopped and slowly set it down on top of the paper bag. He wiped his fingers on a napkin, looked down, then back up at the television before he fixed his eyes on me again.

"About the franchise . . . ," he said.

His rich girlfriend, Brooke, had thrown him out of her condo for screwing the girl from Best Buy. The girl had called his backup cell, and Brooke had answered. Estelle, mother of his noisy child, had refused to take Ramon back, so he was living with his grandfather. He needed money. A hundred and twenty-five grand was sounding good to him.

"The question is, can you shut down this guy's gambling site?"

"It's a piece of cake," Ramon said. "I hacked into the server at the community college and used it to send out the spam for Tommy Pumpkin. I've still got the generator on my computer at home."

"That's good," I said. "Then it sounds like we're set."

Ramon leaned back in his chair, stuck his hands in the pockets of his orange Dolphins hoodie. He had this confused look on his face.

"Let me ask you this," he said. "Are you gonna kill Lansing's father because of what he did to your uncle?"

"To tell you the truth," I said, "I'm not even sure Lansing's father had anything to do with Phil's murder. The way that Gene ran his mouth, he probably told Funderburk about my uncle. Maybe Funderburk tells Lansing Junior and they get this idea that they can use it to lure me in, to get me to bring you in, too. The main thing I'm worried about is getting that three-million-dollar bat from him. That's my top priority."

"But what if it's the truth?" he asked. "Are you gonna kill Lansing's father?"

I had spent some time imagining different scenarios of revenge when I was in prison, and even for a long time thereafter.

"Remember when you said that you have to forget some things in order to keep living?"

Ramon shrugged. "I remember saying something like that, yeah."

"Well, not everybody is wired up to forget. But that doesn't mean you can't keep living."

Ramon looked thoroughly confused. "So that means you *are* gonna kill him?"

I opened the desk drawer and showed him the Ruger forty-four.

"This was my uncle's," I said. "He never fired it, and I've never fired it."

He looked at me for a long time. "That's not an answer."

"You don't need to know everything," I said. "You've got the most important job here. It's our entry. You focus on that, and I'll call the pitches."

He eyed me as if he was considering shaking me off. Finally, he nodded and took a sip of his latte. We both gazed up at the television. Bart Starr was leading the offense onto the field, little puffs of breath exploding through his face mask.

"Let me ask you this," he said. "Do you have a game plan?"

"Have I ever had a game plan?"

He shook his head.

"Well, there you have it," I said.

We sat there a moment, watching Starr sneak across the goal line for the winning touchdown. And then Ramon shook his head. "The season of Gene," he said. "What the fuck was I thinking?"

CHAPTER 28

The one thing I believed I could always trust was my brain. I never thought it would let me down. My mother, she had her problems. And whoever my father might have been, I just assumed I'd gotten his wiring up top. But now it wasn't working so good. And the fuck of it was that I couldn't do anything to fix it. Even the breathing shit was failing me.

I couldn't focus on anything. I'd get a shred of a thought, and then it would slip away and it'd be like chasing a gum wrapper in the wind—lots of gum wrappers, actually. The Vikes weren't helping anymore. I couldn't get enough of them, and my source, Tommy Pumpkin, was still missing. A private investigator working for his old employer had produced a photo of Tommy dunking a basketball during a pickup game.

I was smoking cigarettes at 2 a.m., watching the Roger Maris *Yankeeography* on YES, and trying to concentrate on my breathing. The technique wasn't working anymore, and neither was the Jack Daniel's and NyQuil. No matter what I'd said to Ramon, I needed a plan. I needed the bat, the money, and to make sure that Lansing Junior didn't rip us off, but the wild card of it all was Lansing Senior. How would I deal with him if the time came?

Sometime around three in the morning, I got in my car and started driving in the general direction of Philly. It felt like I had I-95 to myself, so I punched the gas, kept the speedometer up around ninety. It was getting near daylight, and I still wasn't sleepy. Some dumb-shit radio host was talking about this high school football player who'd dropped dead on the playing field, saying how something like this "puts the games into perspective." I called the station's number, got right through, and he put me on the air. I said, "Fuck you. It's just a goddamn ballgame every fucking day. It don't ever mean shit. So take your fucking perspective and stick it up your ass."

I'm not sure when they cut me off, but they must have had a long delay for shit like this because there was a Dial-A-Mattress commercial where my call should have been.

I kept on driving up 95, past Wilmington and into Philadelphia. I'd calmed down a little by the time I got into the city. With the car's interior light burning, I read the MapQuest directions that I'd printed out months ago. I parked in a Brake-O lot across the street from the clinic and sat there smoking cigarettes and drinking 7-Eleven coffee while the sun came up.

"If you're here for methadone, you'll have to wait until I get everything set up."

I caught my faint reflection in the sliding-glass partition at the clinic's counter and realized the man's assumption wasn't a stretch. I looked like hell.

"I'm looking for somebody, actually. Lily Marie Rice."

The man gazed up from the files he'd been riffling. "Does she owe you money?"

"No, I just used to know her a while back. I checked online, saw she was working here."

He settled into his office chair, went back to his files. He had old tattoos on his arms, pockmarks on his cheeks.

"Yeah, well, that page is old. She left a couple years ago. She was stealing money from the clinic. We weren't gonna press charges. We just wanted her to get back in a program, but she left town."

It wasn't like I was surprised (after all, I'd been avoiding this trip for four years). But it still hit me like some hard-assed, Pete Rose–loving base runner charging home from third. There was no air to grab hold of, none anywhere.

"Are you sure you're okay, man?"

The guy was looking up again, his lap full of files.

"Yeah, I'm good. You don't know where she went, do you?"

He shook his head. "Like I said, she just took off when the shit hit the fan. Happens all the time."

Especially with her, I thought.

It came back to me as I was driving home that morning: the episode with the KFC bucket, but it wasn't a chicken bucket.

I was about seven or eight when we took off for Baltimore. I didn't want to go. I remembered that part of it pretty clearly. It was my first year in Little League, and practice was starting the following week. So she told me we were going to Disney World. I'd seen this photo of Space Mountain in the *Weekly Reader* at school.

We left at night. She woke me up, hustled me to the car. It was full of our shit, but I was too stupid to realize what was happening. She'd left a space for me in the backseat, beside the television and a cardboard box. I had my blanket and pillow in my arms.

"Go to sleep," she said. "When you wake up, we'll be there."

"Where?"

Her face hovered above mine. She hesitated, bit her lip. In my memory, she looked so fucking young. She was just a kid herself.

"Where do you think?" she said.

I must have woken up at a rest stop on I-95. The fluorescent lights were shining inside the car, and a man in an orange jumpsuit was pumping gas into the tank. I thought for a moment that we were in Florida. Then I noticed the puffs of frozen breath escaping from the man's mouth, and I realized my mother was singing very softly in the front seat.

I leaned up between the seats and told her I had to go pee. She had a tape playing quietly in the dash, a voice and organ.

"I gotta pee bad," I said.

She lay her cigarette in the open ashtray, which was already stocked with butts, and she looked back like she hadn't known I was behind her. The realization didn't appear to make her happy. The gas pump clicked, and the man in the jumpsuit came to the window. She turned and handed him the money. And then she reached down on the floorboard and came up with an empty bottle.

"Here," she said. "Just go in here. I don't want to get out."

Martini & Rossi, the bottle said. The label had a bundle of red grapes on it.

"I don't wanna pee in the bottle. I wanna go inside."

"Well, I don't want to get out. So pee in the bottle."

"I can't. I gotta use the bathroom."

Her mood, already colored at the edges with anger, sparked to a full burn. She turned away from me, shook her head, and waved her hand toward the building with the bathrooms. "Fine," she said. "Go by yourself. Maybe you'll fucking get kidnapped. Is that what you want?"

I peed in the bottle and screwed the cap back on tightly. I wasn't worried about being kidnapped, but the thought did cross my mind that she might leave me. It felt like a possibility from that moment forward.

I had to scramble to get back to D.C. in time for my lunch meeting. Me, Ramon, Funderburk, and Lansing Junior convened at the Chick-fil-A to work out the details on the hit of Lansing Senior's bookmaking site. Ramon quickly slid into Lansing's side of the booth, leaving me to sit with Funderburk, who was working on a chicken strips salad.

Lansing Junior was telling Funderburk a joke, waving his cigarette around and talking loud.

"So the wife says, 'Wake up, asshole! You're shittin' the bed!'"

Funderburk laughed, threw his head forward, and held his napkin over his mouth like he was gonna spray salad all over the table.

"You gotta tell that one to these two," Funderburk said.

Funderburk reached out to shake my hand. I decided to be a gentleman. Considering my lack of sleep and the disappointing visit to Philadelphia, I was pretty much drained of any strong feelings, including the grudge against my managerial rival.

"So how are your D-Rays doing?"

Funderburk smiled. "Six and zero. And we miss you guys. I'm not shitting you about that. You brought out the best in us."

He paused, stuck a forkful of lettuce in his mouth. "And the worst."

With that painful shit out of the way, we got down to business. Our plan was to use the warehouse as a staging area. Ramon had already set up his tools of trade on my desk. It was an unimpressive site: a no-name PC, a modem jammer, and a dingy keyboard with enough crumbs in it to top a soufflé. I expressed some doubts about the setup's capabilities, but Ramon assured me there was plenty under the hood to get the job done.

We wanted to take down Lansing Senior's website on a Sunday morning when all the NFL bets were being placed. It'd be crucial that they get things up and running quickly, or else they'd be out a lot of cash. Five hundred grand would not seem all that unreasonable in such a situation. According to Junior, the old man kept that much cash at his house in Westport.

"You sure about that?" I asked.

Lansing was chewing his Chick-fil-A. He shrugged off my doubt. "Hey, he's old-school. He believes in cash for emergencies, and we're gonna give him one."

Lansing was going to stay at the garage with Ramon, while me and Funderburk went to New York Sunday morning to make the pickup. The Yanks and Red Sox were playing the season's final game that Sunday at the stadium. There'd be a big crowd, lots of cops. The old man would be instructed to bring the money to Eddie's Sports Bar on River Avenue, across from the stadium. Hundred-dollar bills in a backpack. Just to make sure he didn't blend into the crowd too well, Funderburk suggested we specify that he wear a Sox hat.

Junior got a laugh out of that one. "I'd send him one of my Carlton Fisk jerseys, but he'd know it was me."

"What about firepower?" I asked. "Is your old man gonna be carrying?"

Lansing shook his head. "Even if he is, what the fuck is he gonna do in a crowd like that? He'd be too embarrassed in front of all those people. It wouldn't be sophisticated to shoot someone."

I didn't have much of an appetite, so I pushed my sandwich away and lit a cigarette.

"Are you sure you're up for this?" Lansing asked.

Funderburk nodded. "Yeah, you don't look like you've slept in a week."

I told the both of them to fuck off. And then I asked Lansing how he liked the chicken sandwich.

"Not bad," he said. "The pickle adds a lot."

"Ain't that the fucking truth?" I said.

"Salad's not bad either," Funderburk said.

Fucking asshole, getting a salad. But I bit my tongue. Meantime, Ramon was sitting across the table looking glum. I'm sure the chicken talk was making him think about his recently derailed Pollo Campero franchise. But if all went well, he'd be a hundred twenty-five grand closer to the start-up money come Sunday afternoon.

CHAPTER 29

I'd seen a Walter Payton throwback jersey in the back of Lansing's Acura when we were at Chick-fil-A. I thought Louis might like the jersey, so I bought it for him. I took it over to the house on Friday night, when I knew Theresa would be home. She'd just picked up a load of cardboard boxes at the storage place, and she was starting to pack for Florida.

"You found a place yet?"

"Yeah, Mike found it for us."

"The restaurant guy?"

She nodded, didn't look up. We were sitting at the kitchen table, wrapping drink glasses in newspaper. Louis was back in his room listening to Silkk the Shocker: *"I'm back from hell trying to take you to heaven."* He hadn't been all that excited about the jersey, hadn't seemed to really give a damn about me coming over, even when I asked if he wanted to play a game of *Madden* before I left. All he did was shrug, didn't even bother to talk any shit. I wondered if he'd already struck me off a list, was already on his way to forgetting me. I'd forgotten a lot of people I met as a kid. Had to be done.

A newspaper article caught my attention before I could wrap it around a glass. It was about a mother and daughter who'd been killed in a car wreck. A deer had run out in front of the car.

"Do they have deer in Florida?"

Theresa looked at me like I was crazy.

"So, when are you and Louis leaving?"

She went back to work on the drink glasses. "I'm picking up the U-Haul Sunday, so I'd like to be out of here by Monday afternoon. My neighbor wants to buy the Saturn. He's got a son who just turned sixteen."

"Sixteen? Shit, I used to watch him kick the soccer ball with that kid. He was like five or six."

"You're an old-timer in this neighborhood," she said.

We wrapped some more glasses, and I told her that I'd come over and help load stuff on Monday.

She smiled. "Thanks."

Somehow, having plans for Monday gave me hope that things might go well over the weekend.

"How's Louis feeling about the move?"

"He's fine," she said. "Since I took him out of school, he's not complaining about anything."

"He seems kind of quiet."

She shrugged.

"You think he liked the jersey? I mean, maybe I shouldn't have gotten a throwback. He doesn't remember Payton."

"He put it on, didn't he?"

"Yeah, but he didn't seem too excited."

She set a glass inside the box on the floor, then stopped to look at me for a moment. It was like she'd come very close to figuring me out, was almost there, and didn't really mind what she saw. I wanted her to tell me, and then I could have told her the things that I'd wanted to say since she'd said that she was worried about me. But then she went back to the glasses, back to the pages of newsprint, the sad stories and old ball scores wearing away on the tips of her fingers.

CHAPTER 30

We left D.C. early Sunday morning and headed toward the Bronx. I was piloting my 'Vette with Funderburk riding shotgun, him bitching about my wanting to leave at 7 a.m. even though we weren't supposed to meet Lansing Senior at the bar until noon.

"I wouldn't expect a doctor to know anything about punctuality," I said.

"That's a good one," he said. "Very original."

I was running through the radio stations, finally picking up something good out of Philadelphia. Ghostface was singing: *"Things was deep, my whole youth was sharper than cleats. Two brothers with muscular dystrophy, it killed me."*

An old-timer in the neighborhood, Theresa had said. In my head, I started rolling through all the people who'd come and gone.

Funderburk asked if I needed any more pills.

"Nah, I'm feeling just right. What was that shit you gave me, anyway?"

"Three Xanax and four hundred milligrams of Effexor."

"What the fuck is Effexor?"

"It's an antidepressant. I've been taking it myself. I think it might help you."

"You're a fucking cosmetic surgeon. What the hell do you know about what I need?"

Funderburk looked like I'd hurt his feelings. "It was a gesture of goodwill. I think you might be depressed."

"Go fuck yourself, Dr. Phil."

"Anger is a major symptom," he said.

For some reason—maybe it was the pills—I didn't have the energy to argue with him. So I asked Funderburk if he'd ever met Lansing Senior.

"Geno introduced us when we were putting our plans together for the online pharmacy. Gene tells the guy I'm a cosmetic surgeon, so Lansing comes in and wants me to do some work on him. He's a vain motherfucker. I had to do his eyelids twice. I also did his wife's nose, gave her a little turned-up number like Charlize Theron. She was already a beautiful girl, but he thought she looked a little too ethnic."

"He sounds like a fucking charm," I said.

"You'd never guess he was mob. He's got the Connecticut thing going strong. You'll see."

Funderburk slid his Oakleys onto his nose, shielding his eyes from the morning glare. "But be careful."

"Don't worry. I brought the piece I keep at the garage."

"What is it?" he asked.

"A Ruger forty-four."

I tapped the left side of my leather coat. I'd reluctantly sliced a makeshift holster into the lining at waist level. The jacket was my favorite, a gift from Theresa; it had a nice balance of sophistication and badass.

Traffic was light, and I kept the car at a steady eighty on the turnpike. I hit the G.W. Bridge at ten-fifteen and made a point of not looking in the rearview mirror at the Jersey cliffs. I drove right past Exit 5A, hoping Funderburk wouldn't notice, but he was on top of it.

"You just missed the Cross-Bronx," he said.

I told Funderburk to relax. "I'm taking an alternate route."

He pushed the Oakleys up onto his head. "What the fuck are you pulling here?"

"Change of plans," I said. "We're gonna pay Daddy L a little visit at home."

Funderburk stared at me for a long time. Finally, he pulled his cell phone out of the holster on his khakis. "Fuck this," he said. "I'm letting Junior know what you're up to."

I kept a hand on the wheel and reached into my jacket with the other one. I pulled out the forty-four and let it rest on my thigh, never even bothering to make eye contact with Funderburk.

"Roll down the window," I said, "and toss out the cell phone."

"Fuck you," he said. "I just got an upgrade."

"Didn't you buy the insurance?"

He paused a second. "I've never lost a cell phone before."

"All right, then put it in the glove compartment."

He opened the glove box, tossed the phone inside, and slammed it shut.

"You're going after that fucking bat, aren't you?" he said.

"You just do what I tell you," I said. "We'll get the bat *and* the money."

"Jesus Christ," he said. "You're the last person in the world who needs to be calling the shots in a situation like this."

"You know you've got more talent on the D-Rays," I said. "My boys max out every fucking game. We go a lot further in the playoffs than we have any right to go."

Funderburk seemed to think this was funny.

"What the fuck are you laughing at?"

"You're a regular fucking Billy Martin. But you got no fucking idea how to call a game from behind the plate."

"What do you know about calling a game? You're a fucking center fielder. You spend three hours out in the grass with your thumb up your ass."

"We know your fucking tendencies," he said. "You're impulsive as hell. You throw junk to the Punch-and-Judy hitters and straight fastballs to our power guys. It makes no sense. Your PFD rating is a ten."

I hit the Hutchinson River Parkway, heading toward Westport with the MapQuest directions lying on the dashboard. I'd found Lansing's address through a People Search.

"What the hell is a PFD rating?"

"Potential for destruction," he said.

"Wouldn't it be 'self-destruction'?" I asked.

"We shortened it," he said. "But everybody gets the point."

* * *

Lansing had acreage, the full country estate, a long driveway, stone-façade house and slate roof with dormer windows running across the top. I was guessing five bedrooms, five baths, probably one hell of a multimedia room. I pulled around to the side with the three garage doors. A tennis court out back had been converted into a deluxe batting cage: fully netted, Jugs machine at the ready, practice mound behind a screen. I had to admit I liked what he'd done with the court.

Me and Funderburk stood beside my car taking in the spread.

"Four mil, easy," Funderburk said. "I wonder what his fucking property taxes are on this place."

I started picturing myself living on this type of spread, whacking baseballs around in my personal cage, Louis out there taking his cuts, too. That part of it felt natural. In my vision, Louis was wearing a Bernie Williams jersey, the gray road model.

"Lot of money here," Funderburk said. "Geno told me Michael Bolton lives down the street from Lansing."

A red Audi wagon sat in the driveway. I walked toward it. Funderburk fell in behind me.

"What do you think you're gonna do?" he asked. "Walk right in the front door?"

"It's probably locked," I said. "I got a better idea."

I grabbed the handle of the Audi's driver-side door. As I'd expected, it was unlocked. I reached inside, slid the garage door opener off the sun visor, and hit the button. The middle door rumbled and slowly began to rise.

I gazed back at Funderburk and shrugged. "Let's see what's behind door number two."

"That only makes you one for one," he said. "It's still early."

A yellow Range Rover sat inside the garage, along with a blue Corvette, circa 1967 if my eye was true. I had to pause and admire the car; a very nice sled. It made mine look like a piece of shit.

The door to the house was in the back corner of the garage. I walked over and turned the knob. The door eased on its hinges, and a cool wave of air hit us from inside the house.

"People might as well invite you inside," I said.

We were standing in a basement hallway, though not your typical basement hallway. The carpet was soft and navy blue, the walls an off-white with dark pinstripes. Wall sconces cast a warm light over the space. It felt like the Yankee locker room should be waiting at the end of the hallway. When I heard a voice, I almost expected Joe Torre to walk around the corner.

Instead, Lansing Senior came into view. He was wearing khakis and a striped shirt with a polo horse on the breast. He had a cell phone up to his ear. Needless to say, he was surprised to see us standing there.

"I'll call you back," he said into the phone.

He snapped the phone shut and slipped it into his pants pocket. He looked me right in the eye. Funderburk was practically hiding behind me.

"Who the fuck are you?" he asked.

"I represent the estate of Gene Dellorso."

I reached into my jacket and brought out the Ruger. "I believe you have Mr. Dellorso's bat."

Lansing's gray hair had been trimmed down to a buzz. He was tanned like a nut and looked like he could have been the father of one of those models in the J.Crew catalogs, the guy on the lawn whacking the croquet balls. At first glance, you'd never take him for a street guy.

He craned his neck to try to see who was standing behind me. I stepped aside and left Funderburk exposed. Lansing was none too pleased by the sight of the doctor.

"You fucking cocksucker," he said. "You got some balls walking into my house like this. I've still got partial paralysis in my eyelids because of you."

Lansing shrugged. "It can take time. Everyone reacts differently."

"What the fuck *is* this?" Lansing said. "Everybody and their brother thinks they can shake me down all of a sudden."

"About that," I said. "We'll be picking up the five hundred grand while we're here. It'll save you a trip. They got a lane closed for construction on the Cross-Bronx. The fucking traffic looked brutal."

Lansing was wearing classy jewelry—a stainless-steel Rolex, thin silver chain and cross around his neck—and these delicate little horn-rim glasses.

"I should have known you were in on this Web scam, Funderburk. Who's the jackass with the gun?"

Funderburk couldn't speak. You would have thought Lansing held the weaponry, not me.

The pin-striped wall was lined with framed photos. The one closest to Lansing showed Yogi Berra leaping into Don Larsen's arms after the perfect game in the '56 World Series. The photo had been signed by both men. I took aim and blasted it with the Ruger. The forty-four almost jumped out of my hands. Some of the glass caught Lansing in the side of the face. He flinched, touched his cheek, then checked the palm of his hand for blood.

I pointed to another photo. "I've got plenty of ammo. DiMag and Marilyn are coming down next if you don't get the bat."

Lansing showed me his hands. Judging by the stunned look on his face, I'd say that I had convinced him I possessed more balls than brains. That was not a bad thing in a situation like this.

He led us into the basement's memorabilia room. It had the same carpet and pin-striped walls. There were two rows of light-blue stadium seats in the middle of the room. I guessed they were from the stadium before the 1974–75 renovation. The seats faced a wall covered with photos, shadow boxes, and mounted bats. Standing in front of it all was a mannequin with the girth and facial features of a smiling Babe Ruth. He was dressed in a blousy, yellowing Yankees uniform with a tiny hat cocked back on his head. The mannequin's right hand had been raised as if the Babe was pointing to the center field bleachers. The '32 World Series bat rested across Ruth's shoulder, held in place by the plastic fingers on the left hand.

Lansing stood beside the mannequin as if he and Ruth were on the same side of this dispute.

"Fucking amazing likeness," Funderburk said. "The nose. The mouth."

Lansing eyed his plastic buddy and nodded. "I got a multimedia guy in Manhattan to do it for me. He produced a holographic likeness of the Babe's face from a series of photographs."

"He's gonna look just as good with a different bat on his shoulder," I said. "Now, hand it over."

Lansing was in no hurry. He'd had more than a few guns held on him in his day.

He looked at Funderburk. "My son's in on this, isn't he?"

And then he turned his attention to me. "What do you do, help him sell those stupid jerseys?"

"Not quite," I said. "I told him I'd help him get the five hundred thousand. In return, he told me something that I found very interesting. He said you used to know my uncle, said you two did some business together."

Lansing smirked. "I know a lot of people. Maybe you should be more specific."

"Does the name Phil ring a bell?"

Lansing flicked his eyes at me. There was a glimmer of recognition but not in the way that I'd imagined. He actually smiled.

"You're Phil's nephew?" he said. "How the fuck is he doing?"

Now I was confused.

"He was the best fucking barber in Edgewater," Lansing said. "Stand-up guy, too. He'd be disgusted to know you were in on something like this."

"You fucking idiot," I said. "I don't know any Phil the barber. My uncle was Phil Rice. He owned the Club Level Bar in Cliffside. He also ran a sub-book for your bosses until you killed him."

Lansing went pale, swallowed hard. Almost instantly, he looked about ten years older.

"I should have known," he said. "You're the guy my son was asking about. That was a long fucking time ago, the stuff between me and your uncle."

"Babe Ruth hit that shot against the Cubs a long time ago, too," I said. "But I can see you haven't forgotten."

He took a deep breath, gave Funderburk a pleading look, as if he might stop me from doing whatever I was going to do.

"Hey, Joey," Funderburk said. "Let's just take the money and forget all this other stuff."

I told Thunderturd to shut the fuck up.

"What are you gonna do," Lansing asked, "shoot me right here in my own house, leave my body for my wife and son to find? You think that's gonna make anything right?"

I pulled back the hammer on the Ruger. "Do you think I didn't see Phil's blood all over the floor of the bar?"

"Look," he said, "I don't have a crew anymore. I don't work with muscle. I got three college kids from Hofstra running the online bookmaking. And the loan business has dried up. Why do you think I had to send a deacon and a youth minister to get the bat from Dellorso's wife?"

He slapped the back of his hand into the other palm. "It's not like it used to be. I'm a businessman now."

"So why didn't you just wait and buy the bat at auction? Look at this fucking spread you got. It's not like you can't afford to drop three mil."

Lansing shrugged in a dodgy sort of way. "I've got some tax problems right now. Fucking IRS is crawling up my asshole. The government froze most of my assets."

"What about the property in Maryland, the piece that you promised the church?"

"The Feds don't know about that property yet. If I give it to the church, I get a tax break, 501c3 and all. Plus, it looks good if I go to trial."

He held up his hands, showing me his empty palms. "Only cash I got coming in right now is from the offshore bookmaking."

"So how much are you paying the college kids who run it for you?" I asked. "Are you dicking them like you dicked my uncle?"

"They're compensated quite well, as a matter of fact. One of the little fuckers drives a 911 Turbo. And your uncle's percentage wasn't my doing. I got my orders from above. I did what I was told back then. Those were the fucking rules."

We all stood there for a moment without talking. My silence seemed to make Lansing nervous. He fiddled with his Rolex while I tried to make my next call.

"I'll give you the fucking money," he said. "It's down the hall, on my office desk. A navy blue Adidas bag."

Funderburk nudged me with his elbow. "Come on, man. Do the smart thing. Let's take the money and get out of here."

I didn't trust the way that Lansing kept looking at Funderburk, like he was trying to convince him to turn on me. Not that I'd ever felt the doctor was really on my side at any point in all of this.

Everything was within reach: the bat, the money, Lansing's life. All I had to do was make a decision. Decisions had always been easy for me. I never questioned my instincts. Now I was questioning everything. Maybe it was the pills, or maybe Thunderturd and his fucking PFD theory.

I felt light in the head, nauseous. My knees were swimming. And then I noticed the small photo on the wall, obscured by all the other shit around it: the bats and jerseys and larger pictures. It was Joe Pepitone stretching to make a catch at first base, long hair flapping out the back of his cap.

I breathed in, took my pause, and then let it out.

"Just tell me how it was done," I said. "Tell me how you killed him."

Lansing made an uncomfortable face, glanced away, scratched the top of his head. The Babe was still smiling.

"I sent two guys," he said. "Your uncle, he tried to talk his way out of it again. They said he grabbed a softball bat, started swinging, trying to get out of there. Gave my guys a few bruises. So one of them finally grabs him, the other one takes the bat and gives him a couple to the head."

"A couple?" I said. "There was blood all over the fucking place."

Lansing sighed, finally looked me in the eye. "Listen," he said. "I mean no offense here, but your uncle was no saint. Look at what he exposed you to. I heard about your stint in prison."

"He protected me," I said.

Lansing snorted. "From what? It's like my old man. I wanted to go to ballgames when I was a kid. But what'd he do? He took me to the bar to hang out with his wiseguy friends. He tried to tell me they were heroes. He says to me, 'I got no use for a bunch of overpaid morons catching a ball in a glove.'"

Lansing touched his chest with his hands. "How else was I gonna turn out? I didn't know any other way. But I changed. It took me fifty years, but I did it. I got a family now, a real one. I got tickets at the stadium. Me and my little boy saw Coney throw that perfect game a few years ago. It was the happiest fucking day of my life. I felt like a regular person, like a regular father."

He glanced at the Babe, as if he wanted the mannequin to hear what he was saying. "My fear every day is that something I did in those days is gonna come back and bite me in the ass and take it all away."

I lowered the forty-four and glanced back up at the photo of Joe Pep. Lansing may have been full of shit. I had no way of knowing. But I couldn't take that kind of stuff away from anybody, not even from him.

"My uncle used to take me to Mets games when I was a kid," I said.

Lansing nodded. "That's good," he said. "You were lucky."

"I was a Yankees fan."

I told Lansing I wasn't going to kill him. "Just give me the bat and the money, and I'll make the phone call. I'll get your site up and running again."

He didn't even acknowledge what I'd said. He was too busy looking at Funderburk, eyes narrowed as if he was trying to send him a message.

I was about to raise the pistol again, to ask if he'd even heard what I'd said, when Funderburk blindsided me. He lowered his shoulder and came up into my ribs like I'd been blocking the plate.

I went down on my side, my head banging against the metal armrest of a stadium seat. Funderburk was on top of me, making a play for the Ruger, which I still held firmly in my grip even after the cheap shot. I managed to jab him in the windpipe with the elbow of my free arm. He gasped, grabbed at his throat, and fell to the side of me.

By the time I'd rolled onto my back, Lansing was coming at me with the Ruth bat clutched in his hands. The first thing I noticed was his left-handed grip. Lefties tend to be low-ball hitters, and there I lay on the floor, right in his happy zone.

I rolled onto my side again, whipped the forty-four Mag across my chest, and fired at Lansing's hands. I didn't want to kill him, and despite the fact that I'd only shot the forty-four once in my lifetime—the target being Lansing's Berra-Larsen photo, which was no more than three feet from me at the time—I had as much confidence in my marksmanship as I did on my throws to second base.

But the recoil on that sonuvabitch was even worse than the first time I'd fired it, like taking one of Pedro's fastballs off the wrist. So instead of hitting Lansing's hands, the bullet tore its way through the barrel of Ruth's bat. Next thing I knew, Lansing was standing there with nothing but the nub of the '32 club in his hands, sawed off courtesy of Mr. William Batterman Ruger.

"Oh, shit."

I think I was the one who said it, but it could have been all of us. We had to be thinking the same thing. Lansing was sitting in one of the stadium seats now, still holding the handle of the bat. He closed his eyes tight, then opened them again and looked up like he expected the rest of the bat to still be there. The remnants lay at the plastic Babe's feet; fractured, splintered, and barely recognizable. Ruth was still smiling, pointing at the three of us like he'd just pulled off a clubhouse prank.

Even when the bat had been whole, when I'd taken it from Lansing Junior and when it had been on display in Senior's basement, it had never looked like $3 million to me. I couldn't quite understand how the long splinter might buy Joy a new house, or Gene's old business a new fleet of limos. Now I'd never know what that bat might have purchased.

I stood up, looked down at Funderburk. He was sitting on the floor, rubbing his hand across his throat.

"You're oh for one," I said.

He was looking at the Ruger, not at me, and he appeared frightened by my possible reaction.

"I was trying to save you from yourself," he said. "You shot the fucking bat."

I told him to shut up. I was just about to tell him a few more things, when I heard Lansing say something. He was speaking slowly, in a tired and quiet voice, leaning forward in the seat, elbows on his knees, the bat handle lying on the carpet between his loafers.

"Some people believe Ruth's father sent him to the orphanage because he didn't think a bar was a good place for a kid to grow up. Not that the Babe was ever easy to handle."

Lansing smiled a little, then looked at me. "Do you know how his father died?" he asked.

I shrugged.

"Trying to break up trouble in the bar. He followed a guy outside, got into it with him, fell and hit his head, and that was it. Babe was still playing for Boston then. They say he went home for the funeral but never really spent much time in Baltimore after that."

Lansing asked if I had a cigarette. I reached into my jacket and pulled out my Marlboro Lights. I shook one from the box for him and then handed over my lighter. He lit up and let out a deep sigh, like it had been a long time since he'd enjoyed the pleasure.

"You and me," he said, "maybe we would have been better people if somebody had sent us to an orphanage."

I lit a cigarette myself and took one last look at the wall of photos, bats, and other Yankees memorabilia.

"No father should have to do that," I said.

Funderburk walked over and picked up a shard from the bat. There was plenty more wood left on the carpet. It was like the thing had exploded from within.

"I'm guessing it's not worth three million anymore," Funderburk said.

"Thanks for the diagnosis," I said.

I felt safe enough to slip the forty-four back into the compartment I'd cut inside my jacket. Lansing was still sitting in his stadium seat, all alone, looking stunned and sad.

"We'll take the money and be going now," I said. "Once we're on the road I'll make a call. We'll have your site back up before the one o'clock kickoffs."

CHAPTER 31

I didn't feel like driving, so I tossed the keys to Funderburk. I made him drive back to Virginia. It was the first time I'd ever ridden in the passenger seat of my car. Once we were on the turnpike, I called Lansing Junior to let him know that we had the money. I told him to have Ramon lay off the website.

"Did you count the cash?" he asked.

"It's all here," I said.

"So what'd he act like? A real prick, isn't he?"

"What the fuck do you want me to say? I got the money, so let's just do our business and be finished with this partnership."

We were rolling down the turnpike, listening to John Sterling call the last game of the regular season. The Yanks already had the division sewn up, so I kept dozing off, catching my head as it dropped forward.

Funderburk glanced over, asked if I had money for the toll booth. I handed him a five, went back to staring out the window, back to breathing and feeling the sunlight.

"Listen, about what happened back there," Funderburk said. "I was only trying to keep things from escalating. I thought you were gonna shoot the sonuvabitch."

For some reason I let the matter lie. Instead, I asked Funderburk if he was married.

"Divorced." He paid the tollbooth lady, rolled up the window and accelerated. "It was a contributor to my financial situation. You know, getting involved with Gene's business."

"Any kids?"

"I've got two daughters, eight and eleven. They're both in the TAP program."

"Dance class?" I asked.

"No, it's a talented and gifted program. They're smarter than me."

He laughed at his own joke, and I laid off the open shot.

John Sterling was doing his "*Yankees win*" routine. Funderburk shook his head, snapped off the radio.

"Do your kids live nearby?"

"Nah, my wife remarried. They moved to Boulder. That's why I wanted to move to Vegas. I'd be a lot closer to my girls, could hop over for a weekend. I'd hate to give up the D-Rays. That team's a part of me, something I live for. But . . ."

He shrugged, looked straight ahead at the road and the cars changing lanes all around us, people jockeying for better position, saving a second here and there.

"This friend of mine's moving to Florida," I said. "I'm gonna help her pack up the truck tomorrow."

I lit a cigarette, cracked the window, and flicked the ash against the edge of the glass. "She told me she was worried about me."

Funderburk looked over and smiled. "So, you tapping that ass, or what?"

All I could do was shake my head. "Jesus Christ, it's fucking impossible to carry on an intelligent conversation with you."

I'd planned to have Funderburk pull over right before we got to the garage. I was going to lift the forty-four, stick it in his face, and ask him, point blank, if he and Lansing Junior were scheming to take all the money. I'd felt confident I could scare the truth out of him, one way or the other. But after the ordeal with Lansing Senior, the destroyed bat, and the three and a half hours in the car, I didn't have the energy for any more confrontations.

That was not a good thing. As it turned out, Funderburk was the least of my problems. When we walked into the garage, there was our favorite bearded accountant, the Spork, parked in a folding chair with the *Robb Report* open on his lap. Ramon was sitting beside him, next to the computer, with his arms crossed. He looked like he'd just blown a twelve-run lead.

"What the fuck are you doing here?" Funderburk asked.

The Spork smiled, pulled a nine-millimeter out from under the magazine, and stood up. "Drop the gym bag and kick it over here."

Funderburk didn't even hesitate. He gave the money to Witherspoon.

That's when I heard the expensive sneakers squeaking on the concrete floor behind us. It was Lansing Junior walking around from behind a BMW 745i that was in the garage for detailing. He had a nine of his own leveled off on me and Funderburk. The Spork and Lansing had firepower aimed at us from both directions.

Funderburk looked like he'd had his feelings hurt. "We're teammates," he told Witherspoon.

"Teammates, my ass," Witherspoon said. "You cut my innings in half this season, and that's after you raised the fucking registration fee by fifty bucks. I know you pocketed the extra money, asshole."

"You can't prove that," Funderburk said. "And as for your innings, your knuckleball's as flat as a fucking pancake. Even Rice hit one of 'em out of the park."

I told Funderburk to shut the fuck up, and then I asked Lansing to explain just what the hell was going on.

He stepped closer to me and Funderburk.

"This is a matter of respect," he said. "You come into my fucking house like you own the place, show me no respect at all, then take something that doesn't belong to you. I'd say there has to be retribution for that."

"So, what are you gonna do, shoot us and take all the money?"

He smiled. "You throw in a triple homicide and things start to get complicated. I think we'll just tie you up and take all the money. As I heard someone say once before, it looks like you're getting the short end of the cut."

"You'll be better off," the Spork said. "You know what they say: more money, more problems."

I turned to Witherspoon. "Thanks for the advice, Biggie Smalls."

Lansing told me to take off my jacket and drop it on the floor.

"You're not taking my fucking jacket," I said. "It was a gift."

"Fuck you," he said. "I saw you slip that fucking cannon in there this morning. Now, slide it off real slow."

I glanced at Ramon, tried to get a read from the look in his eyes. Sometimes, during a game, I could tell what he was thinking, what pitch he wanted me to call. When we were on the same page, when he wasn't shaking me off, things always turned out well. Now I thought I read confidence. He knew what I was thinking. He *had* to know. Then again, maybe it was just the Xanax and Effexor talking.

Instead of removing my jacket, I reached into the lining and calmly brought out the forty-four Mag. "Is this the one you're talking about?" I pointed it right at Lansing.

Lansing actually took a step back, a sure sign that I'd gotten into his head with the move. He had the more powerful weapon, and he had the Spork covering the other end of the room. But I'd leveled things out. I'd turned it into a guessing game with the off-speed pitch.

"Why don't you get some fucking sense?" Lansing said.

"Yeah," Funderburk whispered. "Don't get nuts again."

"I've got a hunch you're not willing to die for five hundred grand," I told Lansing. "Now, tell the Spork to drop the nine and slide it over here on the floor. Then you and I can talk this over in a sensible fashion."

Lansing's eyes were darting all over the place, his chest moving up and down, his breathing erratic. "This thing is semiautomatic," he said. "I can fire off four shots before you get one out of that antique."

"Oh, yeah? Well, I'm so full of pills I probably wouldn't even feel the first four shots."

"I can vouch for that," Funderburk said. "He's got enough shit in him to bring down an elephant. He actually shot the Babe Ruth bat. Destroyed the fucking thing."

The Spork asked Funderburk what the fuck he was talking about.

I told Lansing that we had paid a visit to his old man's house.

"I should have known you'd do something stupid," Lansing said.

"I didn't kill him."

"No shit," Lansing said. "The fucking asshole has been calling my cell phone for the past two hours. I finally had to turn it off. Just what did you tell him about our deal?"

"I didn't tell him shit. He put two and two together, said he knew you had to be involved."

"Where's the goddamn bat?" Witherspoon asked.

"He's got a helluva batting cage out back," I said.

"Fucking douche bag," Lansing said. "He put that in for his kid. Twelve fucking thousand dollars, and he can't even swing five grand to help me pay my fabric suppliers."

"Fuck the batting cage," Witherspoon said. "Where's the bat?"

"I told you already," Funderburk said. "Mister PFD over here turned it into a box of toothpicks with that fucking cannon he's carrying."

"Bullshit," Witherspoon said. "It's in the fucking car, isn't it?"

Lansing turned to Witherspoon, actually pointed the nine at him for a second, and told the accountant to shut the fuck up.

"I told you to forget about that fucking bat," Lansing said. "We got a half million in that bag over there. Now, let's figure out how the fuck we're gonna do this."

The Spork was still holding the gun on Ramon. He was pissed, wired, and determined; a little too much of each, judging by the way his hands were shaking. He actually appeared more nervous than Ramon. My lanky right-hander was chewing a piece of gum nice and slow, arms crossed over his chest.

"I'm not leaving without that fucking bat," Witherspoon said.

"Just shut the fuck up for a second," Lansing said.

"You want me to shoot the Cuban?" Witherspoon asked. "I'll do it. I'll fucking do it."

"Fuck you," Ramon said. "I got a fucking name, asshole."

Lansing took a moment to think things through. "All right," he said finally. "How do you want to do this, Rice?"

"Like I said, tell the Spork to drop the gun and kick it under the Beamer. That way, nobody can make a play for it."

"This is a stupid idea," Witherspoon said. "I'm not dropping shit."

"Just do it," Lansing said. "You're not standing here like I am."

I swung the Ruger in Witherspoon's direction. "How do you like the view now?" I asked.

Witherspoon took a moment to consider the possibilities now that

I had *him* in my sights rather than Lansing. Finally, he bent over, set the gun on the floor, and kicked it under the 745i.

I glanced at Funderburk. His face had gone pale. Out of habit, he'd put on his fucking Oakleys.

"Okay," Lansing said. "Now what?"

I thought about it, but I didn't really know where to go from this point.

"I don't know," I said. "You got any ideas?"

Ramon spoke up. "Me and Spork can count the money. We put Lansing's piece in a separate bag, and they can take it with them."

"Bullshit," Witherspoon said. "I'm in for at least twenty percent of the take."

"What the fuck kind of risk did *you* take?" I asked.

"Me and Lansing are partners. We're pooling our resources to open an eBay shop."

I looked at Lansing. "You're in business with this idiot?"

He shrugged. "I'm trying to diversify. Besides, he's got some good business ideas. We just did a Chuck Norris bobblehead that's selling like fucking hotcakes."

"All right," I told Ramon. "For the sake of getting this the fuck over with, give them twenty-five percent. You and Funderburk can take it out of my cut."

"Forty," Witherspoon said.

"Fuck you," Ramon said.

"Yeah, you little prick." Funderburk gave him the finger.

"Thirty-two five," Lansing said. "We meet in the middle. It's the art of the deal."

Ramon rolled his eyes. "Fuck you, Donald Trump."

"Then I'm not budging from forty," Lansing said. "We can fucking start a war right now if you want."

"All right," I said. "Calm down with the fucking war stuff. You got some kind of hard-on for saying that. I'll do thirty-five percent, but that's it. The negotiations are over."

"What the fuck?" Ramon said. "You're negotiating the wrong way."

"Just count the money," I said.

Ramon and Witherspoon sat at the desk and went to work, leaving our bills in the Adidas bag. They emptied out Gene's old bat bag and dropped Lansing's and Witherspoon's cut in there. As it turned out, the accountant wasn't such a great counter. He even lost track a couple times and had to start over.

"Hurry the fuck up," Lansing said. "I've already spent too much time in Virginia. It's depressing the shit out of me."

"Like you're so fucking New York," I said. "You and your old man in your townhouses and mansions, drinking your fucking Smoothie Kings. We got that same shit down here. They got it everywhere, in case you haven't noticed."

"Did you say something?" Lansing asked. "I couldn't hear for all the cows mooing."

Once the money had been divided, Witherspoon and Ramon stood up. The Spork zipped up Gene's old bat bag. And then he got a stupid idea. He took the bag full of money and flung it into Ramon's gut. The move temporarily stunned Ramon. With Ramon wondering what the fuck was up, Witherspoon made a run at me. I was still holding the forty-four on Lansing, feeling he was the biggest threat. But the Spork jumped up, kicked me in the chest, and knocked me to the floor. He'd obviously been taking some sort of martial arts classes and having more success than he'd had with the knuckleball.

Witherspoon's kick felt like a sack of bricks compared to Funderburk's bony shoulder back in Westport. I was on my back, trying to catch my breath and barely holding on to the forty-four. The Spork was on top of me biting my hand and trying to pry the Ruger from my grip.

"Get the fuck off me," I said.

Lansing had suddenly developed a case of happy feet, hopping around our perimeter and looking all bug-eyed but still pointing the nine-millimeter at me.

"Shoot him!" Witherspoon yelled.

"I can't. I don't have a clear shot."

"Put it to his fucking head."

Witherspoon had barely gotten the words out of his mouth when Lansing fired the nine. It let out a crack like a bullwhip. I knew he'd missed me because the only pain I could feel was the Spork's teeth in my hand. The bullet *zinged* off the cement and clanked into the warehouse's metal roof.

The Spork had locked on to my paw like it was a strip steak. It was my broken hand, to boot. My other arm was pinned to my side, and I couldn't pull it free to go after his windpipe.

Finally, Ramon came up with Big Red clutched in his hand. It might not have been the Babe's $3 million wood, but I was glad to see Geno's favorite bat in play; thirty-four inches and thirty-one ounces of magnesium-enhanced alloy with a super-thin handle for extra whipping power through the strike zone.

Ramon took a home-run swing, missed Witherspoon entirely, and caught my left knee. It felt like I'd been clipped by a Cadillac.

"Fuck," I said. "Hit him, not me."

Lansing fired at Ramon and missed. He couldn't have been more than three feet from him. The bullet punched its way into the passenger-side door of the BMW. I was staring right at it.

"Goddammit," I said, "you're paying for that, Junior."

Ramon ditched the baseball swing and went with the wood chop. This time, he caught the Spork flush in the middle of his back. Witherspoon let out a soft moan, turned my hand loose, and rolled off me.

The next thing I heard was Funderburk telling Lansing to drop his piece. I looked up and saw him standing behind Lansing with the other nine pressed to the back of the little shit's head. The good doctor had reached under the car during the scuffle.

Lansing lowered the weapon, offered a barely audible word (I'm pretty sure it was "fuck"), then dropped his gun on the floor.

Ramon scooped up the weapon while I inspected the teeth marks on my hand; four puncture wounds, bright red and stinging like I'd been injected with some kind of lethal accountant venom. Of course, it didn't hurt so bad because of the pain in my knee.

"What the fuck?" I asked Ramon. "How could you miss him?"

Ramon shrugged. "I'm not a low-ball hitter."

What could I say? I'd seen him hit, and it was true.

Witherspoon had made it to his knees. He was groaning and spitting on the floor.

"Watch it," I said. "This ain't a fucking barn."

I stood up, grabbed the bat bag, and stared at Lansing.

"You really shit the bed on this one," I said.

Lansing swallowed hard. “Let’s be reasonable here. There’s no need for violence.”

“You just shot at me, asshole.”

“It was a heat-of-the-moment thing,” he said.

Ramon raised the bat over his head. “I’ve got some heat for you,” he said.

I held up my hand and told Ramon to calm down.

“What were you thinking,” I asked Lansing, “coming in here with this sort of bullshit? And then giving a gun to an idiot like Witherspoon. He’s a fucking biter, for Christ sake.”

“I’ll admit,” Lansing said, “this whole thing got out of hand. But I need this money. I’ve got suppliers threatening me with lawsuits.”

“So your solution is to take the Spork on as a business partner?” Ramon asked.

Lansing shrugged. “He’s been helping me out with a tax problem.”

“IRS?” I asked.

“They got me on the employee taxes,” he said. “I’m small potatoes for these assholes. I don’t even know why they’re coming after me.”

“It’s your name,” I said. “Your old man told me he’s in deep shit, too.”

Lansing’s mood appeared to brighten. “Good for him.”

Funderburk still had a tight grip on the back of Junior’s T-shirt, the nine-millimeter pressed up against his ear. I told him to turn Lansing loose. He let go of the T-shirt and backed away but kept the nine on him for good measure.

I tossed Gene’s bat bag at Lansing’s feet. “Just take your money and your accountant and go the fuck back to New Jersey.”

Lansing was slow to pick up the cash. He reached down with a measure of unease, as if he expected Ramon or Funderburk to put a cap in him the second he touched it. The Spork was already standing beside Lansing. He held out his hand as if Junior might want him to carry the bag.

“Fuck you,” Lansing said. “You ain’t getting a dime of this. It’s going back into the business. You and your fucking karate bullshit.”

CHAPTER 32

"The thing about Vicodin," I told Ramon, "is that it doesn't get rid of the pain. It just makes me not give a fuck."

He was sitting beside me at the desk, working on a chicken thigh. "What the fuck are you talking about?"

I wasn't sure, exactly. But before I could figure it out, I asked Ramon how he'd feel if I didn't get a new team going in the spring.

He set down the piece of chicken. "Are you serious?"

"To be honest, I haven't really missed it all that much."

"Me either," he said. "You know, out of sight, out of mind."

He polished off his Heineken, leaned back in the folding chair. He told me I could have the last breast, but I didn't have much of an appetite. It had been a long day. Knocked on my ass twice, having my hand gnawed, dealing with two generations of shitheads. And, of course, accidentally shattering a $3 million baseball bat.

"I've been thinking I could find something better to do with my free time," I said.

"Like what?" he asked.

"I haven't figured that part out just yet."

He tipped his chair back on two legs, pulled open the Adidas bag, and looked inside.

"What if we invested in a Pollo Campero together?" he asked.

The proposal had some appeal. After all, it was a product that I loved. I asked Ramon what a venture like this might cost.

"About two hundred fifty grand," he said. "Of course, we've only got two hundred thousand between us, thanks to your negotiating skills."

"I gotta give my share to Joy. After what I did to the bat, it's the right thing."

Ramon shook his head. "I can't believe you shot the fucking bat."

"You wouldn't believe the kick on that fucking Ruger."

That said, I didn't want to dwell on the bat. I started thinking about the Pollo Campero franchise again. This proposed partnership had its possibilities.

"Just how much did you say the L.A. store did in its first month of business?"

"Seven million in sales," Ramon said.

"You know," I told him, "between the detailing and the ticket business, I've got some customers who have more cash than they know what to do with. If I show them numbers like that, we might get some extra investors. You put up the first hundred grand, and then I'll go after the rest."

He set his chair down on all fours and steadied himself. "Are you serious?"

"Yeah, I'm serious. We'll give our little slice of the world some flavor."

"Damn right," he said.

We went back to talking about Lansing and Witherspoon and how they'd tried to screw us out of our money.

"Funderburk really stepped up," Ramon said. "It was a tight spot, and he had our backs."

"I didn't expect it from him," I said. "Not after the shit he pulled in Connecticut. I guess you never know who you can count on."

"That's right," Ramon said. "You think you got somebody figured out, and then . . ."

I drove out to Joy's house later that night. I wasn't looking forward to telling her about the bat.

She looked pretty, wearing white Adidas warm-up pants with no shoes. She stepped onto the front stoop in a New York Giants T-shirt, arms crossed against the chill.

There was a big full moon up in the sky, a crispness about the air. It felt like playoff time. There was an urgency to things.

She leaned in to kiss me, but I held up my hand and stopped her.

"I've got some bad news. The bat was destroyed."

Her reaction was soft. She simply tilted her head a little, pulled her dark hair behind one ear.

"Are you okay?"

I had my hand stuffed in my jacket pocket to hide the Spork's teeth marks.

"Yeah, I'm good."

"What do you mean the bat was destroyed?" she asked.

"I shot it."

She narrowed her eyes, confused. "I don't understand."

"Lansing Senior attacked me with it. Funderburk had knocked me down. It was a big fucking brawl. I took a shot at Lansing. I wasn't trying to kill him, just stop him, but I missed."

She stepped back, looked down at the ground like she was trying to picture the scene. All she managed to say was, "Huh."

I pulled the Adidas bag off my shoulder and held it out for her. "It's only seventy-five grand," I said. "I know it's not much, but I thought it might help you. I'm real sorry about the bat, Joy."

She looked inside the bag. "Where did you get this?"

"All this shit is over. You won't be hearing from those guys anymore."

She closed the bag and reached to hand it back to me. "I don't care about the money."

"What are you talking about? It could help. I don't know how much Gene owes on the house, but it could buy you time, maybe until you can refinance."

She dropped the bag at my feet, crossed her arms again, and looked away from me. She had one foot crossed over the other, like a little girl.

"I don't want to live here anymore," she said. "I don't even like these people. Who am I kidding? I don't belong here. We don't belong here."

It would have been natural to assume she was talking about her and little Gene when she said "we." But I got the feeling I was part of the equation.

I pulled my cigarettes out of my jacket, lit one, blew out the match, and stuck it in my pocket.

She held out her hand. "Let me have one of those."

I lit one for her. She took a long drag, blew her smoke up at the moon. "I went to church Sunday."

"That's good," I said. "I'm glad you didn't quit because of me."

"I took little Gene to his Sunday school class and dropped him off, and then I got back in the car and drove around for an hour. I couldn't sit through another fucking sermon."

"Coffee," I said. "You gotta try the coffee. I had a vanilla latte at Gene's funeral. The barista at that church does excellent work."

A car rolled down the street, turned in the driveway next door. The automatic garage door rumbled and lifted, and the car disappeared inside.

"Do you want to come in?" she asked.

The door was half open, and the walls looked warm in their six coats of paint.

"I gotta be somewhere early." I handed her the Adidas bag again. "You keep this for now. I'll stop by in a couple of days. I got some ideas about what we could do with the cash. We'll talk."

She opened her mouth but didn't say anything. She was looking past me, out at the pale split-level across the street. It was similar to hers and Gene's, almost a reflection.

"What do you think about little Gene?" she asked. "I'm worried he's not the most likeable kid around."

"What? He's very likeable."

It was a tough sell. I hoped I'd been convincing.

"Besides," I said, "all kids go through some rough stages. I went through one myself."

"How old were you?" she asked.

"About thirty-four," I said.

She smiled. "He likes you," she said. "He asked when you were going to take us to another ballgame."

A vision of Theresa and Louis rushed into my head: Theresa in her bed, Louis sleeping on the floor beside her, boxes packed and lined up against the walls. There they were, spending their last night in my neighborhood.

"Season's over," I said. "Maybe we'll go opening day, next spring."

She took one last draw on the cigarette, flipped it out into the yard.

"Seriously," she said, "do you think he's going to turn out all right?"

I was watching the butt smolder in the brittle grass. I finally realized she was looking right at me.

"Why are you asking me?"

She shrugged. "Who the fuck else am I gonna ask?"

CHAPTER 33

I picked up coffee and bagels at Starbucks for breakfast, grabbed fresh boxes of Froot Loops and Frosted Flakes at 7-Eleven, and sat in my car across the street from Theresa's place until I saw the light go on in the kitchen.

I gathered up the food and drink and the Best Buy bag that I'd brought along for Louis, and then I headed to the front door.

"Jesus," Theresa said, "how long were you out there?"

"Not long," I said. "I wasn't sure what time you wanted to get started."

It was just beginning to get light outside. The porch bulb was burning, and I could still see my breath. The house was warm, furnace running with a dusty smell. That was something we had in common. We liked a warm living space.

Theresa took a sip of her coffee. "Thanks. I already boxed up the coffeemaker."

I set the 7-Eleven bag on the kitchen counter and Theresa looked inside. She shook her head.

"That's a lot of carbs and sugar," she said.

"Hey, it's moving day. It's a stressful time for a kid. Fuck the protein."

She smiled, rubbed her eyes. We both stood there looking at each other. U-Haul boxes were stacked around us.

"There's an art to packing a moving truck," I said. "If you know what you're doing, you can pack the contents of a five-bedroom house in a twelve-foot U-Haul."

She nodded. "I'm glad you know what you're doing."

"I never said I knew what the fuck I'm doing. I just said it was an art form."

She was still smiling, wearing the pale blue Whip Spa T-shirt I'd given her. It was wrinkled, hanging down to her thighs. "Well, at least you brought coffee," she said.

I walked over, pushed her hair off her face, moved in to kiss her lips. And then, at the last instant, I kissed her cheek instead. It wasn't like she turned away. It just felt like the right thing to do.

"Nice T-shirt," I said.

She looked down. "It's a throwback."

"Yeah, I heard they got contracted out of the league."

Theresa noticed the bite marks and reached out for my hand. "What the hell?"

I pulled away before she could take a closer look.

"This fucking schnauzer down the hall from me. He thinks he's a pit bull."

I took the bagels out of the bag, started spreading cream cheese. She appeared to be scanning my body for other signs of damage.

"I did mean it," she said.

I stopped spreading the cream cheese, looked up. "Mean what?"

"That I worry about you."

I handed her half a raisin bagel. "Light cream cheese, right?"

She took a bite of hers. I took a bite of mine. We stood there chewing and looking at one another.

"Listen," I said, "you should be careful with that U-Haul. They don't handle so well, and they've got blind spots on them. Don't go changing lanes all the time."

"You asked me the other night," she said, "and I never answered. I just wanted you to know."

"And watch for those fucking deer," I said. "Those little cocksuckers will dart in front of you before you know it."

"You always said things that made me feel good about myself. I appreciate that."

And then she opened the drawer where the silverware used to be and pulled out a baseball wrapped in a plastic bag.

"What's that?" I asked.

She smiled, pulled the ball out of the bag, and handed it to me. "It's for you. Signed by your favorite author."

I checked the signature. Sure enough, Joe Pepitone had scrawled his name right on the sweet spot.

"Well, I'll be god damned," I said. "Where'd you get this?"

"EBay. Louis helped me find it. He said you were always saying eBay was full of counterfeiters and rat bastards, so we made sure it had a certificate of authentication."

"It's fucking true," I said. "Nevertheless . . ."

All I could do was stand there running my fingers along the laces, staring down at Pepitone's dark blue signature. I hadn't taken the combination of pills Funderburk gave me before the Connecticut excursion. I wanted to get through this day as clean as possible. That meant five Vikes before I came over and five more in my pocket for the midway point of the furniture moving. I'd take all I needed, plus the Effexor and Xanax, when I got back home. I'd drink some Heinekens, watch a *Yankeeography* on YES, maybe turn down the volume and listen to a little Beny Moré.

At the moment, five Vikes weren't doing the job. My pulse quickened, my fingertips went numb. I hadn't been concentrating enough on my breathing that morning. Now I couldn't even take a breath. Words flooded my head, drowning any hope of rational thought.

"What if I adopted Louis?" I said. "We could all live together."

Theresa had lit a cigarette. She'd just begun to exhale, the coils of smoke floating amid the first darts of sunlight streaming through the window.

She paused, let the rest of the smoke drift away from her lips. She looked at me but didn't say anything. The tiny silver cross around her neck glinted in the sunlight.

I understood that she was giving me time to work my way out of the jam. Like Joy, she had some measure of faith in a God. And in this one instance, she had faith in me. I didn't let her down.

"Maybe in a few years," I said. "You know, if things don't work out for any of us."

She smiled, nodded. "Sounds like a plan," she said.

I got to work moving boxes out to the truck, stacking them against the back of the cab. Louis came out in his old McNabb jersey. The thing had faded from dark green to teal. He was wearing a hooded sweatshirt under it.

"She says I gotta help you."

He had his hands rolled up under the bottom of the jersey. He looked half asleep and half pissed off.

"Don't worry about it," I said. "Did you see the shopping bag?"

He shook his head. "What's in it?"

"It's a network adapter for your PS2, so you can play other assholes online."

He didn't say anything.

"I got one, too," I said. "You can still whip my ass, even from Florida."

He looked back at the house like Theresa had called him, even though I hadn't heard anything.

"I gotta go eat breakfast," he said.

"All right. There's some Froot Loops and Frosted Flakes in there."

He turned to go back in the house, then stopped, looked back at me.

"I won the Super Bowl in franchise mode last night."

"That's not too hard with McNabb," I said.

"Wasn't with McNabb. I was the Cardinals. All-*Madden* level, too. Threw for 360 yards against the Patriots."

"Shit, that's impressive."

"I know it is."

He stood there a moment longer. I couldn't think of anything else to say. He finally went back in the house to eat his cereal, and I sat there thinking that I'd get online back at my place and order him a new McNabb jersey, definitely a size larger—maybe the black alternate model—and send it to him in a couple of weeks. I'd put some money in the package, too—maybe a couple grand—because I knew Theresa wouldn't take any if I tried to give it to her now.

I stood on the back ledge of the truck, not yet up for going back inside and lugging the heavy stuff. I pulled the rest of the pills out of my jacket pocket and washed them down with coffee. The cool air was light and hollow, the sun dulled by haze and clouds. Traffic hummed two blocks away, but Theresa's street was still and quiet. She came out of the house carrying the big mirror from the foyer with the glass facing out. She held the wooden frame on either side like she was dancing with it. I could barely see her eyes over the top. She moved unsteadily, small steps, swaying a little this way and that. With each jerk of movement, the mirror picked up a different image: a bush, a mailbox, the neighbor's truck, the plastic bags at the curb filled with the few things she was leaving behind. And finally, as she got closer to the truck, there I was: leather jacket, warm-up pants, bite marks, and all.

"Hey," she said. "Are you going to take it, or not?"

I caught myself, reached out for the top of the mirror, and carefully pulled it toward me. She was still holding the other end.

"Don't drop it," I told her. "I think that's bad luck, or something."

Printed in the United States
By Bookmasters